Domesday Books

ph Delchard and Gervase Bret are commissioners, appointed by liam the Conqueror, to look into the serious irregularities that ne to light during the compilation of Domesday Book, the great vey of England. Delchard is a Norman soldier who fought at the tle of Hastings, and who does not suffer fools gladly. Bret, a talented yer, comes from mixed Saxon and Breton parentage. They make a hly effective crime-fighting team in a violent and unstable period history. Each of the books in the series takes them to a different glish county.

ward Marston was born and brought up in Wales. He read Modern tory at Oxford then lectured in the subject for three years before oming a full-time freelance writer.

v.edwardmarston.com

The Domesday Books:

The Wolves of Savernake

The Ravens of Blackwater

The Dragons of Archenfield

The Lions of the North

The Serpents of Harbledown

The Stallions of Woodstock

The Hawks of Delamere

The Wildcats of Exeter

The Foxes of Warwick

The Owls of Gloucester

The Elephants of Norwich

THE RAVENS OF BLACKWATER

EDWARD MARSTON

DOMESDAY BOOK 2

Ostara Publishing

Originally Published 1994

A CIP reference is available from the British Library

ISBN 9781906288167

Printed and Bound in the United Kingdom

Ostara Publishing
13 King Coel Road
Lexden
Colchester CO3 9AG
www.ostarapublishing.co.uk

To my beloved daughter
Sister Helena Rose
of the Convent of St. Prudentia

Fortiter in re, suaviter in modo

Now was the time when those who were doomed should fall. Clamour arose; ravens went circling, the eagle greedy for carrion. There was uproar upon the earth.

—The Battle of Maldon

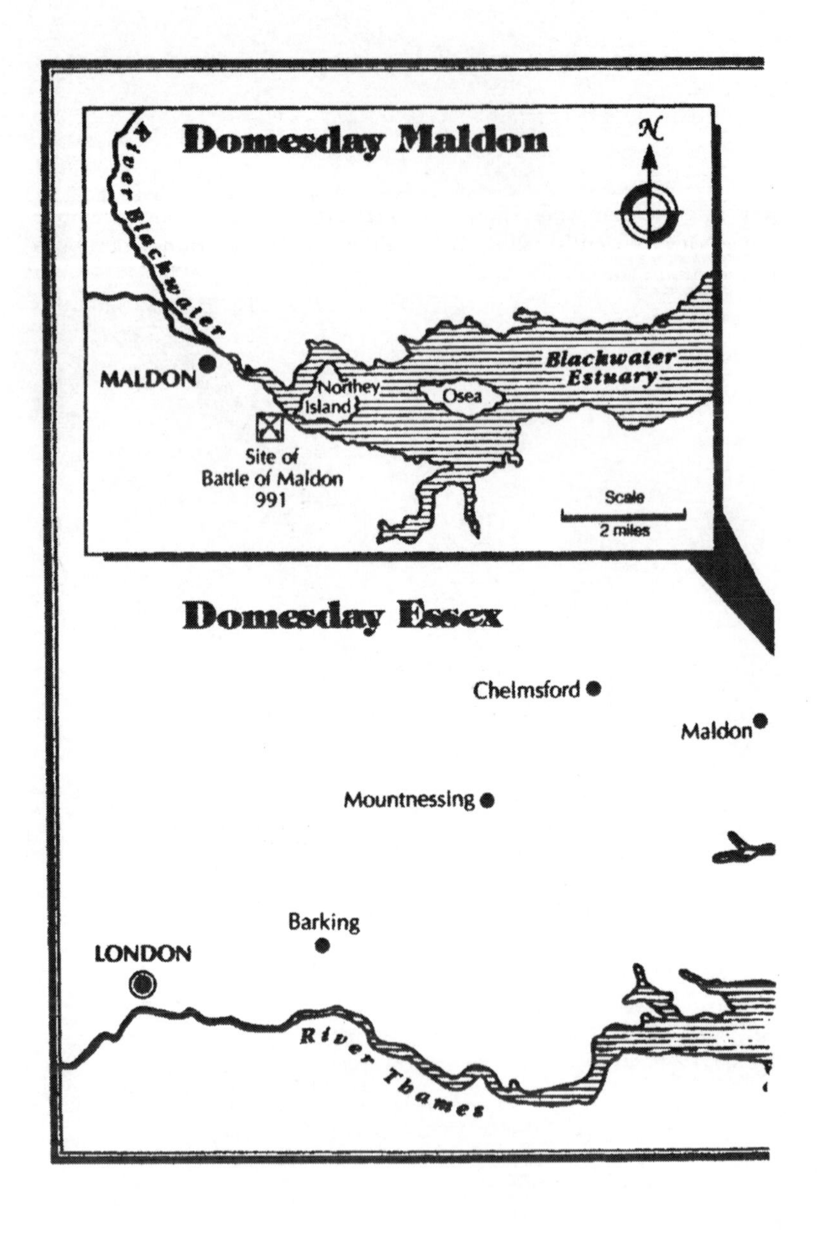
Domesday Maldon
N
River Blackwater
MALDON
Northey Island
Osea
Blackwater Estuary
Site of Battle of Maldon 991
Scale
2 miles
Domesday Essex
Chelmsford
Maldon
Mountnessing
Barking
LONDON
River Thames

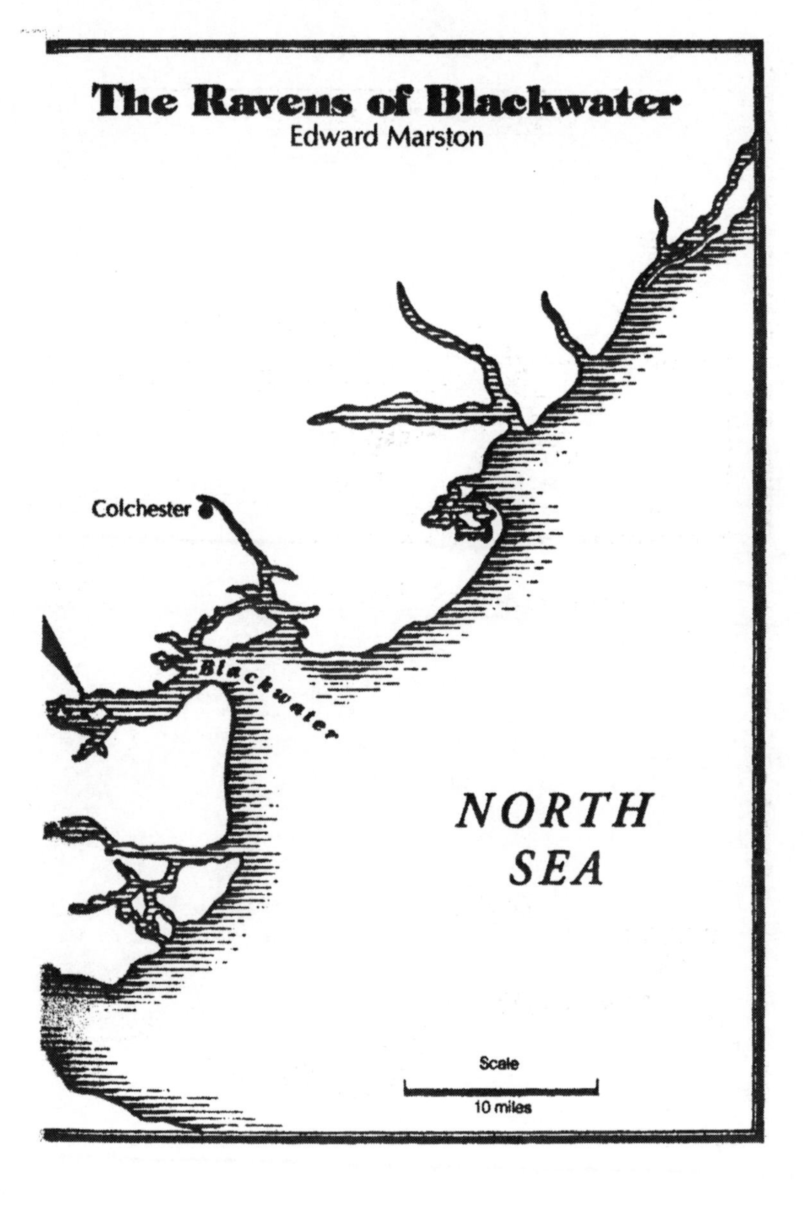

The Ravens of Blackwater
Edward Marston
Colchester
Blackwater
NORTH
SEA
Scale
10 miles

Prologue

BLACKWATER HALL SEEMED TO HOVER LIKE A BIRD OF PREY OVER THE RIVER estuary whose name it held in its eager talons. Built on a grassy knoll, it stood a mile or so below the town of Maldon and commanded a superb view of the battlefield where the Danes had won a famous victory almost a century earlier. Northey Island looked much now as it did then, a triangular lump caught in the very throat of the river and linked to the mainland by the slender causeway across which the invaders had surged at low tide. Saxon courage had not been able to withstand the might of the Danish army and Northey was a sad memento of defeat. Beyond it was the oval shape of Osea Island and beyond that the River Blackwater pursued its serpentine course past a succession of creeks and inlets, which were fringed with marshes, mud flats, saltpans, and sandbanks.

The house was imposing. Most of the dwellings in Maldon and the surrounding area were built of timber and roofed with thatch or shingled wood. They were simple structures. Blackwater Hall bore no resemblance to the long, low manor house that it had so comprehensively replaced. Constructed of stone, imported for the purpose from Caen, it was proud and tall with a menacing solidity. Its ground floor was used for storage. The main hall was on the first floor, reached by an exterior flight of stone steps. Above the hall was a gallery off which the various apartments ran. Narrow arched windows looked out with cold disdain. A tiled roof added to the sense of strength and invincibility. Blackwater Hall was like the keep of a Norman castle, an impression that was reinforced by the outbuildings, which were grouped around it to form a courtyard and by the high stone wall, which enclosed the whole property. It was at once built for defence and poised for attack.

Algar despised the place. As he stood there shivering in the courtyard, he had no time to admire the house or to enjoy its splendid view. Nor did he wish to be reminded of the Battle of Maldon even though he had named his son after one of its most noble heroes. Wistan, the Saxon warrior, had killed three Danes before being overwhelmed; Wistan, the fifteen-year-old boy, was being forced to watch his father's punishment. Algar could cope with his sickness and could endure the pain that was coming, but he could do neither if his only son was there to witness his humiliation. It was too much to bear. In the bright sunshine of a summer afternoon, Algar was shaking uncontrollably.

"Hold him still!" ordered the steward.

The soldiers tightened their grip on the hapless slave. When Wistan took a protective step forward, a mailed fist knocked him unceremoniously away. His face was on fire and blood trickled from his nose but there was nothing he could do. The steward had four soldiers to help him and a dozen more within earshot The handful of villeins who lurked by the stables were too frightened to protest, let alone to interfere. They were creatures of the lord of the manor and he had taught them their place. Another lesson was now about to be handed out.

"Where is the rogue!"

"Here, my lord."

"That miserable bundle of rags?"

"His name is Algar."

"I can smell his stink from here."

"He refuses to work."

"He has no *right* to refuse!"

Guy FitzCorbucion was striding arrogantly towards them from the house. At his side, with a quieter tread and a more composed manner, was his younger brother, Jocelyn. They were the heirs of Blackwater, the sons of the mighty Hamo FitzCorbucion, a Norman knight who had fought with such ferocity and distinction at Hastings that he had been rewarded with substantial holdings in Essex as well as in other countries. Hamo lived in Maldon and held his honorial court there. When his father was absent—Hamo had returned on business to his native Coutances—Guy was in charge of the estate. It was a role that he relished.

He confronted the miscreant with derisive contempt.

"Look at this pile of ordure!" he sneered. "The cur cannot even hold himself like a proper man."

"The fellow is ill," noted Jocelyn with a distant sympathy. "He has the ague upon him."

"No!" said Guy. "He is trembling with fear and so he should! I have important concerns here at Blackwater. I do not like to be troubled by a lazy, good-for-nothing slave."

"I am not lazy, my lord," croaked Algar.

"Be quiet!" yelled Guy.

"Fever has made me weak and—"

"Silence!"

The command was accompanied by a kick in the stomach, which made the Saxon double up in pain. Wistan's anger stirred but he stood rooted to the spot. He and his father were the lowest of the low, mere slaves on the estate of a Norman lord, tied to an existence of unceasing and unvarying toil. They had no freedom, no hope, no right to reply. Hamo FitzCorbucion owned them. His sons could treat them like the beasts of the field mat they were.

Algar mastered his distress and pulled himself upright He wanted at least to offer a token show of defiance in front of his son, but his strength failed him. Worn out by work on the land, Algar had now been wasted by fever. He was barely forty, yet he looked like a decrepit old man. He managed to throw a glance of hatred at Guy FitzCorbucion. The young man exemplified the family name. Corbucion. The raven. A harbinger of death. Guy had the same jetblack hair, yellow eyes, and beaklike nose as his father. His voice was the same insistent caw. He fed on carrion like Algar.

Guy flashed a look of disapproval at the steward.

"Why do you bother us with this offal?" he said.

"I warned him, my lord."

"You should have beaten him soundly."

"Why, so I did," said the steward, "and the marks are clear upon him. But still he would not give service. I told him that he would be brought before you. He ignored me."

"Vile wretch!"

"He feigned illness."

"Saxon cunning."

"He will not work."

"Wait till *I* have finished with him!" said Guy darkly. "The insolent dog will *beg* me to let him work."

He turned back to Algar with a malevolent smile. The slave shuddered. He knew what to expect. Norman overlords were a law unto themselves. They dispensed summary justice on their estates. Guy FitzCorbucion was typical of the breed and symbolised the hideous changes that had afflicted the county. When the manor had belonged to Earl Derwulf, there were freemen and smallholders in abundance. Algar had been a cotter on the estate, rendering service to his lord in return for a cottage and a tiny patch of land. Now he had been reduced to the status of a slave. Since the Conquest, everybody in Maldon was worse off. Freemen lost their freedom, sokemen surrendered their rights, and smallholders had their land confiscated.

While Algar shivered in his rough woollen tunic, two young Normans stood over him in their rich mantles. While the peasant and his son struggled to survive, the ravens of Blackwater lived in luxury. Algar felt that he was no longer a true man. His bones had been picked clean by the invaders.

Guy indicated a post on the far side of the courtyard.

"Tie him up!" he snarled. "I'll whip some obedience into his miserable carcass!"

"Wait!" said Jocelyn, hand raised to stop the soldiers from dragging their cargo away. "You are too harsh, Guy."

"Keep out of this, brother."

"It is a matter for Father."

"Father would run the man through with his sword."

"He would at least hear the fellow speak."

"A slave refuses to work. That says all."

"Suspend judgement until Father returns."

"And let them call me weak?" said Guy vehemently. "Never! I hold the reins here. When an animal falters, it must feel the lash of my displeasure." He leaned in to glare at his brother. "You are too soft, Jocelyn. They will not respect you for it. Saxons only understand one thing." He pointed once more to the post. "String him up!"

But Algar would not submit to an ordeal that he knew would kill him. Guy FitzCorbucion was a big man with a strong arm. The whipping would be merciless. Algar was not going to be flayed in front of his son. He wanted to leave Wistan with a sense of pride in his father and there was only one way to do that. Therefore, as the two soldiers tried to pull him away, he summoned all of his remaining energy and struck. Breaking free of their hold, he flung himself at Guy and got angry hands around his throat. It was a bold bid but it was doomed to failure.

The young Norman reacted with speed. Incensed that the slave should dare to attack him, he beat him to the ground with pummelling fists, then reached down to lift him bodily into the air. Algar was held briefly above Guy's head and was then dashed into a trough with ruthless violence. There was a loud crack as the slave's head hit the thick stone and his whole frame sagged lifelessly into the brackish water. Wistan ran forward to help his father but he was far too late. In trying to escape one death, Algar had met another, but at least he had done so with a degree of honour.

Wistan lifted his father gently from the trough and embraced the sodden body. Tears ran down the boy's face but rebellion was burning inside him. Algar's death had to be avenged and Wistan made a silent vow to his murdered father. However, when he looked up to direct his venom at the culprit, Guy FitzCorbucion was no longer there. Laughing aloud, he was sweeping towards the house with his dark mantle flapping behind him like a pair of wings.

Chapter One

IT WAS LATE WHEN THEY REACHED LONDON AND THE SONOROUS BELL OF ST. MARTIN'S-le-Grand was signalling the curfew as their horses clattered over the wooden bridge, which spanned the broad back of the Thames. A long day in the saddle proved exhausting and all that most of them sought was simple refreshment and a comfortable bed. Early the next morning London awakened them with its urgency and clamour. It was a large city with almost fifteen thousand inhabitants, all of whom, judging by the uproar, seemed to have converged on the various street markets to buy, sell, haggle, or solely to contribute to the general din. Visitors used to the quieter life of Winchester were at first startled by the boisterous activity. After a hasty breakfast, they went out to take stock of this deafening community.

Ralph Delchard's attention went straight to the Tower.

"Look at it!" he said with an appreciative chuckle. "A perfect monument to our victory over the English."

"It's a sign of fear," said Gervase Bret.

"Normans fear nobody!"

"Then why build such a fortress, Ralph, unless it be to have a place in which to hide in safety?"

"We have no need to hide, Gervase. All this is ours. We *own* London. The Tower was built to remind its citizens of that fact. Besides," he added, waving a dismissive hand at the dwellings all around them, "would you have King William live in one of these wood and wattle huts that will blow over in the first strong wind? A conqueror's head cannot lie beneath a roof of musty thatch. He demands a castle."

"In order to feel secure."

"In order to proclaim his position."

"And fend off apprehension."

"No!"

Ralph Delchard did not like to be contradicted at any time, even by such a close and valued friend as Gervase Bret. The former was a Norman lord, the latter a Chancery clerk; they worked supremely well together in the royal service but there were occasions when their differences showed through. Ralph tried to win the argument by pulling rank.

"I fought at Hastings," he said.

"So did my father," countered Gervase.

"Indeed, he did—God rest his soul! A mere Breton, he may have been but he chose the right leader to serve. Your father died in battle, Gervase. I went on with Duke William to complete the Conquest of this troublesome land."

A deep sigh came from the younger man. "Yes, Ralph. You have recounted the story often."

"Not often enough, it appears," said the other, "for you have forgotten some important details. We marched north from Sussex towards London and Duke William, as he then was, asked to be admitted, but the city was full of stubborn Saxons and the portreeve refused to open the gates to us. That made William angry. So he led us in a great circle around London, destroying and burning everything in our path. The city found itself at the centre of a ring of fire and devastation."

"It will never forget that—or forgive it."

"When William came back to London, they let him in."

"Only in return for a charter that guaranteed their ancient liberties. His welcome was conditional."

"I was *here*, Gervase," said Ralph, grinning proudly at the memory. "We entered the city like conquerors."

"Then built fortresses to skulk in."

"No!"

"We spent the night in one of them," observed Gervase with a glance over his shoulder. "Castle Baynard. Close by it stands Montfichet Tower. Even they and this stronghold in front of us are not enough to calm the Conqueror's nerves for he built another castle downstream at Windsor."

"Be careful, lad. Do not mock the King."

"Then do not overpraise him."

"We are his servants, Gervase, and that demands loyalty. You sometimes forget which side you are on."

"I am on the side of justice."

"*Norman* justice," said Ralph. "Rights of conquest."

There were seven of them. Accompanied by five men-at-arms, Ralph Delchard and Gervase Bret were sitting astride their horses in Cheapside, the main thoroughfare and marketplace of the city. People thronged and gave them the usual collection of resentful looks and watchful stares. Ralph was a big, powerful man with a mailed jerkin beneath his mantle and a sword and dagger at his belt. The knights, all part of his personal retinue, wore the helms and hauberks, which were now such familiar sights all over England. Gervase was of medium height and slighter build than his companions. The studious air and the sober attire of a clerk concealed a wiry body, which was well able to take care of itself in physical combat. Ralph and the others were essentially Normans; however, Gervase came of mixed Breton and Saxon parentage. He saw things through somewhat wider eyes.

The Tower of London dominated the city. It was a three-storeyed palace-keep with dressings of Caen stone and it rose to a height of ninety feet. At its base, the walls were fifteen feet thick although they narrowed slightly as they climbed up towards the turrets. Work still continued on the interior of the building but its chill message was already delivered by the daunting exterior. The Normans were there to stay. In the most uncompromising way, the Tower announced the strength of the invaders and the irreversibility of their daring conquest. Ralph Delchard thought it made the surrounding Saxon and Viking architecture look rickety and insubstantial. In his heart, Gervase Bret would always share the feelings of the underdogs.

Ralph chuckled and clapped his friend on the back.

"Come, Gervase," he said. "Let me show you the sights."

"I have been to London before, Ralph."

"Not to this part, I warrant."

He threw the remark to his men, who guffawed at the private joke. They knew where they were going and what they expected to find there. Ralph's knees nudged his horse forward and he cut a path through the crowd for the little cavalcade. They went past tables loaded with fruit, baskets filled with vegetables, stalls festooned with animal skins, and cages alive with squawking poultry. Pungent smells blended into a universal stench that assaulted the nostrils. The cacophony was unrelenting. Ralph struck off to the left and took them through a maze of streets and alleys whose names made no attempt to disguise the nature of the business that was transacted there. Gropecuntelane brought a blush to Gervase's cheeks and a chortle of approval from those who could translate the blunt Anglo-Saxon into its vulgar equivalent in Norman-French.

They turned into an alleyway that was no more than a strip of mud between a series of thatched huts, which clung to each other for mutual support like drunken revellers. Ralph rifted a hand to bring them to a halt, then he drew his sword and went on alone at a rising trot, slashing at the doors of the stews with cheerful brutality and yelling at the top of his voice.

"Come on out, you lechers! Out, out, out!"

Response was immediate. Protests and abuse were thrown in equal measure and the contents of a chamber pot missed the intruder by a matter of inches. As Ralph hacked at the last door with his sword, it swung open to reveal an ancient priest who was pulling on his cassock over a naked and scrawny body. In the blindness of his panic, he ran straight into the flank of Ralph's horse and bounced off it before looking up with contrition and crossing himself three times.

"There was sickness in the house!" he gabbled.

"Then you'll have caught a dose of it!" said Ralph.

He and his men roared with amusement as the old priest scurried off in the hopes of outrunning eternal damnation. Faces had now emerged from other houses and three of them belonged to the remaining members of the armed escort. As they pulled on their helmets and buckled their sword-belts, Ralph upbraided his men with mock annoyance. They soon mounted their horses and took their places behind him. All ten of them now cantered out of the alley and woke up anyone who had so far managed to sleep through the barrage of noise. Gervase rode beside his colleague.

"How did you know where to find them?" he asked.

"They are soldiers," said Ralph easily. "They take their pleasures where they can find them."

"But there must be dozens of such places here."

"These were the ones I recommended."

Gervase was shocked. "You *sent* them here?"

"This is London. I could not stop them. If they seek enjoyment in the stews, they might as well get the best." He laughed as his friend coloured again. "The King is my lord and master in all things, Gervase, and I learn from him. He has raised castles to secure the kingdom and monasteries to sing the praises of the Almighty, but he has not neglected the baser needs of mankind. William the Conqueror owns three brothels in Rouen alone. I'll show you around them one day."

"No, thank you!"

"It will broaden your education, Gervase."

"I'll take your word for it."

Ralph enjoyed teasing him. Gervase was no stranger to lustful urges but he would never satisfy them in the houses of resort, which existed in all the major cities and towns. Alys was waiting for him back in Winchester and the thought of her was enough to keep him pure in body if not in mind. Ralph had many sterling qualities but there was a sensual side to him, which could tip too easily into coarseness. Gervase was grateful when the bulk of St. Paul's Cathedral loomed in front of them to distract his friend. Two figures stepped out of a shadowed doorway.

"You are late," scolded Canon Hubert.

"A few of my men were delayed," said Ralph.

"Keep a firmer grip on them."

"Someone else was doing that."

Ribald laughter came from the knights. Canon Hubert shot them a look of disgust, then let Brother Simon help him to mount the spindly donkey he always rode. Hubert and Simon completed the party. While the others had spent the night at Castle Baynard—or in the arms of the city whores—they had sought shelter with the regular canons at St. Paul's. Despite an outward show of piety, Edward the Confessor had not turned London into the centre of Christianity he had envisaged. Apart from St. Paul's, the only religious house in the city was St. Martin's-le-Grand and even that had worldly associations. There was a decidedly secular tenor to London and it had not pleased Canon Hubert and Brother Simon.

"Let us ride out of this sinful city," said Hubert.

Ralph shook his head. "If you had a horse instead of that ass, we could quit the place a lot faster."

"A donkey was good enough for Jesus Christ."

"I did not realise you intended to travel exactly as Our Lord travelled," said Ralph. "We will wait for you here while you walk on water across the Thames."

Hubert snorted. "This is no time for blasphemy!"

"When is?"

The soldiers laughed irreverently and the prelate swung the head of his donkey around so that he could face them all. Canon Hubert was a short, fat, fussy, middle-aged man who had acquired extra layers of pomposity with each year that passed. Brother Simon, by contrast, was a walking skeleton in a black cowl, a nervous, reticent, and inoffensive soul who echoed all that Hubert said and who challenged nothing. The prelate rid himself of a burst of self-importance.

"Please bear in mind, sirs," he said pointedly, "that I was chosen for this assignment by the King himself, plucked from my sacred work in Winchester to perform this temporal office. I deserve and demand total respect. In short, sirs, *I* lead where the rest of you but follow."

"One moment," said Ralph, bridling. "You take too much upon yourself, Canon Hubert."

"Someone has to show a sense of responsibility."

"*I* am appointed to lead this commission."

"You but take the chair," said Hubert with flabby condescension. "It is I who lend spiritual weight and substance to our dealings." His voice rose to quell the general snigger from the escort. "I insist on obedience."

"Then you must earn it," said Ralph, determined to win the tussle for power. "My men answer to me, Hubert."

"And you answer to the Church."

Brother Simon actually spoke for once without being prompted. "Canon Hubert represents the Church."

"There is a faint resemblance, I grant you," said Ralph.

"Cease this mockery!" hissed Hubert.

"Then do not try my patience. You may stand for the Church, but I have the State at my elbow and that puts me in complete control. If you question my authority again, we will ride on without you and discharge our business accordingly."

But the prelate made no reply. It was neither the time nor the place to pursue the argument. Seated on a small donkey amid a cluster of knights on their huge destriers, he was at a severe disadvantage. His attempted rebuke had failed so he would have to assert his authority in other ways at a later date. Ralph Delchard celebrated his small victory with a broad grin.

"We see eye to eye at last," he said. "Let us have no more battles between Church and State, if you please, because I will always win. Look at the Tower of London over there," he advised with a flick of his hand. "It is the emblem of power of the State. King William and his army subdued this land. Swords and arrows won the prize, not prayers and hymns. See that Tower and you see true Norman might. What part does the Church have in that?"

Gervase Bret did not wish to undermine Ralph's argument or he would have pointed out that the Tower of London had, in fact, been designed by Gundulph, a monk from Canon Hubert's old monastery in Bec. Church and State were more closely intertwined than Ralph Delchard cared to admit and the uneasy relationship between them was reflected in the constant jousting between him and Canon Hubert. Gervase did not want to throw fuel on the flames of another debate. Therefore, as the party set off, he held his tongue and contented himself with one last glimpse of the Tower. It was as grim and intimidating as ever, standing at a spot on the river that had been chosen for strategic importance, and maintaining close surveillance both of the city itself and the main approaches to it. Gervase noticed that it now contained a feature, which had not been there before, that caused a slight shudder to run through him.

Perched on the turrets with a proprietary air were a dozen or so large, black ravens, and many more were circling the building, which had become their natural home. It seemed to him an omen.

Essex was curiously isolated from London. The River Lea with its variegated courses and its undrained wetlands near the Thames served as a most effective barrier. Most of inland Essex was characterised by heavy clay and extensive woodland. As soon as they left Stratford, the travellers encountered the lower reaches of a royal forest, which stretched in a wide swathe almost as far north as Cambridge. Royal forests were subject to forest law whose harsh statutes were savagely enforced, as Ralph Delchard and Gervase Bret had learned in Wiltshire, when their work took them to the town of Bedwyn and the Savernake Forest Their new assignment was carrying them to a coastal region but they would have to negotiate a great deal of woodland on the way. It was a fine day and birds celebrated the sunshine with playful sorties among the trees and sporadic bursts of song. The mighty oaks and beeches, the cool glades, and the sudden patches of open land reminded Gervase very much of Savernake, but Ralph was thinking only of their destination.

"I hate the sea," he confided.

"Why?" said Gervase.

"Because you can never control those damnable waves. In the last resort, you're always at their mercy. That was the only part of the invasion that frightened me—crossing the channel. I'll fight any man on dry land without a qualm but do not ask me to sail into battle again."

"Is that why you stayed in England?"

"It is part of the reason."

"You inherited estates back in Normandy."

"Yes, Gervase, beautiful pastureland near Lisieux but there were richer pickings over here. And no voyage to endure across choppy waters."

"You will never make a sailor, Ralph."

"The very sight of the sea makes my stomach heave."

"Then you'll have a queasy time of it in Maldon."

"That is why I am so keen to get there, discharge our business as swiftly as possible, and leave."

"It may not be as simple as that."

"We must *make* it simple."

"There may be problems and delays."

Ralph slapped a thigh. "Sweep them aside."

They were riding slowly in pairs past a copse of silver birch. Ralph and Gervase led the column. Behind them were four soldiers followed by Canon Hubert and Brother Simon. Four more soldiers brought up the rear with baggage-horses trailing from lead reins. Ralph and his knights were all mounted on destriers, sturdy war-horses that had been trained for battle and had already proven themselves in combat. The animals could run straight at a mark without guidance from their riders and they could be trusted not to bolt during a charge. Like his men, Ralph sat in a padded war-saddle with high guard-boards at the front and the back to protect his waist and loins. When business had drawn them to Savernake, they had only ventured into the neighboring county and four knights had been deemed a sufficient escort. This time they were striking out much further from their base in Winchester and Ralph had selected eight of his best men to accompany them into a county known for its hostility towards the Normans.

Gervase Bret rode a hackney, a brown beast that was sound in wind and limb but lacking any of the breeding so evident in the destriers. Canon Hubert's donkey was picking its way beside Brother

Simon's pony, a gaunt, flea-bitten creature from Devonshire that matched its rider perfectly in its shuffling angularity. Simon was trying to minimise the discomfort of travel by meditating on the psalms but Hubert had more earthly concerns.

"We should reach Barking Abbey soon," he said. "I hope they will have suitable refreshment for us."

"I am not hungry, Canon Hubert."

"Food keeps body and soul together."

"Will we stay there long?" asked Simon anxiously.

"As long as I deem necessary. Why?"

"I do not like the company of women."

"They are holy nuns."

"Females unsettle me."

"Fight hard, Brother Simon," urged Hubert with a stern countenance. "Subdue your fleshly desires. Be true to your vow of chastity and control your lewd inclinations."

The monk was thrown into disarray. "But I *have* no lewd inclinations!" he exclaimed. "I have never known what lust is nor ever wished to learn. All I am saying is that I seek and prefer the company of men. I feel safe among them. I have an appointed place. With women, I have no idea what to say and how to say it. They unnerve me."

"Even when they are brides of Christ?"

"Especially then."

Brother Simon took refuge once more in the psalms and buried himself so deep in contemplation that he did not even notice the buildings that began to conjure themselves out of the trees in the middle distance. Painful experience had brought him around to the view that the best way to deal with members of the opposite sex was to pretend that they were not actually there. His own mother—now long dead—had herself been consigned to the realms of nonexistence. Simon preferred to believe that he had been brought into the world by a more spiritual agency than the female womb.

The thriving village was one of the earliest Saxon settlements in Essex. Situated at the head of Barking Creek, it was largely a fishing community but religion had invested its name with a greater significance. Barking Abbey was the most famous nunnery in England and its distinguished history went back over four centuries. Erkenwald, Bishop of London, had built abbeys at Chertsey and Barking. While he himself ruled at the former, his sister, Ethelburga, became abbess of the later, partly to serve God more dutifully and partly to avoid marriage to the pagan King of Northumbria. Both brother and sister were later canonized and their relics produced a steady crop of miracles over succeeding years. Ethelburga was not the only nun whose path to sainthood at Barking Abbey involved a detour around an unwanted husband.

Ralph Delchard was the first to spot the place.

"Here we are at last!" he said. "A house of virgins! I wonder if there will be enough to go around."

Gervase suppressed a smile. "Show them some respect."

"I will so. I'll thank them afterwards most respectfully." He lowered his voice to a confidential whisper. "It is one experience I have never tried, Gervase. To lie with a nun for the good of my soul."

"Do not jest about it."

"Celibacy is a denial of nature."

"That is its appeal."

Ralph gave a ripe chuckle then made his horse quicken its pace and drag the column along more speedily. They were soon entering the main gate of the abbey and looking up at the great, stone-built, cruciform church, which towered over the whole house. When they had dismounted, the soldiers were taken off by the hospitaller to be fed in the guest quarters. Ralph Delchard, Gervase Bret, Canon Hubert, and the now terrified Brother Simon were conducted to the parlour of Abbess Aelfgiva. She was a stately figure of uncertain age but her virtue was so self-evident that even Ralph's jocular lasciviousness was quelled. Abbess Aelfgiva accorded them a warm welcome and a light meal of wine, chicken, and bread was served. Simon was too busy reciting the twenty-third psalm in Latin to put anything else into his mouth but the other travellers were grateful for the repast.

"Where is your destination?" asked the Abbess.

"Maldon," said Hubert, assuming immediate authority now that they were on consecrated ground. "We are dispatched on the King's business."

"It is a pity you did not arrive an hour earlier."

"Why, my lady abbess?"

"Because you could have accompanied my other visitors," she said with mild concern. "They had but four men by way of an escort. A detachment of Norman knights would have made their journey a lot safer, I think."

"Where are they headed?" said Ralph.

"Maldon Priory."

Hubert was surprised. "The town has a priory?"

"A recent foundation. This abbey is the motherhouse."

"How many nuns does it hold?"

"Only a token number at the moment," she explained, "but it will grow in size. Mindred will ensure that."

"Mindred?"

"The prioress. She spent the night here with one of her nuns. They set out within the hour."

"Then we may overtake them," said Ralph. "Ladies travel slower. If we coax a trot out of Hubert's donkey, we might run them down before the end of the afternoon. We will be pleased to offer them our protection."

"That reassures me greatly."

"Then let us not tarry," suggested Gervase. "We must press on as far as we can today."

"Yes, yes," muttered Brother Simon, still puce with embarrassment at the thought of being inside a nunnery. "We must go at once."

"All in good time," said Hubert, devouring the last of the chicken and washing it down with a mouthful of wine. "I must have further conference with Abbess Aelfgiva."

"Then I will leave you to it while I round up my men in readiness," decided Ralph, getting to his feet. "Eight lusty knights set loose in a nunnery—I must call them to heel before they are converted to Christianity."

Hubert shot him a look of reproof but the abbess gave him a discreet smile from inside the folds of her wimple. When Ralph expressed his thanks for her hospitality and withdrew, Simon saw his opportunity to follow suit. Gervase remained in the parlour with the others. Highly aware of Hubert's many shortcomings, he was not blind to the man's abilities and these were now put on display in the most convincing manner.

Barking Abbey was not just another Benedictine house dedicated to the greater glory of God. It was the spiritual centre for the whole region and the repository of an immense amount of news and information. When anything of importance happened in the county of Essex, the abbess soon heard about it and time spent in her company was highly rewarding if a way could be found to draw her out. Canon Hubert did it with consummate skill, first whining her confidence with a soft but persuasive flattery and then extracting all that he needed to know. It was done in such a swift and painless manner that Abbess Aelfgiva hardly knew that it was happening. When the two men finally bade her farewell, they were armed with a deal of valuable intelligence about the shire through which they were travelling.

Ralph Delchard took the column of horses off on the next stage of its journey. Riding beside him, Gervase talked of the cunning interrogation he had just witnessed.

"Hubert was masterly."

"I refuse to believe that."

"He turned the abbess on like a tap and information poured out of her. It was a striking performance."

"Between Hubert and a woman! Never!"

"We heard much praise of Maldon Priory."

"Spare me the details, Gervase."

"And much criticism of Hamo FitzCorbucion."

"Now, that *is* more interesting," conceded Ralph. "We will have to call Hamo before us on many charges. What did the noble lady have to say on that disagreeable subject?"

"Exactly what the documents tell us," said Gervase as he patted the leather satchel, which was slung from the pommel of his saddle. "FitzCorbucion is a notorious land-grabber, feared by all and sundry, rejoicing in that fear. He is entirely without scruple and will fight over every inch of land and blade of grass we try to take from him."

"Then we must fight harder."

"Abbess Aelfgiva warned us to move with care."

Ralph was scornful. "We have a royal warrant to support us," he said. "That means we can slap down any man in the land if he obstructs our purpose. The abbess may treat Hamo with caution but I will stand for none of his antics. I am not riding all this way to be thwarted by a robber baron." He relaxed slightly and tossed a glance over his shoulder. "What did you think of the place?"

"Barking Abbey? I was most impressed."

"So was the Conqueror," said Ralph. "He stayed there until they had built enough of the Tower of London for him to be accommodated in the city. It is one of the reasons why he acknowledged all of the Abbey charters. Barking lost none of its holdings."

"Unlike Waltham."

"Yes, Gervase. Unlike Waltham."

Barking Abbey was one of the wealthiest of the nine English nunneries. Only Wilton and Shaftesbury had richer endowments and a larger annual income. The Conquest had inflicted little damage on these houses but the same could not be said for Waltham Abbey, which lay not far north of Barking. The college of secular canons was founded by King Harold and punished because of that association. Before he succeeded to the throne, Harold was Earl of Essex with over thirty manors in the county. William the Conqueror seized these, along with the estates formerly owned by Waltham Abbey, feeling that he had just cause to strip the latter of its bounty. Gervase Bret reminded his companion why.

"King Harold was buried at Waltham," he said.

Ralph tensed. *"Who?"*

"King Harold."

"Edward the Confessor was the last king of England."

"Apart from Harold Godwinesson."

"He was a usurper."

"Not if you are a Saxon."

"Do not provoke me, Gervase," said Ralph wearily. "Only those who win battles are entitled to write about them. We did not defeat a lawful sovereign at Hastings: We killed an upstart earl with too little respect for Duke William's claim to the throne. Harold was hit by a Norman arrow and cut down by Norman swords. It was no more than he deserved."

"That is a matter of opinion."

"And a statement of fact."

"Whatever you may say, he ruled as King of England."

"Well, he was not buried with the honour due to a royal person," said Ralph. "His mistress, Edith Swan-neck, had to scour the battlefield to find his mangled corpse. It was she who brought the bag of bones all the way back to Essex."

"This was King Harold's county," said Gervase with quiet compassion. "It has suffered cruelly as a result."

"It will suffer even more when we get to Maldon!"

As soon as he spoke the words, Ralph wished that he could call them back because they did not represent his true feelings. He was fiercely proud of the Norman achievement in England and determined to do all he could to enforce it, but that did not mean his view of the Saxon population was completely heartless. Gervase had caught him on the raw by reviving the eternal argument about Harold's right to be called the King of England. In fact, Ralph had some sympathy for the people of Essex. There was no shire in the realm where the hand of the Conqueror had fallen more heavily. They were riding through dispossessed territory.

The party made good progress, breaking into a trot from time to time and increasing it to a canter when they came to suitable terrain. After a couple of hours, they paused to water the horses, stretch their legs, and empty their bladders. Then they were back in the saddle again. Another hour had passed before they heard the commotion ahead of them. At first they thought it was the sound of a hunt, pursuing deer or wild boar through the forest, but the scream of a young woman suddenly cut through this illusion. Ralph's sword was in his hand on the instant and he raised it aloft.

"Follow me!" he commanded.

He spurred his mount into action and his men galloped after him with their weapons drawn. Gervase Bret went with them and Canon Hubert was left behind with Brother Simon. The two of them kicked maximum speed out of their unwilling animals and wobbled off after the others. Ralph and his men thundered through the undergrowth as if they were in a cavalry charge, their harnesses jingling and the hooves of their destriers sending up such a flurry of earth that the ground was pitted for hundreds of yards. The noise ahead grew louder and the scream took on a new intensity. Snapping off branches and scattering leaves, the soldiers rode hell-for-leather towards the sounds of a brawl and the cries of distress.

When they came out of the trees, they found themselves in a field that sloped gently away towards a coppice below. A dozen or more figures were engaged in a bitter struggle and the clang of steel rang out across the grass. In the very heart of the melee were two nuns, clinging for dear life to their horses and totally at the mercy of the violence that raged around them. Ralph Delchard assessed the problem at a glance. The visitors who had left Barking Abbey were the victims of an ambush. Instant rescue was needed to save their lives. Letting out a piercing battle cry, Ralph held his sword straight out like a lance and his men fanned out in a line behind him. Destriers bred for battle could finally show their paces. Men-at-arms who were trained for combat felt their blood race with excitement. The troop came hurtling down the slope like an avenging army.

Down by the coppice, there was a break in the fighting. The attackers were burly men in nondescript armour and an array of helms. Their ambush had been successful. They had hacked one of the armed guards to the ground and wounded another so badly that he was hardly able to defend himself. But they had reckoned without interference, especially of so fearsome a nature, and they rightly judged that they would be no match for the posse of Norman knights now descending upon them from the trees. Their leader barked an order and they fled at once. Deprived of the chance to fight, Ralph vented his spleen by berating them for their cowardice. He and his men pursued them for half a mile but they had too big a start and too good a knowledge of the woodland to be overhauled. Ralph eventually called a halt and the sweating steeds dug their hooves deep into the ground.

When the knights got back to the coppice, they found Gervase Bret kneeling over the fallen man and Brother Simon attending to the wounded rider. Canon Hubert was trying to comfort the two nuns who had dismounted from their horses and were holding on to each other. Ralph came up to be introduced to Prioress Mindred and Sister Tecla, both of whom were still shaking at their ordeal. The prioress was a tall woman in her fifties with a nobility of bearing that soon reasserted itself and skin as white and shiny as a bowl of melted wax. Pale blue eyes shone out of the glowing mask. Sister Tecla was a slim young woman of middle height with delicate hands that fluttered like anguished butterflies. Even the wimple could not fully conceal the haunted beauty of her little face.

When Ralph gave her an admiring smile, she lowered her eyes in confusion.

"Who were they?" he asked.

"We do not know," said Mindred.

"Were they hiding in the coppice?"

"They took us unawares."

"What were they after?"

"What every band of robbers is after," said Hubert testily. "Money. Those villains had no respect for God. They were ready to lay violent hands upon two sacred ladies."

Ralph ignored him. "We arrived in the nick of time," he said. "Did you carry anything of particular value?"

"No, sir," said the prioress. "Except for a few items we picked up at Barking Abbey."

"Items?"

"A holy relic and a number of books."

"Such things are of priceless value," noted Hubert.

"Only to us," she said, then afforded herself a gentle smile. "What we carry is some of the precious earth taken from the spot where St. Oswald was killed in battle against the heathen. It is the merest handful, but its power saved us from harm. It brought you to our rescue."

Four guards had escorted the nuns, lightly armed Saxons who were overwhelmed by the surprise attack. The man on the ground was unconscious and severely injured, but Gervase was confident that he would live. Brother Simon was already binding the gashed arm of the other man to stem the flow of blood. It was important to get the wounded to a place where they could be given proper treatment and the nuns clearly had no enthusiasm for much further travel that day. Ralph announced that they would head for the nearest village and one of the Saxon guards named the place.

"We will spend the night there," said Ralph, "and give you the opportunity to recover from this vile assault. You need have no more worries about safe conduct to Maldon."

"We are deeply obliged to you," said Mindred.

"And to St. Oswald," added Hubert.

"Will you stay long in Maldon?" she asked.

"Unhappily, no," said Ralph, flicking a wistful glance at the demure Sister Tecla. "We are royal commissioners on urgent business. When we have banged a few heads together, we must be on our way. There is nothing, alas, that will delay us in the town of Maldon."

As the royal commissioners proceeded with their charges, a boat nosed its way slowly into the shallows of the River Blackwater near Maldon. After one more pull on the oars, the man hauled them into the craft and let it drift through the thickening reeds and the lapping water. When he hit something solid, he thought he had reached the bank but he turned round to find himself still several yards away from dry land. Something else had stopped the boat, a piece of driftwood perhaps or some other obstruction that had floated into his path. He clambered up to the prow of the boat and peered into the gloom, using one of the oars to prod about in the water until he encountered what felt like a solid object. It was nothing of the kind. When he pressed down hard, it sank briefly into the mud of the River Blackwater, then shot back to the surface and bobbed there defiantly. He was petrified. Lying on the water in front of him, hideously disfigured and staring up with sightless eyes, was the half-naked body of a man.

Chapter Two

PROGRESS WAS SLOW. ONE OF THE WOUNDED MEN WAS ABLE TO SIT ON HIS MOUNT but the other remained unconscious so they had to build a crude framework of branches interlaced with osiers. Its raised end was slung by ropes from the unconscious man's horse and he was dragged along on the makeshift bed. They had been able to do little more for him than stem the bleeding from his assorted injuries and it was important not to aggravate his condition by trying to press on too fast. But a slight increase in speed was possible when they left the meandering woodland track to join a firmer and straighter thoroughfare. It was the old Roman road between Colchester and London, one of the many that radiated out from the city in the northeast of Essex, which the legions had chosen as their capital.

An hour or so brought them to Shenfield, but it was no more than a straggle of small houses and did not really answer their needs in any way. The party rested there while word was sent to the village of Hutton, a couple of miles to the east, for the local priest. He eventually arrived on his ancient grey mare and at once revealed his medical skills by examining, treating, and redressing the wounds. The priest strongly advised that both injured men stay in Shenfield until they recovered more fully. Ralph Delchard accepted this counsel and left another of the Saxon bodyguards to watch over the two casualties. Now able to move at a swifter pace, the travellers were keen to use the last few hours of daylight to reach a place that could accommodate all of them in reasonable comfort.

Ralph stayed at the head of the column this time. On the journey to Shenfield, he rode beside Sister Tecla in the hopes of drawing her into conversation, but the trials of the ambush and her own natural reserve meant that he got no more than an occasional nod or a shake of the head from her. Gervase Bret rode beside him, having taken advantage of the lengthy stop to consult the documents he carried in his voluminous satchel.

"Shenfield is held by a subtenant from Count Eustace of Boulogne," he said. "Like whole areas of this shire."

"Count Eustace always was a greedy pig," said Ralph.

"He owns about eighty manors in Essex."

"Do they include Hutton?"

"No, they do not. Hutton belongs to St. Martin's."

"In London?"

"In Sussex."

"Battle Abbey?"

"The same."

"Good!" said Ralph. "In my view, that is the only kind of monastic foundation that has any real purpose. Battle Abbey was raised to mark a Norman victory. The rest of the religious houses that litter this country are full of eunuchs like Brother Simon who like to hear the sound of their own high voices singing Mass." He turned to Gervase. "And what of this village we ride to now?"

"Mountnessing?"

"Count Eustace or Battle Abbey?"

"Neither," said Gervase. "I checked the returns made by the first commissioners. Mountnessing is held in lordship by Ranulf, brother of Ilger. The manor runs to nine hides, which is well over a thousand acres. Then there's a further two hides and more held from Ranulf by William of Bosc."

"It lies to the northeast, they told us."

"We shall soon have to leave this road and head off into the woodland again." Gervase glanced warily around. "I hope that there is no second ambush awaiting us."

"Those cowards would not dare to attack us!" asserted Ralph. "We could have cut them to ribbons. They only fight when the odds are in their favour."

"This county is full of outlaws."

"Outlaws?"

"Yes," said Gervase sadly. "Dispossessed men who've had everything taken from them except their urge to fight back. Before the Conquest, they had lands to work and homes in which to raise families. Now they lead lives of servility."

"You sound as if you pity the wretches."

"I find it hard to blame some of them."

"Saxons are losers, Gervase. Never forget that. If they had invaded Normandy and destroyed *us* in battle, you would shed no tears then for those whose lands were confiscated. In any case," he said blithely, "did not these same hairy Englishmen whom you count among your forebears once invade this country and take it from the Romans who had themselves seized it by force from the Britons? Might is right. Pity has no place in the breast of a conquering army."

"And what about mercy?"

"I'd show none to rogues who ambush ladies."

"No more would I, Ralph," said Gervase. "They deserve to be caught and punished for that outrage. What I say is that I do have some sympathy for those who are driven into the wilderness and forced to live as outlaws."

"But these were not outlaws."

"How do you know?"

"The way they rode, the fashion in which they fought."

"I took them for Saxons by their apparel."

"You were intended to, Gervase."

"What do you mean?"

"Those were not renegades who preyed on passing travellers," explained Ralph. "They were trained soldiers who knew how to lay an ambush. When their captain gave the command, they beat an ordered retreat. No, do not feel sorry for any fellow-Saxons, my friend. They were Normans."

"Can you be sure?"

"I'd stake my finest horse on it."

"A roving band of soldiers?"

"No, Gervase. Knights from a lord's retinue. Sent for the express purpose of launching that attack. They might disguise themselves as Saxons but their breeding showed through. Norman warriors?"

"From where?"

"That is what we must find out."

"Why ambush two nuns and their escort?"

"Answer the first question and the second will answer itself." Ralph glanced over his shoulder at the two women who rode further back in the cavalcade. "One thing that I do know, Gervase. Those men were not robbers. If all they wanted was booty, they would simply have set their ambush and grabbed the two sumpter horses before riding off. But they showed no interest at all in the baggage."

"What, then, were they after?"

"The two ladies. When we came out of the wood, they were trying to overpower the escort in order to get to Prioress Mindred and Sister Tecla." He gave a chuckle. "Given the choice, I'd have taken Sister Tecla myself. She could keep any man warm on a long, cold night."

Gervase was puzzled. "The *ladies* were the target?"

"They or something that they carried."

"But they are holy nuns—they have nothing."

"Look more closely, Gervase," suggested Ralph. "Sister Tecla may have nothing except an aura of sanctity about her but those leather pouches that sit astride Prioress Mindred's palfrey are bulging. With what?"

"Gifts from Barking Abbey. Books and a holy relic."

"What else?"

"That is all. The prioress told us."

"Then she is lying."

"Shame!"

"Consider the facts," argued Ralph. "Would a troop of soldiers go to such lengths to steal a few sacred texts and a handful of earth? And if that *is* all that those pouches contain, why does the prioress keep them beside her instead of on one of the sumpter horses?" He warmed to his theme. "We did not only rescue two noble ladies in distress back there, Gervase. We stumbled on an intriguing situation. Prioress Mindred and Sister Tecla went to Barking Abbey to collect something of great significance."

"The books and the relic of St. Oswald."

"There has to be more than that. Remember that the ambush was not laid on the outward journey from Maldon but on the return. When they had picked up their cargo."

"Indeed, it was," said Gervase thoughtfully. "Your reasoning begins to make sense. Those attackers must have wanted their prize very badly."

"A prize that is hidden in those leather pouches."

"What could it possibly be?"

"Who knows?" said Ralph with a grin. "But we will have pleasure trying to find out. It will give us something to exercise our mind on the journey. Ride with Sister Tecla tomorrow and question her. I got no word at all out of her but you have a lawyer's skill in making people talk. She is your quarry now. I will tackle the prioress."

"Do not be too rough with her."

"I will probe softly till I catch her off guard. You must do the same with her sweet companion. Oh, and while you are about it, Gervase, bear one thing in mind."

"What is that?"

"Nuns tell lies," said Ralph. "All the time."

Jocelyn FitzCorbucion was sitting in his apartment at Blackwater Hall. On the table before him were manorial accounts that required urgent study, but Matilda was pushing a more immediate problem in front of his nose.

"He has been gone for days now, Jocelyn!" she said.

"That does not concern me."

"Guy is missing. We should search for him."

"He has been missing before, Matilda," said her brother easily. "Do not worry about him. Sooner or later, Guy always comes back—unfortunately."

"Something may have happened to him."

A rueful nod. "Yes, and we all know what it is!"

"Guy may be in danger."

"He is well able to take care of himself."

"But he has never been gone this long before."

"All that means is that he hunts further afield."

"Go after him, Jocelyn."

"He would hardly thank me for that!"

"If he *is* in trouble ..."

"Forget about him," said Jocelyn impatiently. "Guy has gone where he always goes. Our brother is a rutting stag who has galloped off in search of a fresh doe!"

The force and the bluntness of his rejoinder brought a faint blush to Matilda's cheeks. She was a short, shapely young woman of seventeen in a russet gown that was held at the waist by a gold-braided belt. Matilda had the lustrous black hair of the FitzCorbucions but its bluish tinge was more pronounced. Held in a gold fillet, her hair was brushed away from her face to reveal its oval beauty and luminous skin. She had a gentle demeanour that was quite out of place in Blackwater Hall. Although she found it hard to love her elder brother, she could still be anxious over his prolonged disappearance. Alarm clouded her soft green eyes and furrowed her shining brow. Her tenderness could even reach out to someone as unworthy of it as Guy, who always treated her with cool indifference. She nevertheless cared. Matilda FitzCorbucion was truly a dove among ravens.

Jocelyn saw her distress and rose from his stool to take her into his arms by way of apology. He did not want to hurt Matilda but he could not pretend to share her fears for their brother. Guy often went astray for a night or two and Jocelyn was glad of these moments of respite. It enabled him to get on with his work without the inevitable interruptions and arguments. Matilda saw it all rather differently and her brother should have respected her feelings. He held her by the shoulders as he tried to explain.

"Father is due back from Normandy any day now," he said, "and I have promised to master these accounts. I can do that much better when Guy is not here to distract me."

"That may well be," she replied, "but Father will be very angry if he returns home to find Guy is absent."

"It could be an advantage, Matilda."

"Advantage?"

"To have Guy out of the way while they are here."

"Who are you talking about?"

"The royal commissioners."

"Commissioners?"

He gave her a patronising smile then led her across to the door. "Why not leave it all to us?" he said indulgently. "We will sort everything out between us. There is no need for you to be involved in any way."

"But I *am* involved," she said firmly, breaking free and holding her ground. "I am Guy's sister and I have a sister's fear for his safety. Who are these commissioners and why do you wish to keep him away from them?"

"Because he might antagonise them."

"He has a short temper, I grant you."

"Yes," said Jocelyn with a sigh. "If he loses it in front of them, he could cause us all grave embarrassment. We have to present our case with discretion."

"Case? What case?"

"Matilda ..."

"And do not try to fob me off!" she protested. "I am not an idiot, Jocelyn. I can read, write, and hold a civilised conversation. I speak the Saxon tongue better than any of you and I have a deeper insight into their customs. More to the point, I am old enough to be told about anything that threatens our future here at Blackwater Hall." She took a step closer to him. "A case, you say? Are we to be put on trial in some way?"

"There will be judicial process."

"Why?"

"Because the Conqueror has decreed it." He took a deep breath and gave her the salient details as succinctly as he could. "When another Danish invasion seemed likely, King William needed to know the extent and disposition of the wealth of this country. He ordered a description of all England so that he could see how best to raise taxes and secure knight service. Teams of commissioners were sent all over the land to gather the relevant information."

A memory stirred. "Have we not already had such visitors to Maldon?" she recalled.

"We have, indeed," he said, "and Father appeared in the shire court to answer all their questions before a sworn jury. When they completed their work, they went away."

"What has brought them back?"

"Suspicion."

"Of what nature?"

"We will not know until they arrive," said Jocelyn. "All that we received was a letter to warn of their approach. This great inventory is being drawn up by the Exchequer clerks in Winchester. They have seen a number of irregularities in the returns for Maldon, enough to justify the sending of a new team of commissioners. Father has the major holdings in this part of Essex so our demesne will come under review. We must be able to defend ourselves with sound argument and legal charter."

Matilda understood. Guy was altogether too headstrong for the niceties of judicial process. Jocelyn, at once more shrewd and conscientious, would be a far better advocate even though he lacked his brother's iron will. The most effective lawyer of them all was Hamo FitzCorbucion, a man who combined the aggression of one son with the skill of the other while adding a cunning tenacity that were all his own. He would not be cowed by royal officials.

"We need Father here," she said. "He holds the land."

"I can deal with them," boasted Jocelyn.

"What are these irregularities of which you speak?"

He gave a noncommittal shrug. Matilda had the all-too-familiar feeling that something of importance was being kept from her for no better reason than that she was a woman. It was exasperating. She knew little of the administration of the estate and even less about any illegalities that had taken place. But one thing was as clear as crystal to her: Royal commissioners would not make such a long and arduous journey to Maldon unless there were serious mistakes to rectify. Blackwater was definitely under threat.

"How much do we stand to lose?" she asked levelly.

Jocelyn said nothing but his patent discomfort was an answer in itself. She sensed acute problems. Before she could press for details, however, there was a loud banging on the door. Her brother was relieved by the intrusion.

"Come in!" he called.

The door opened and the steward came quickly into the room. When he saw Matilda, he stifled his news and stood there with an expression of grim dismay.

"Well?" said Jocelyn.

"It concerns your brother," muttered the steward.

Matilda was alerted. "Guy?"

"Where is he?" asked Jocelyn. The delay irked him. "Speak up, man. You may talk in front of Matilda. She has a right to hear anything that touches on Guy."

The man nodded. "He has been found, my lord."

"Where?"

"In the River Blackwater."

Matilda gasped. "Was he drowned?"

"No, my lady," said the steward. "Murdered."

The decision to ride on as far as Mountnessing proved to be a wise one. Its manor house was large enough to accommodate the six main guests and the soldiers were housed for the night in nearby dwellings. The weary travellers were given a cordial welcome. When a meal had been served and eaten with gratitude, Prioress Mindred and Sister Tecla excused themselves and withdrew to their chamber. Gervase Bret noticed that the older woman kept the leather pouches within reach at all times and took them with her when she left. He himself was sharing a chamber with Ralph Delchard. When the two of them retired for the night, he raised the topic with his friend.

"You have aroused my curiosity, Ralph," he said. "I would dearly love to take a look inside those pouches."

Ralph beamed. "Canon Hubert has already done so."

"The prioress showed him?"

"No, but he contrived a quick peep."

"How?"

"By sheer persistence," said Ralph. "I heard the story from him as we sat at the table. He wanted to know what books had been given to Maldon Priory by way of gifts. Hubert was really testing the noble lady and sounding out the depths of her knowledge. She surprised him."

"How?"

"With the readiness of her answers. Our prioress is highly educated and well versed in these sacred texts. Canon Hubert was duly chastened."

"That will do him no harm." They shared a laugh. "Do you remember the names of any of the books?"

"I took particular note of them, Gervase, because I knew that you would ask. Now let me see ..." He lay back on his mattress with his hands behind his head and pondered. "The first was *De Consolatione.*"

"Boethius."

"Historia Ecclesiastica Gentis Anglorum."

"The Venerable Bede."

"*De Miraculis Christi.*"

"Isidore of Seville."

"Then there was a book of tropes, two psalters, a gospel book in English, a summer lectionary, a winter lectionary, and the *Cura Pastoralis* of Gregory the Great. Yes, I think that was all."

"No hymn books?"

"None, Gervase."

"No missals, no breviary, no book of homilies?"

"Nothing more. Ah—wait," said Ralph, as he prised one last name from his memory. "*Liber Officialis Amalarii.* Did I recall that all right? Is there such a volume?"

"Indeed, there is. By Amalarius of Metz."

"Are these works valuable?"

"Extremely."

"I have listed each one that Canon Hubert mentioned. He was most precise. Prioress Mindred not only let him have a glimpse at them, she proved by learned discourse that she had read each and every one herself."

"Then she is indeed a devout Christian," said Gervase. "But I am bound to wonder what the nuns of Maldon have done to deserve such bounty. Their priory is reputedly tiny yet they have been given the makings of a library that would not disgrace a much larger foundation."

"It was an act of charity by the Abbess of Barking."

"There may be more to it than that."

"There is, Gervase," agreed Ralph, then he yawned aloud, "but I have no energy to discern what it is. Sleep calls me. We can get no further in our speculations tonight. Tomorrow may reveal more. In the meantime ..."

But the words were lost in a second yawn. He turned on his side, made himself comfortable, and then drifted off. Gervase settled down on his own mattress but he slept more fitfully, dreaming fondly of Alys and waking intermittently to ponder anew the mysteries that surrounded their female companions. The ambush had certainly enlivened their day and the journey on the morrow would be far more interesting now that they were escorting two nuns from Maldon Priory. He mused on the paradox that underlay all of the nunneries. They were the exclusive preserve of the aristocracy, of women from wealthy families who could afford the large dowry that was necessary. Nuns paid for the privilege of taking the vow of poverty. Those who were already poor had no chance of gaining admission to the religious houses. Only the rich qualified.

As was customary Ralph Delchard awoke just before dawn. He was keen to get them on the road early so that they could make full use of daylight. When he shook the drowsiness from his head and sat up, he saw that Gervase Bret was already awake, poring over some documents by the light of a candle and talking soundlessly to himself. It was no more than Ralph expected. When they reached Maldon, it was the young lawyer who would lead them into battle against any malefactors. Like an experienced soldier, Gervase knew the value of careful preparation and the importance of keeping his mental weaponry in good working order. Ralph was duly impressed by his colleague's diligence.

"You must know those documents by heart," he said.

"It helps."

"How can you plough through all mat heavy detail with such enthusiasm? Latin confuses me. Facts bore me. Figures make my eyes cross."

"You have to read between the lines, Ralph."

"No, thank you," said the other, hauling himself to his feet. "I leave those interminable scribblings for you to interpret. What interests me are the people."

Gervase smiled. Some of the names that had been thrown up in the returns for the county of Essex had caught his friend's imagination. Godwin Weakfeet, Robert the Perverted, Tovild the Haunted, and Roger God-Save-Ladies had all diverted him but there was one favourite, which Ralph was bound to mention first. Gervase braced himself.

"Humphrey Goldenbollocks."

"The Latin is more tactful."

"Who wants tact?" said Ralph. "*Aurei testiculi.* That's how this Humphrey is set down. Goldenbollocks."

"A crude translation."

Ralph chuckled. "He sounds like a crude fellow and one after my own heart. I look forward to meeting this Humphrey of the Heroic Appendages." He nudged Gervase. "How do you suppose he got such a name?"

"I dread to think!"

"Perhaps they glow in the dark!"

"Ralph ..."

"What a blessing of nature that would be! Those bollocks are worth their weight in gold. That is how the name arose. Humphrey has probably fathered a dozen children. Fifty. A hundred. A thousand."

"There may be an easier explanation."

"King Midas slept with him and touched his balls."

"Perhaps this gentleman simply has red hair."

"Then he'd need red bollocks to match it, Gervase, and the document styles him *Aureis testiculi.* Red is not gold. I will raise the matter with Canon Hubert."

"Heaven forbid!"

"I have it!" decided Ralph. "Our translation was too literal. Goldenbollocks does not refer to their colour so much as to their status. They have been elevated above the common stock because they have a feature that gives them the quality of precious metal." He flashed a broad grin. "Humphrey has *three* of them!"

Gervase gave way to mirth for a few moments then guided his friend back to the more seemly subject of the two nuns. Ralph was confident that he would be able to divine their secret before they reached Maldon but Gervase had doubts. If such a skillful interrogator as Canon Hubert could extract no more than a list of books from the noble lady, then Ralph's own efforts were doomed. Prioress Mindred was self-possessed and supremely well defended. Even such a master of siege warfare as Ralph Delchard would not take this citadel.

The guests at the manor house ate breakfast together then joined the armed escort that was assembling outside. Canon Hubert and Brother Simon had been up before dawn to visit the little Saxon church, which stood nearby. It. was now the turn of the two nuns to offer prayers for a safe journey. Gervase Bret slipped quietly after them into the church and lowered himself to the cold stone. Prioress Mindred and Sister Tecla were kneeling at the altar rail in attitudes of supplication. They were only a few yards in front of him and their low chant in unison was quite audible. Gervase was shocked. Expecting the same Latin phrases that he himself was reciting in silence, he was astonished to hear the words of an Anglo-Saxon charm in which Christian and pagan elements were curiously intermingled.

I chant a charm of victory, I bear a rod of victory;
Word-victory, work-victory; may they be of power for me
That no nightmare hinder me, nor belly-fiend afflict me
Nor ever fear fall upon my life;
But may the Almighty save me, and the Son and the Holy Ghost,
The Lord worthy of all glory,
And, as I heard, Creator of the heavens.
Abraham and Isaac, Jacob and Joseph,
And such men, Moses and David,
And Eve and Hannah and Elizabeth,
Sarah and also Mary, Christ's mother,
And also the brethren, Peter and Paul,
And also thousands of the angels,
I call upon to fend me against the fiends,
May they lead me, and guard me, and protect my path.

Gervase could not believe his ears. The charm was such a compound of faith and ignorance that it seemed incongruous on the lips of two educated nuns. There was a rustle of skirts as the women rose to their feet and Gervase bent his head lower and kept his eyes shut. As they walked softly past him, something brushed his shoulder and he realised that it was the leather pouches carried by the prioress. Even in church, she would not be parted from them. For a few more minutes, Gervase concentrated on saying his own prayers, then left the dank shadows of the church to step back out into the light. Ralph Delchard chided him for keeping them all waiting and hurried him to his horse. The two nuns were already mounted on their palfreys. Gervase looked across at Prioress Mindred to be met by a cool, steady, inscrutable gaze, which was mildly unsettling, but it was when he glanced at Sister Tecla that he got a sharp jolt. She was staring at him with a mixture of interest and apprehension, subjecting him to a frank appraisal that was tempered by a natural timidity. As soon as their eyes locked, she turned her head away like a startled fawn and lowered her lids. Gervase was strangely excited. It would indeed be an intriguing journey.

Oslac the Priest was old enough to remember what life in Maldon had been like before the Conquest and young enough to adapt successfully to its harsh consequences. The three hides of land that he had once owned had been summarily confiscated by the Normans, but Oslac was philosophical about it. He still retained his Church of

All Souls' and his pastoral role in the community. Much of his work consisted of trying to protect his flock from a tyrannical landlord, which meant that he was constantly in dispute with the powerful Hamo FitzCorbucion. Ironically, he had now been summoned to Blackwater Hall in order to direct his sympathy and advice there.

"*Why?*" asked Matilda, pacing the room and twisting the ends of her belt between nervous fingers. "Guy was so young and full of life. Why did he have to die?"

"Because he was called by God," said Oslac quietly.

"For what reason?"

"Ours not to question the Almighty. We must accept His right to take us away from this world whenever and wherever He chooses. Your brother's death is a deep loss but it was ordained by divine will."

Matilda stopped in front of him with her challenge.

"Can divine will be so *cruel?*"

"My lady ..."

"Can it be so brutal and pitiless?"

"It only appears so."

"My brother was *murdered*, Father Oslac."

"I regret that as much as you."

"He was battered to death and thrown into the river. Guy was in the water for days before they found him." She spread her palms wide in her bewilderment. "Are there not kinder ways for God to summon his servants? Can such hideous slaughter really be part of a sublime plan?"

"Yes, my lady. There is a reason in all things."

"Then what is the reason here?" she demanded.

"It will emerge in time."

They were in the main hall and Oslac was finding it difficult to console Matilda FitzCorbucion. Most women in her situation collapsed into helpless grief but she was responding with anger and protest. That was a healthy sign in one way but it put the burden of justification on the shoulders of the priest. Accustomed to offer condolences in his gentle voice, Oslac was instead caught up in a spirited argument about the nature of death. Matilda would not be calmed with soft words. She wanted straight answers.

Oslac was a big man of solid build with a face that had weathered countless setbacks, yet one that still retained its essential kindness. He had cause to hate the FitzCorbucion family as much as the rest of Maldon did, but he had come to Blackwater Hall in the spirit of Christian love and his presence was a comfort of sorts. Matilda bit her lip and shook her head in apology. She offered her hands and he took them between his own.

"You need rest, my lady," he counselled.

"How can I sleep at a time tike this?"

"I have a potion with me that will aid slumber."

"Save it for a needier case," she said. "I am too full of ire to take to my bed. I cried all my tears when our mother died. There are none left for Guy. I cannot weep for his death because the horror of it has enraged me. I want to know who killed him—and *why*?"

"That is understandable."

"The murderer must be brought to justice."

"He will be."

"I must know his *reason.*"

Matilda broke away and paced restlessly once more. Oslac watched her. She had grown up in the four years since her mother's death. On that occasion she had been distraught and vulnerable, grieving over the loss of the one person in Blackwater Hall whom she could love and trust. Matilda was now the lady of the house and she had matured into that position. Oslac could see aspects of her parents blending perfectly in her. The tenderness of her mother was allied to the robustness of her father, the natural grace of the one with the single-mindedness of the other. Matilda also had something of Jocelyn's questing intelligence but none of the characteristics of her other brother. When Oslac scrutinised her, Guy was invisible.

"How may I best help?" he asked.

"You have done much for us already."

"Call on me for anything."

"Track down the killer."

"Others will do that better than I."

"Then at least tell me his name." Matilda confronted him again and he shifted his feet uneasily. "Do not hide it from me, Father Oslac. I know the rumours. I have heard the whispers. Guy had many enemies but one in particular longed for his death. Who was he?"

"There is such a person," he admitted.

"What is his name?"

"He may be completely innocent ..."

"His name!" she insisted.

Oslac hesitated to tell her the truth. While she was still stunned by the death of her brother, it seemed callous to point out that Guy himself—if reports were true—had himself committed a murder. The priest had conducted the burial service for Algar only a few days earlier and he knew that the man's demise was not the accident the steward of Blackwater claimed it had been. The wretched slave was not the first casualty of Guy FitzCorbucion's rage but he would certainly be the last. Matilda had been kept ignorant of the whole business and Oslac saw no value in adding to her distress.

He began to fashion an excuse but it never even left his lips. The door opened and Jocelyn came striding into the hall with the steward at his heels. He looked tired and flushed but there was little indication of grief. Indeed, he seemed to be enjoying his sudden promotion to the position of authority. It had made him decisive.

"We have sent for the sheriff," he said. "This is work for Peter de Valognes."

"He will find the culprit," said Oslac.

"That task may be done before he gets here."

"What do you mean?" asked Matilda.

"We have examined all the evidence," said Jocelyn, "and we have taken statements from a number of people. They all say the same thing. Two of them overheard him swear revenge. Others speak of his violent nature. It must be him."

"Who?" said Matilda.

"A boy with a reason to kill."

"A boy?"

"His name is Wistan. I've sent men to arrest him."

It was over an hour before Gervase Bret managed to elicit a complete sentence out of her. Sister Tecla was reticence incarnate. As they rode along side by side, he tried every conversational gambit that he knew to provoke her into comment but she stayed beyond his reach. Up ahead of them, Ralph Delchard and Prioress Mindred were chatting volubly and even sharing an occasional laugh. The prioress had far too subtle a mind for Ralph, saw through his purpose at once, and used language to construct a wall of words around her, but at least she was talking. Most of the replies that Gervase got came from the birds or the horses. It was only when he asked the most obvious question of all that he finally broke through the nun's studied silence.

"Are you named after St. Tecla?" he wondered.

She was amazed. "You have heard of her?"

"Of course."

"But she is a Saxon saint."

"So are Oswald and Aldhelm and Botolph," he observed, "but I have heard of them as well. My mother was a Saxon."

"Yet you are in the service of the Normans."

"The King of England is my master. He rules over all the people of this land, whatever their origin. That puts us on an equal footing as his subjects." He felt that a smile was worth trying. "Tecla was a remarkable woman. She was a nun at Wimborne in Dorset, I believe."

"That is true."

"Her abbess sent her to help Boniface in his missionary work in Germany. She was much loved and respected. Her fame spread throughout Germany. When she died, a shrine was built there. Miracles occurred." His second smile was more confident. "You bear the name of an outstanding lady."

"I am proud to do so."

"What other saints do you revere?"
"All of them."
"A Benedictine house must surely love St. Benedict."
"So we do, sir."
"Then there is St. Oswald."
"St. Oswald?"
"The martyr," he said. "Oswald, King of Northumbria. It was a holy relic of his that took you to Barking Abbey. That was the purpose of your visit, was it not?"
"Why, yes," she said uncertainly.
"How much earth are you carrying with you?"
"Earth?"
"From the place where Oswald fell in battle."
"A tiny amount, that is all." She was mildly flustered but soon recovered her poise. "You are very well informed about our English saints."
"So I should be. The master of the novices used to beat us soundly if we did not learn our lessons properly."
Curiosity made her turn to him for the first time. "You were a postulant?" she said. "At which monastery?"
"Eltham Abbey."
Disappointment showed. "A Norman foundation."
"It had due respect for native saints." To subdue her reservations, he gave her further proof. "St. Oswald was much admired at Eltham. Our abbot took such an interest in him that he actually visited the battlefield where the saint was struck down by Penda, the pagan King of Mercia. The place is in Shropshire, although its name eludes me."
"Maserfield."
"Thank you, Sister Tecla."
"Miracles took place at the very spot where he fell."
"Yes," said Gervase. "Praying with his last breath for the souls of the bodyguards who were slain with him. Our abbot told us that so many people have been to Maserfield to get some of the precious earth that they dug a deep trench. St. Oswald's power reaches well below ground for we have seen how the particles that Prioress Mindred carries are still able to work their magic."
"They brought you to us in our time of trial."
"Perhaps they, too, had heard of the miracles."
"Who?"
"The men who attacked you."
An involuntary shiver. "I have tried to forget them."
"They must have been after something," he probed.
"It was terrifying."
"Did they try to snatch the holy relic?"

"I thought we would all be killed."
"Did they grab at the sacred books?"
"Then you saved us."
"What did those men hope to get?"

But the directness of his question brought the exchange to an end. Sister Tecla shot him a look of betrayal then urged her horse forward at a trot until she caught up with Prioress Mindred. Safe under the wing of the older woman, she was clearly not going to stir from there for the remainder of the journey. Gervase cursed himself for having blundered. At the very moment he was establishing a rapport with her, he had thrown it away by rushing the procedure. What had been gleaned, however, was confirmation of their earlier suspicion. The men who laid the ambush on the previous day had been after a specific prize and neither of the nuns was ready to disclose what it was. They had something to hide. Gervase Bret spent the rest of the morning wondering what it could be.

Wistan knew that they would come for him. As soon as the body of Guy FitzCorbucion was found in the waters of the River Blackwater, the boy feared for his safety. Word spread quickly through the estate and there were several who raised a cheer or said a prayer of thanks at the news. The most loathed member of a loathsome family had been murdered and that was a cause for celebration. If it had been left to those who lived and worked on the demesne, the killer would have been rewarded with instant sainthood. He had overcome a veritable force of evil.

He moved swiftly. Wistan had lingered until darkness fell, then he ran for his life. The river was cold but he was a strong swimmer and he cleaved his way with powerful arms towards the distant blob of Northey Island. Once there, he sought cover and felt marginally more secure. Nobody would search for him at night. When morning came, he went deeper into the island and scooped himself a hiding place in the long grass. The sun soon dried his wet clothes and the fruit he had brought filled his belly. All he could do now was to lie low and hope that they did not find him.

Wistan had aged considerably. Within the space of little more than a week, a fifteen-year-old boy had turned into a full-grown man. When his father had been killed in front of him, the iron had entered his soul; when Algar was buried in his miserable grave, the boy had renewed his vow of revenge. As he hid in his lair and kept on the alert, Wistan felt more embittered than ever, but there was one consolation. Guy FitzCorbucion was dead. The man who had killed Wistan's father had himself been cut down without mercy. It was no more man he deserved. Wistan burst into silent laughter and rocked happily to and fro.

His grisly mirth was short-lived. Something on the mainland caught his eye. Deep in his burrow, he saw a distant column of smoke rising into the clear blue sky and he knew instantly what it meant. They were searching for him. They had seen that he had fled and so they set fire to his hovel. The little wooden hut that he had shared with his father all those years was being destroyed out of sheer spite. Thatch burned well and the smoke was now billowing. Wistan was unmoved. He was not afraid of them any longer. They had simply given him one more reason to hate the ravens of Blackwater.

Chapter Three

LONG BEFORE THEY REACHED MALDON, THEY SAW IT RISING MAJESTICALLY BEFORE them in the distance. Surrounded by fertile farm land, it sat on the top of a steep hill, which overlooked the estuary and the lower reaches of the Chelmer and Blackwater valleys. It was a prosperous town of well over a thousand inhabitants, most of whom were engaged in agriculture or related occupations, but with a sizeable number who made their living as fishermen and coastal traders. A few, with larger crafts and greater ambitions, sailed across to France and the Low Countries to develop international commerce. Maldon's position, high on a tidal estuary, made it one of the key ports in the region. Apart from Colchester, it was the only place in Essex that had been given borough status and its preeminence was marked by three churches, a royal mint, and a flourishing market. After a painstaking journey from one small village to another, the travellers were glad to see a real town dominating the horizon and to know that they would reach their destination before nightfall.

Ralph Delchard was pleased with their achievement.

"I feared we might not get here before dark," he said, "but those nuns sit on fine palfreys that will trot for hours on end. I have never seen religion ride so fast."

"They were as anxious to reach Maldon as we were," said Gervase, beside him. "We questioned them too closely and that lent spurs to their heels."

"Prioress Mindred gave nothing away."

"Nor did Sister Tecla."

"We will have to be more guileful with them," decided Ralph. "They are certainly concealing something from us and I intend to find out what it is."

"All will be revealed in time."

"Conduct them safely to their priory, Gervase."

"Why me?"

"Because I am not ready to ride into the town."

"But that hill should give us a wonderful view."

"That is my fear," admitted Ralph. "A wonderful view of the sea. I am too weary to cope with that now. It would turn my stomach and prevent my sleep."

"Take heart, Ralph," said the other. "All you would see from Maldon is the river estuary. The sea itself is miles away from the town."

"Water is water. I prefer the sight of land."

Gervase Bret was puzzled. Ralph Delchard was such a courageous man—and had proved it on so many occasions—that it was difficult to believe anything could actually frighten him. With a sword in his hand, the Norman lord would meet any adversary without flinching but the arts of war could not subdue the rolling waves. Gervase could think of only one reason why the sea should exert such power over his friend. Ralph could not swim.

When they got within half a mile of the town, the party divided into two. The commissioners were staying at a nearby manor house. After a flurry of farewells and an expression of sincere gratitude from the prioress, Ralph Delchard went off with Canon Hubert, Brother Simon, and four of his men while Gervase Bret continued on the road to Maldon with the rest of the company. Shadows were lengthening by the time they had climbed the hill, but there was still enough light left for the visitors to take stock of the place. The returns made by the first commissioners showed that Maldon had one hundred and eighty houses, most of them belonging to the King and held directly from him by local burgesses. What Gervase had not gleaned from his documents was the fact that the vast majority of dwellings were built of timber. High Street was one long avenue of wood and thatch with only the occasional stone structure to counter the distinctive feel of an old Saxon burh.

Far below them, the Blackwater estuary was patrolled by gulls, oystercatchers, and honking geese. The thick ribbon of water twisted leisurely towards the sea and Gervase could pick out a couple of small boats navigating their way past Osea Island against the tidal flow. The priory stood on a patch of land near the lower end of High Street and thus overlooked the Hythe, the town's harbour, and its adjacent Church of St. Mary's. He was fascinated to see the little convent, which seven nuns shared with Prioress Mindred. It was a single-storey building of wood, reinforced with stone and set at right angles to a tiny stone-built chapel. The houses in the town had almost no land attached to them but the priory boasted the best part of an acre, most of it given over to a walled garden. Gervase realised why the property had not been recorded by the first team of commissioners. When they visited Maldon a year or so earlier, the priory had not existed. It was one of many features of the town that the original survey had perforce omitted.

Fatigued by the journey himself, Gervase knew that the two women must be exhausted but there was no sign of it in their gentle smiles and their upright posture. As travelling companions, they had been pleasant and uncomplaining, although he was still none the wiser about the true purpose of their visit to Barking Abbey. When they reached the gate, Gervase dismounted quickly so that he could help the prioress down from her horse. She thanked him profusely and he turned to perform the same service for Sister Tecla, holding her mount with one hand while offering her the support of the other. Although she said nothing, there was such warm gratitude in her manner that he was amply rewarded. He was no longer being blamed for his earlier overeagerness in questioning her. Sister Tecla had clearly forgiven him.

The gate of the priory opened and a stout figure of middle height stepped out to greet the two women. Her body seemed about to burst out of her habit but her face was so completely enclosed by her wimple that only a few inches of flesh were visible around a pair of steely eyes. Prioress Mindred allowed no more than a token kiss but Sister Tecla was given a welcoming embrace. It was not extended to Gervase Bret. As the nun's gaze fell on him, it hardened into abstract hostility.

"This is Sister Gunnhild," introduced the prioress.

"I am pleased to make your acquaintance," he said.

Gervase inclined his head politely but he got no more than a curt nod in return. Sister Gunnhild was too old to bother with pretence and social nicety. She disliked men.

Like its eccentric owner, Champeney Hall was a weird mixture of Norman and Saxon, with a strong bias towards the former held in check by an unexpected nostalgia for the latter. To all outward appearances, the manor house was the archetypal dwelling of a thegn, a long, low building that was constructed of heavy timber and roofed with shingled wood. Internally, it bore no resemblance to the home that had served the Saxon lord who built it. In those days, the hall was divided into a series of bays, which acted as separate living quarters for the thegn, his family, his servants, his farm labourers, and even some of his livestock. Gilbert Champeney made radical alterations to that scheme of things. His home was neatly partitioned by stone walls with solid doors and he had raised the slope of the roof at the rear of the property so that it was possible to move around each chamber without banging a head against a rafter. A large, two-storey, stone-built wing had been added so that the simplicity of the Saxon hall was offset by the brooding sophistication of a Norman keep.

Gilbert himself was a generous and willing host.

"My home is yours, sirs," he said.

"We are indebted to you, my lord," said Canon Hubert.

"Indebted," repeated Brother Simon obsequiously.

Looking around, Ralph shrugged. "Why not burn the whole place down and build a proper Norman manor house?"

"Because this is not Normandy," replied Gilbert with a nervous laugh. "There is no point in destruction for its own sake. Preserve what is worth preserving—that is my belief. Our king follows the same precept. The Saxons had an established legal code so he largely kept it. They had a sound currency so he retained its organisation. They had an excellent system of taxation so he extended it." The nervous laugh was more of a snigger this time. "And it is that which has brought you all to Maldon. Taxation. Saxon common sense refined by Norman efficiency. Just like my home."

Gilbert Champeney was a short, bustling, bald-headed man with watery blue eyes and a mobile face. Now well into his fifties, he still had the boyish enthusiasm for any project in which he was engaged and an uncomplicated ability to enjoy his life. Looking at him now, it was hard to believe that he had, like Ralph, fought with the Conqueror at Hastings. Ralph still had the unmistakable stamp of a soldier, but Gilbert seemed too soft and affable ever to have borne arms. Twenty years of living in Essex had infected him with a fondness for the nation he had helped to displace. The visitors were quick to note that his tunic had a Saxon cut to it and that he was in the process of trying to grow a beard.

"You will no doubt be hungry," he said.

"Yes!" replied Ralph.

"Famished," said Canon Hubert.

"Then I have a treat for you. Although I have kept a Saxon reeve to run my estate and Saxon men to work it, I felt I could not survive without a Norman cook. He is at this moment roasting some steaks of beef on a spit and preparing a sauce with red wine, juice of Seville oranges, and a pinch each of ground black pepper and ginger."

Hubert's stomach rumbled in appreciation. "With a sprinkling of cinnamon?" he said hopefully.

"Of course."

The canon could believe in Heaven once more.

Gilbert first called for servants to conduct the men to their respective chambers so that they could deposit all the baggage that they had brought with them. The soldiers were also shown to their quarters, much more cramped, but adequate for their purposes. Gervase Bret arrived with the other half of the armed escort in time to join his colleagues for the sumptuous meal. He warmed to their host at once. Gilbert Champeney's hospitality had been sought because he was one of the few Norman magnates in the area who was not involved in their investigation. While others grabbed what they could and defended their illegal acquisitions with lies, forgeries, or open aggression, the lord of this manor was content with what he possessed. He had a quality that set him apart from other Norman barons. He needed to live in harmony with the Saxon people. Gilbert wanted to be liked.

"How long will you stay in Maldon?" he said.

"For as long as your cook will favour us," said Hubert as he stuffed boiled cabbage into his mouth. "We had not thought to find such quality in the food."

"I cannot eat a thing," said the emaciated Simon.

Hubert grunted. "Then you are a fool."

"Self-denial is a virtue."

"Well-fed men have more strength to serve God."

"You have said that indulgence is a sin, Canon Hubert."

"Yes, Brother Simon," conceded the other. "But this is not indulgence. To refuse the offer of such a repast is an insult to the kindness of our host."

"I go along with that," said Ralph, sipping wine from his cup. "Hubert and I have at last found something about which we can agree." He turned back to Gilbert. "To answer your question, my lord, we will remain here until we have finished our allotted work. It is quite straightforward."

"Whom does it mostly concern?" asked Gilbert.

"Hamo FitzCorbucion."

"Then it is not straightforward at all, I fear."

"Why not?" asked Gervase.

"Hamo has not yet returned from Coutances."

"Then his elder son must speak for him," said Ralph.

"That, too, presents a slight complication."

"What is it?"

Gilbert Champeney picked at his teeth and waited till he had their full attention. He enjoyed delivering tidings that would have such an important bearing on the work of the royal commissioners. Another nervous laugh slipped out.

"Guy FitzCorbucion has been murdered."

"Why are they calling it Domesday Book?" asked Matilda.

"That need not trouble you," said her brother.

"I wish to know, Jocelyn. Tell me."

"When I have more time."

"It is a simple question."

"And I will give you a simple answer. In due course."

"Now," she insisted.

"Matilda ..."

"*Now!*"

Jocelyn FitzCorbucion clicked his tongue in irritation. He and the steward were about to leave Blackwater Hall when his sister intercepted them. Matilda was now standing in the doorway to obstruct their exit. The dove-like softness had been shed in favour of a hard-faced persistence. She was frustrated at being excluded from everything of importance that happened on the estate. It was time for her to find out exactly what was going on. Matilda folded her arms and stuck out a combative chin.

"Well?" she demanded.

The two men exchanged a glance. Jocelyn heaved a sigh.

"Explain it to her, Fulk," he said.

"Very well, my lord."

The steward was a fleshy man in his thirties with a smirking politeness. He had been employed on the demesne long enough to learn all its dark secrets and he was as adept at enforcing his master's writ among the villeins and serfs on the estate as he was at dealing with the finer points of the manorial accounts. Fulk was not used to having to answer to a woman. It put the merest hint of annoyance into his voice.

"King William calls it a description of England," he said, "but it is known as the Domesday Book in the shires because it is like the Last Judgement. These commissioners want to know *everything*."

Jocelyn was brusque. "There, Matilda. You have had your explanation. Now, stand aside."

"One moment," she said.

"You are in our way."

"The Last Judgement will weigh our sins. Is that why you are being arraigned? For some sinful acts?"

"We are not being arraigned," he said defencively.

"Indeed not," added Fulk smoothly. "Your brother and I merely attend a meeting at the shire hall this afternoon. The town reeve has summoned all people of consequence in Maldon so that we may hear what these commissioners have to say." He gestured towards the door. "If you prevent us from leaving, we will be late for the gathering and that might be interpreted as a deliberate affront to them."

She stood her ground. "Who are these commissioners?"

"Powerful men with a royal warrant," said Jocelyn.

"Father would keep them waiting."

"I will handle this my way, Matilda."

"He'd send a dusty answer to the King himself."

"We have to leave. Please excuse us."

Jocelyn tried to brush past her to get to the door but she shifted her position to block his way once more.

"Where are these commissioners staying?" she asked.

"At Champeney Hall."

She recoiled slightly at the name and her resistance faded at once. Matilda stepped aside to let them pass and stood pensively in the open doorway as they went down the stone steps into the courtyard. Jocelyn was angry at having been challenged in that way in front of the steward. For the first time in his entire life, he was in a position of real authority at Blackwater Hall and it was being eroded by a mere woman. He loved his sister and he wanted to help her get over the shock of their brother's sudden death but he could not tolerate such interference. It weakened his standing. He tried to pass off the incident with a forced laugh.

"Women!" he moaned. "They have to be humoured."

"Sometimes, my lord."

"Matilda will not be able to hinder us much longer. When my father returns, he will have a surprise for her."

"I know."

"He went to Normandy to arrange a marriage for her. Father will bring back the name of her future husband."

"She needs a man to control her," said Fulk.

The steward's tone was deferential but there was an implied rebuke for Jocelyn in his comment. Fulk was more accustomed to the forcefulness of a Hamo or the arrogance of a Guy. He was not so far impressed by the softer edge of Jocelyn FitzCorbucion. The latter winced inwardly and resolved to show greater firmness.

His opportunity came immediately. Grooms had the horses saddled and waiting for them. As the two men mounted, there was a clatter of hooves and eight knights came cantering into the courtyard on their destriers. They reined in their mounts, who stood in a sweating half circle around Jocelyn.

"Have you caught him yet?" he snarled.

"No, my lord," said the captain.

"Search harder."

"We have been out since first light."

"Find that boy!"

"Wistan ran off the night before last," explained the captain. "The lad has strong legs. He could be several miles away by now."

"Widen the search. I want him hunted down."

"Yes, my lord."

"Question the other slaves."

"We have done so."

"They must know where he is."

"All of them deny it."

"Beat the truth out of them!" ordered Jocelyn, waving a fist. "Take more men and continue the search at once. That boy killed my brother. He will pay dearly for that. Get back out there. Look under every stone in the county until you find him!"

Wistan had chosen his escape route well. They would not expect him to be on the island. Throughout the night, the causeway was submerged by the tide and the dark water would deter anyone without a boat and a knowledge of the currents. A whole day had come and gone without any sign of pursuit. Evidently, they were searching on the mainland for a boy who could run instead of on Northey for one who could swim. Well into a second day in hiding, he began to feel a little safer. The island was large and the population sparse. He had over five hundred acres in which to roam. When his food ran out, he could forage for more. Wistan would live from day to day. Survival was all.

With a vague sense of security came a tattered dignity. He had deceived them. The son of a slave had outwitted the knights from Blackwater Hall. He could never take them on in direct combat because he was hopelessly outnumbered, but he could wrest some smattering of honour from the contest. Wistan could make his father proud of him from beyond the grave. He remembered why Algar had given him his name and what its significance was at the Battle of Maldon. Wistan was a hero. The Vikings had bided their time at the very place where he himself was now lurking. When they were allowed to cross at low tide by means of the causeway, they came up against the full strength of the Saxon fyrd, the army that had been raised to defend the town. Wistan had been at the forefront of the struggle. He had accounted for three Vikings before he was cut down by the invaders.

Guy FitzCorbucion was an invader and he was dead. The boy felt a warm glow inside him every time he savoured that thought. He wanted to destroy all the ravens of Blackwater. They might catch him in the end but he hoped to take full revenge first. Like the Wistan of old, he intended to fight to the death and take some of the vile invaders with him. His own father had shown him the way. Algar had gone down with a last brave show of spirit. As the boy recalled it now, it buttressed his resolution. He thought about the way that he would best like to kill Hamo FitzCorbucion.

A snuffling sound brought him out of his reverie and he huddled into his hiding place in the long grass. They were searching for him on the island, after all. He could see nothing from his burrow but the sound was slowly getting closer. Wistan grabbed the crude knife that was tucked in his belt. He would have to live up to his namesake sooner than he had anticipated but he was not afraid. Excitement made his heart thud and his temples pound. He held his breath as the snuffling got louder and the grass was trampled. He lay curled in a ball until his adversary was almost upon him and then he unwound like a spring, rising up on his knees and using the knife to jab with vicious force.

He caught the sheep a glancing blow on its shoulder and blood oozed swiftly into its fleece. With a leap in the air and a bleat of pain, it went careering across the field to join the rest of the herd. Wistan was both stunned and relieved. He was sorry to have wounded the animal but glad that he had not been run to earth. There was no sign of a human being but sheep were now grazing all over the area. It was time to find a new hiding place. Gathering his meagre belongings, he crept through the grass with the stealth of a fox. Wistan was the quarry in a murder hunt but that prospect did not trouble him any more. It had started to be exhilarating.

The shire hall occupied a prime position near the junction of Silver Street and High Street. Timber-framed and roofed with thatch, it was a large building with a murky interior that smelled in equal parts of dampness, decay, and some unspecified farm animal. A sparrow was hopping along the rafters and spiders had turned the whole of the ceiling into a continuous and interconnecting series of elaborate webs. The walls were roughly plastered and some attempt had been made to decorate them with simple patterns. There were several windows but they seemed to keep out more light than they admitted. The hall was built solely for communal use. Comfort and decoration were afterthoughts.

"I wonder if he will turn up," mused Ralph Delchard.

"Who?" said Gervase Bret.

"Humphrey Goldenbollocks."

"Keep your voice down!"

"We could do with him in tins gloom," observed Ralph with a glance around. "He can stand on the table here and shed light on the whole business by displaying his golden orbs. The meeting will be illuminated by bollock light. Yes, I do hope that Humphrey will come."

"I am more interested in someone else," confessed Gervase.

"Sister Tecla, by any chance?"

"No, Ralph!"

"She liked you, I could tell."

"I will probably never see her again."

"She'll contrive a tryst somehow," teased the other. "Nuns do not place their affections lightly." The musty atmosphere made him cough. "So who are you interested in meeting in this miserable cave of a hall?"

"Tovild."

"Who?"

"Tovild," said Gervase. "He is mentioned in the returns a number of times. Tovild the Haunted."

"What is it that haunts the man?"

"I have no idea."

"Could it be Humphrey Goldenbollocks?"

"He is too busy haunting Ralph Delchard!"

They traded a laugh and took their seats as Canon Hubert and Brother Simon made their way towards them. The town reeve had been busy. He had not only summoned all interested parties to the meeting, he had arranged for the shire hall to be prepared in readiness for the event. Trestle tables had been set up at one end of the room for the commissioners and chairs had been placed behind them. Ralph took up a central position to reflect his status as leader of the quartet. Gervase sat to one side of him and Hubert to the other. Simon was on the fringe of it all with parchment and writing materials in front of him. Acting as the scribe to the proceedings, he was trying to make himself as invisible as possible. Canon Hubert, by contrast, was more rotundly self-important than ever after another delicious meal at Champeney Hall. He bulked large.

The four of them arrived well before the meeting was due to start so that they could settle in and study once more the various documents relating to the ownership of property in the region. Ralph Delchard also took care with the disposition of his knights. Two of them were stationed outside the main door while the other six stood guard just inside it. Their chain mail had been cleaned, their helmets polished, and their swords freshly sharpened. They made an imposing sight and every visitor would be able to read the message that was implicit in their presence. The royal commissioners were there on serious business.

"Are we ready to receive them?" said Ralph, looking from one colleague to another and receiving affirmative nods from each. "Very well. Let us fight the Battle of Maldon."

He gave a signal to the captain of his guard and the man stepped out into the street. The townspeople then began to drift in. A clerk had been positioned near the entrance so that he could record the name of everyone who attended. First came the burgesses, local men who owned a house, land, or both and thus had a recognised status in the borough. Only a proportionate number had been invited by the town reeve but others came along out of curiosity and apprehension. Royal commissioners were always bad news. The earlier team had caused immense upset in the town with the vigour of their enquiries and the threat of higher taxation. Saxon burgesses were justifiably resentful. Norman overlords had already seized their property and bled them dry. They wished to know what new impositions this second group of royal officials brought with them.

Benches had been set out and the burgesses took those near the rear of the hall, leaving the ones at the front for persons of greater rank. Many of the Norman magnates were absentee landlords and men like Ranulf Peverel, Hugh de Montfort, and Richard FitzGilbert were represented by their subtenants. Peter de Valognes also had some holdings in the area but they were not under investigation by the commissioners. When the Sheriff of Essex finally came to Maldon, therefore, it would be to investigate the murder of a prominent Norman and not to quibble over property rights in the shire hall.

The major landowners who put in an appearance did so with a show of defiance, sweeping into the hall with a clutch of manorial officials around them and lowering themselves onto the front benches with muted truculence. During the visit of the first commissioners, the shire hall had echoed with accusation and counteraccusation and the barons were clearly prepared for further acrimony. Gilbert Champeney was one of the few people present untouched by the prevailing mood of suspicion. Although not called before the commissioners, he nevertheless came to the meeting out of interest and tossed amiable greetings to all and sundry as he made his way to a seat. He was accompanied by his son, Miles, a young man who seemed to have inherited all his father's good qualities while being spared some of his physical shortcomings. Miles Chanpeney was tall, slim, and poised with a quiet handsomeness that was enhanced by a shock of curly fair hair. His tunic and mantle were very much those of a Norman but, like his father, he seemed at ease among the largely Saxon gathering.

"That *has* to be Gilbert's son," whispered Ralph.

"He was away on business last night," said Gervase.

"If I was that young and that good-looking, I would be away on business every night!" said the other with an envious chuckle. "So that is Miles Champeney, is it? He seems a fine, upstanding fellow. I judge him to be a fit companion for you, Gervase."

"For me?"

"He can take you out wenching in the long evenings."

"Ralph!"

"I was like that once, you know. Young and lusty."

"You still are," said Gervase. "That is the trouble."

Ralph let out a peal of laughter that gained everyone's attention. He waved happily in acknowledgement then looked across at the doorway as a newcomer arrived. It was the man for whom they had all been waiting. Jocelyn FitzCorbucion was only the second son of the fearsome Hamo but he still sent a rustle through the entire hall when he stepped into it. With Fulk at his elbow, he stalked to the front of the hall and took a seat directly in front of the table. When Gilbert gave him a smile of welcome, he replied with a pleasant nod but his manner altered dramatically when he saw Miles Champeney. The two young men glared at each other for a second as if engaged in a private tussle, then Jocelyn turned his head away with the faint leer of someone who felt he had won the encounter. Gervase Bret took particular note of their open antipathy.

Ralph did not need to be told that a FitzCorbucion had answered their summons. It was time to begin. He slapped the table and the heavy murmur died instantly.

"Gentlemen," he said in a voice at once friendly and admonitory, "let me thank you all for giving us your time this afternoon. We are royal commissioners who have been sent from Winchester on a most important errand. You have a right to know what that errand is and what manner of men have been dispatched to this pleasant town of yours. My name is Ralph Delchard," he said, "and I am here to judge the fairness of all proceedings that take place. On my right is Canon Hubert of Winchester, a most learned scholar and a most just man. On my left is Gervase Bret, an astute lawyer who will guide us through any disputes with due respect for legality. And at the end of the table is Brother Simon who is our scribe and our touchstone of righteousness." Gilbert Champeney laughed and Simon blinked in meek astonishment. "We are here to perform a vital task," continued Ralph. "If you are honest in your answers and straight in your dealings with us, we will not need to remain here too long. Canon Hubert will explain."

Ralph turned to the prelate, who shuffled his papers.

"I will be brief," he said.

"Praise the Lord for that!" muttered Ralph.

"You will all remember the visit of the first team of royal commissioners." There was a mutinous growl from the body of the hall and he raised his voice to smother it at birth. "Our predecessors were industrious men who laboured hard to produce the returns for the county of Essex. Those returns were sent to the Treasury in Winchester where they will, in the course of time, be transcribed." He increased the volume of his address even more. "*When* certain irregularities have been dealt with. I speak of the illegal acquisition of land."

More rumblings broke out and Ralph had to thump the table to restore calm. He glanced meaningfully at his men to remind his audience that he had the strength of his knights to enforce order upon the proceedings. When a surly silence fell once more on the hall, Canon Hubert resumed.

"The county of Essex is a quarrelsome place," he said with unconcealed distaste. "Shire juries and Hundred juries have heard endless cases of invasions, occupations, ablations, and general misappropriations. The work of our predecessors confirmed this distressing picture. An examination of the returns that they made to Winchester has revealed a pattern of random annexation and nowhere is this more evident than in Maldon." Murmurs of agreement started, but he rode over them like a ship cresting a wave. "King William has sent us here to right any injustices that have come to light. When we have done that, the returns can be amended before being transcribed by the Exchequer clerks to take their place alongside the records of other shires."

Ralph let him speak for another ten minutes before he interrupted the garrulous canon. "We are empowered to call any witnesses," he warned sternly. "No man is too mean to be ignored in our deliberations and no lord too great to refuse our summons." To emphasise the point, his eye rested for a moment on Jocelyn FitzCorbucion and there was a crackle of enmity between the two of them. "We will begin taking the evidence tomorrow. The following persons will be summoned."

Gervase Bret took charge and read a list of names from the document in front of him. The burgesses listened with gathering fascination. Every person mentioned was a Saxon whose land had been forcibly annexed by Hamo FitzCorbucion. The lord of the manor of Blackwater had seen off the first commissioners with an amalgam of bluster and easy duplicity. Could four men with a bundle of documents really uphold the rights of dispossessed Saxons against such a mighty Norman presence? Hamo was omnipotent. Hope nevertheless stirred in the shire hall. Ralph Delchard's force of character, Canon Hubert's open denunciation of illegality, and Gervase Bret's steady litany of injured parties served at least to inspire a guarded confidence. Blackwater Hall was no longer the irresistible force it had been for the last twenty years. Hamo FitzCorbucion was in Normandy, his elder son lay dead, and Jocelyn was as yet unproven in a role of authority. Saxons were encouraged to take heart.

"That concludes our business for the afternoon," said Ralph when the list of witnesses was finally completed. "We start here tomorrow at ten o'clock and we insist on punctuality."

The meeting broke up in an excited babble and the burgesses streamed into the street to compare their reactions to what they had just heard. Some of the Norman landholders and subtenants also departed, peeved that they had been summoned to the hall for such a perfunctory meeting, but reassured by the fact that the investigations were not directed at their property. A few barons stayed to complain and bicker, but Ralph Delchard waved them away with brisk unconcern. Jocelyn FitzCorbucion was not so easily sent on his way. He stood up to confront the commissioners and he spoke with glacial composure.

"I am here on behalf of my father, Hamo FitzCorbucion," he said. "When will we have to appear in person before you?"

"When you are called," said Ralph.

"We require ample notice."

"It is up to us to decide any requirements."

Jocelyn was unruffled. "Do not try to bully us, my lord. We are not mindless Saxons who can be herded like sheep. If you wish for cooperation, you will have to ask for it with sufficient courtesy or your request will be denied. We are not at your beck and call."

"Indeed, you are!" asserted Ralph, rising to his feet. "If you do not come before us when summoned, I will send my men to demand the reason."

Jocelyn raised a mocking eyebrow. "Eight bold knights? Really, my lord! What can you hope to achieve? If your eight dare to venture near Blackwater Hall, they will find ten times that number asking them their business in round terms. You will need a whole army if you intend to offer force."

"We are here by royal warrant!"

"Why so are we, my lord. My father sailed from Normandy in the Conqueror's own ship. He fought at Hastings and he was granted his estates in Maldon as part of his reward. We have charters with the King's seal upon them." He gave a shrug. "They are a form of royal warrant, are they not?"

Ralph was taken aback by the bland assurance of the reply and Jocelyn preened himself. He could see that he had put the commissioner on the defensive and, in the process, he had gained the admiration of his steward. Fulk was pleasantly surprised at the lordly tone that Jocelyn was taking. He had always thought him rather weak and ineffective in the past because he was so easily overshadowed by Guy, but he had clearly underestimated him. Jocelyn might not be as intimidating as his father or as contemptuous of opposition as his brother, yet he had the FitzCorbucion pugnacity, albeit it in a more civilised form.

Gervase Bret came quickly to Ralph's assistance.

"We are not concerned with land that was granted to your father in 1066," he said to Jocelyn. "Our interest is in the frequent annexations that have taken place in the past twenty years."

"They, too, can be supported by charter," said Jocelyn.

"We will put that claim to the test."

"When we decide to call you," added Ralph firmly.

"We will vindicate ourselves," came the confident reply. "If, that is, we decide to answer your summons."

"Would you offer an insult to the King!" growled Ralph.

"He is not here to be insulted, my lord."

"We speak for him!"

"I think you exceed your authority somewhat." Jocelyn was almost taunting them now. "Your predecessors did the same and my father had to teach them some geography. Maldon is a very long way from Winchester."

Ralph went puce with indignation. "Do you *dare* to flout royal commissioners?" he roared.

"God forbid!" exclaimed the other. "I simply remind you that you are in FitzCorbucion territory here. If I summon our men, they will come running in their dozens: If you call for the Conqueror's soldiers, your voice will not reach all the way to Winchester."

"Do not threaten me—*boy*!" said Ralph vehemently.

"I merely suggest that you treat us with respect."

"And I warn you to do the same to us."

"Of course."

Jocelyn gave him a thin smile and a gentle bow. He was relishing his taste of power and felt completely in control of the situation. Before Ralph could upbraid the young man for his impudence, Gervase intervened to deflect them. An argument with the FitzCorbucion family at this stage was pointless and it would not advance their cause in any way. He therefore introduced a more diplomatic note.

"We are sorry to learn of the tragedy at Blackwater Hall, my lord," he said. "That will be borne in mind."

"Why, yes," said Jocelyn, reminded of something that had gone completely from his mind. "It weighs heavily upon us."

"Then we will try not to add to your burden. You have our sympathy and we will show some forbearance." Ralph gurgled at his elbow. "Has the sheriff been informed?"

"Word was sent yesterday to Colchester."

"Is he on his way to the town?"

"Alas, no," said Jocelyn uneasily. "Peter de Valognes is in the middle of Hertfordshire at this time, over three days' ride from here. We cannot look for his assistance yet. We may not, in any case, need it."

"Why?" asked Gervase.

"Because we have identified the killer."

"Is he in custody?"

"He soon will be," said Jocelyn, anxious to discard a topic that had subtly robbed him of the initiative. "But this is a private matter for our family and does not concern you in any way. Excuse us." He mustered his dignity and strode away with Fulk at his heels, pausing in the doorway to deliver a final comment. "We will not obstruct your work here in Maldon as long as you do not, in any way, intrude upon our grief."

They went swiftly out and left Ralph Delchard fuming.

"*I'll* intrude upon his grief!" he vowed. "Give me a sword and I'll add to it. Who does this young upstart think he is? Damnation! He's barely old enough to shave his chin."

"You were wrong to bandy words with him," said Canon Hubert censoriously. "It is Hamo FitzCorbucion that we must stalk and not this whelp. Why waste time on a cub when we need to kill the lion itself?"

"I'll take no lectures on hunting from you, Hubert," said Ralph with asperity. "When did *you* ever track down an animal? This boy had to be put in his place."

"Then it is a pity you did not do it."

Ralph simmered and Gervase stepped in to prevent yet another argument between the two commissioners from getting out of hand. A few inquisitive burgesses still lingered near the door and the town reeve was hovering with a document in his hand. It was important to present a united front to the people of Maldon and not to squabble in front of them. Canon Hubert allowed the tactful intervention but his reproaches were only postponed. When he and Ralph were next alone, he would tax him with his shortcomings. Hubert rose to his feet with a disapproving smile and swept off towards the door with Brother Simon scurrying after him and trying to poke the last of the documents hastily into his leather satchel.

Gervase beckoned the reeve and took the document from him before dismissing him with polite thanks. The soldiers cleared the stragglers out of the hall so that only the two commissioners remained there.

The becalmed Ralph Delchard was rueful.

"It pains me to admit this but—Hubert was right."

His friend nodded. "You should not have lost your temper with that young man."

"He *annoyed* me, Gervase."

"Deliberately."

"I had to respond."

"Not in that way."

"God's tits, I'll not let anyone dictate terms to me!"

"That is why he tried to do so."

"Jocelyn FitzCorbucion threw open defiance at me."

"Couched in moderate language," noted Gervase. "He is a clever advocate who knows the value of keeping a cool head. I look forward to meeting him in legal argument."

"If he will deign to grace us with his presence," said Ralph with heavy sarcasm. "Did you hear what that verminous rogue actually dared to do? He threatened us."

"No, he gave himself away."

"What do you mean?"

"He used his weapon of last resort first, Ralph. If he was that secure in argument, he would not need to thrust his superior numbers at us."

"That is true enough."

"I think he was simply aping his father."

"Yes, Hamo FitzCorbucion is the real malefactor here."

"He is expected back very soon," said Gervase, "so we will be able to take on father and son together. When they have buried another member of the family." His face puckered in thought for a moment. "That was another curious thing. When I asked him about his brother, he needed a second to remember that Guy FitzCorbucion was dead. Would you so easily forget a brother who had been cruelly murdered?"

"I'd not shake off the loss of any loved one," said Ralph soulfully. "When my wife died trying to bring our son into this world, I mourned for a year or more. Nothing could console me, Gervase. I was destroyed."

"You could not say the same of this Jocelyn. He warned us not to intrude upon a grief that did not exist until I jogged his memory about it. What does that tell you?"

"He hated his brother."

"It may go deeper even than that."

"In what way?"

"I have this feeling ..."

"You are missing Alys!"

Gervase ignored the affectionate gibe. "We must look into this murder very closely," he said. "It will tell us a great deal about the FitzCorbucion family and it may—if my instinct is sound—have a direct bearing on our work here."

"How?"

"Wait and see."

"But Jocelyn told us he had already solved the murder."

"He was at pains to make us think he had, Ralph."

"Why?"

"So that he could brush the subject aside," reasoned Gervase. "Put yourself in his position, Ralph. Would *you* have attended a meeting such as this when a brother had recently been killed?"

"I'd have sent my steward to represent me."

"Then why did Jocelyn turn up?"

"To show off his claws and threaten to scratch."

"To prove himself," said Gervase. "Guy's death is not the source of grief it would be for any other brother. It is just a convenient excuse that can be used against us."

"I take your point. There is matter here."

"We must probe it to the full."

"We will," said Ralph with a hollow laugh. "When they have the funeral for Guy FitzCorbucion, I will wait until the gravedigger has done his office and then borrow his spade."

"His spade?"

"To dig up all the other bodies that Hamo has buried."

"There will be enough of them, Ralph, I promise you."

They made to leave and Gervase glanced at the document that the town reeve had given him. It was the list of all the people who had attended the meeting in the shire hall and he ran his eye quickly over it. Disappointment made him purse his lips and shake his head sadly.

"What is the matter?" said Ralph.

"He did not come to the meeting."

"Who?"

"Tovild the Haunted."

"You are obsessed with this man, Gervase."

"A passing interest, no more." He handed the list to his companion. "*Your* friend, however, was here."

"My friend?"

"Humphrey *Aureis testiculi.*"

"You jest with me."

"He was here, I tell you. Look at those names."

Ralph did so and one of them jumped right out at him.

"Humphrey! He exists! He was in this very room!"

"And you did not even notice him," chided Gervase.

"I was too busy," said Ralph, almost distraught. "He was here in front of my nose and I missed him. I will not rest until I *know.*" He executed a dance of delight. "By all, this is wonderful! Goldenbollocks is *real!*"

"He is—and they are."

"You saw him?"

"He was not difficult to pick out."

"In the *flesh*?"

"Humphrey sat in the middle of the hall," said Gervase with mock seriousness, enjoying a chance to tease Ralph for a change. "I singled him out at once."

"But the place was full of people. How ever did you recognise my Humphrey in that crowd?"

"Easily."

"By intuition?"

"No," said Gervase. "Latin translation."

Ralph Delchard shook with mirth for fifteen minutes.

Chapter Four

Maldon Priory was a recent foundation, which had blended so quickly and so easily into its surroundings that it seemed always to have been there. The regular tolling of its little bell was almost as familiar a sound in the town as the incessant cries of its gulls and it was taken for granted in the same way. Some nunneries were simply a part of double-houses and Mass was celebrated by a resident staff of chaplains under the supervision of a chapter priest, but the priory was essentially a female enclave. There were those who maintained that women should be spared the full rigours of the Benedictine Order with its regime of self-denial and its emphasis on the importance of manual labour. Prioress Mindred did not share this view and made few concessions to soften the lives of her nuns. Eight times a day, they entered the miniscule chapel to sing the sequence of offices and each one of them accepted Chapter Forty-eight of the Rule with its unequivocal stipulation—"Idleness is the enemy of the soul. Therefore, the brothers should work with their hands at fixed times of day, and at other fixed times should read sacred works." What was prescribed for the brothers, the prioress believed, should also apply to holy sisters. They, too, had souls.

"Has all been well in my absence, Sister Gunnhild?"

"Yes, Reverend Mother."

"Have you met with any problems?"

"None."

"No misbehaviour to report?"

"Not while I have been in charge here."

Prioress Mindred was alone in her quarters with the stout Sister Gunnhild, who was far and away the most senior and experienced nun at the convent. Gunnhild was a Dane and old enough to remember when a Danish King, Cnut, sat on the throne of England and ruled the country with a mixture of harsh statute and Christian precept. She had been a bride of Christ infinitely longer than Mindred herself and was far more qualified for the office of prioress, but she did not dwell on that thought and instead bent herself readily to the latter's command. Lady Mindred was the widow of a Saxon nobleman, who had left her with substantial wealth and a deep emptiness at the centre of her existence. Since it was her money that founded the priory, she was the natural choice as its first mother and she was delighted when the Abbess of Barking assigned Sister Gunnhild to Maldon to assist her. Mindred's high ideals and Gunnhild's practical experience were a potent combination.

"We are pleased to have you back, Reverend Mother."

"Thank you, Sister Gunnhild."

"How did you find them all at Barking?"

"In good spirits. The abbess sends you her love."

"I hope you conveyed mine to her," said Gunnhild.

"To her and to the holy sisters. You are greatly missed there." The prioress smiled. "But what they have lost, we have certainly gained. You are a foundation stone, Gunnhild."

"I serve God in the way that He chooses for me."

"You are an example to us all."

"So are you, Reverend Mother."

Gunnhild's face was still so hidden by her wimple that only her nose and eyes could be properly seen. Some of those who had come to the priory were still too bound up in the vanities of the world and they had to be taught to neglect their beauty, conceal their hair, and subdue any bodily charms behind the black anonymity of their habits. The severity of a Gunnhild was the desired target to which all the sisters—with greater or lesser degrees of success—endeavoured to aim, but not all of them were fired with the same devotion as the Danish nun. Some had resorted to the cloister because they could find no earthly bridegroom or because they needed a refuge from the continuing turmoil of Norman occupation. Prioress Mindred—herself a late convert to the notion of living in a religious house—was determined to allow no laxity in her tiny community and to turn her nuns into truly spiritual beings, whatever their original motives for taking the veil. In this work, as in every other aspect of the daily round at the priory, Sister Gunnhild's help was absolutely crucial.

A scrunching noise took their attention to the window, which looked out on the garden. They caught a glimpse of bodies bent in toil with rake and hoe. Noblewomen who had never before done manual work of any kind were going about their allotted tasks in the warm sunshine. There was the faintest whisper of complacence in Mindred's voice.

"We are moving forward," she said. "We had to employ carpenters to build this priory and some masons to erect the chapel but our holy sisters have created the garden out of a wilderness. Our kitchens already cook vegetables that we have grown ourselves and our own fruit trees will yield their harvest in a year or two." She glanced across at the embroidered portrait, which hung on the wall. "St. Benedict was right. Idleness is truly the enemy of the soul."

"Work has its own dignity," said Gunnhild humbly, "and women may learn its value in the same way as men."

"Work and study. It is the perfect life for all." She indicated the books that lay on the table beside her. "We brought these gifts back from Abbess Aelfgiva. They will enrich our minds and provide spiritual nourishment."

"May I see them, Reverend Mother?"

"Please do."

"Our library is expanding," said Gunnhild, picking up the books one by one in her pudgy fingers to examine them. "These are exceptional gifts. I look forward to being able to peruse these works in detail. They are suitable additions to our stock and will guide the minds of our holy sisters in the right direction. Especially Sister Lewinna."

"Sister Lewinna?"

"I caught her reading Aesop's *Fables* again."

"That is no disgrace. I donated the copy myself."

"Sister Lewinna was *laughing.*"

"Aesop has a strong sense of humour."

"There is no place for laughter here," said Gunnhild earnestly. "I had to impress that upon Lewinna. She still has much to learn. Aesop was no Christian and his tales of animals may lead a lighter mind astray."

Prioress Mindred did not entirely agree but she had no wish to take issue with Sister Gunnhild. The library helped to shape the character of the nuns. Lady Mindred was an educated widow who had presented an English translation of Aesop because she felt its harmless stories embodied eternal truths about the human condition. Gunnhild was a cultured nun who had read the author in the original Greek and found it streaked with a levity she thought unbecoming. It was one small instance of the differences that existed, at a deep and largely unacknowledged level, between the two women.

There was work to do. During her absence, the prioress had left all the administrative chores to Gunnhild but she now had to take up the reins herself. It was time to go through the priory account book, a volume of such functional solemnity that it was in no danger of provoking Aesopian amusement. As Gunnhild took her place at the table beside her prioress, she touched on a subject that had caused her deep anxiety.

"Sister Tecla has told me of your ordeal," she said.

"It was most unfortunate."

"The world is not safe when holy nuns can be set upon by a band of robbers. I beg of you not to stir from here again unless it be with a larger escort."

"The journey was imperative, Sister Gunnhild."

"I appreciate that."

"And we did have the strong arm of St. Oswald to guard us on our way home. He saved our lives."

"God bless the noble saint!"

"Honest men came to our rescue."

"So I heard from Sister Tecla."

"They were kind and considerate to us," said Mindred as she recalled me commissioners. "I am a true Saxon with a natural fear of Norman soldiers but nobody could have offered us finer protection or more congenial company."

"Perhaps too congenial."

"Why do you say that?"

"Out of concern for Sister Tecla." Gunnhild voiced her criticism in tones of complete humility. "It is not for me to question your decisions, Reverend Mother, because my duty is to obey at all times and I do so willingly. When these men came to your aid, it was natural for you to express your thanks and accept their protection. But Sister Tecla should not have been exposed to conversation with them. She took the veil to avoid the world of men and she was distressed by the closeness of their questioning."

"She did not complain to me."

"Sister Tecla preferred to suffer in silence."

"Is that what she told you, Sister Gunnhild?"

"Not in so many words," admitted the other, "but that is what has emerged. I saw the young man who brought you back to the priory. He troubled her. I sensed it. He helped her down from her horse too readily."

"Only after he had helped me," said the prioress. "His name is Gervase Bret and he was charming."

The word slipped out before she could stop it and it brought a momentary flash of disgust into Gunnhild's eyes.

"Charming?" she repeated dully.

It sounded like an obscenity on her lips and had even less place in a convent than a copy of Aesop's *Fables*. Yet another hidden difference between the two of them had briefly surfaced. Although Mindred had committed herself totally to the religious life, she had not yet expunged all traces of her former existence. One word had proved that. She could still take pleasure in male company and find the attraction of a young man worth an admiring comment. It was inappropriate and she regretted it at once. To cover her embarrassment, she opened the account book and pretended to read through the latest entries.

Sister Gunnhild was able to apply some gentle pressure.

"We must do all we can to help Sister Tecla over this."

"I will pray with her."

"It may take more man prayer, Reverend Mother."

Prioress Mindred could see what she was being asked. Sister Gunnhild was in an attitude of submission but she was still applying tender force. Her exaggerated humility could be a strong weapon and the prioress was for once unable to deflect it by asserting her own authority. A silent battle of power went on for a couple of minutes before Mindred eventually capitulated.

"Very well," she said. "You must look after her."

Sister Gunnhild was content.

Ralph Delchard took a cheerfully irreverent view of those in ecclesiastical office and it made his relationship with men like Canon Hubert one of fluctuating tensions. As a Norman soldier whose life had been shaped by victory on the field of battle, he also had a haughty disregard for the conquered Saxons and considered their language, customs, and appearance to be markedly inferior to those of his own nation. Oslac the Priest disarmed him completely. Here was an ecclesiastic whom it was impossible to deride and a Saxon whom it was difficult to dislike. Ralph could not but admire the man's bearing, forthright manner, and ability to look anyone in the eye. He had none of the awkward deference or dumb insolence of his compatriots. Conquest had not subdued him in any way. It had simply altered the circumstances in which he lived. Oslac had the kind of flinthard integrity that no invading army could destroy.

They walked the short distance from the shire hall to the Church of All Souls' and found the priest alone in his vestry. The town reeve had told them that the body of Guy FitzCorbucion lay in the mortuary chapel. It was enough to take Ralph Delchard and Gervase Bret there in search of information about the murder. They introduced themselves to Oslac and were given a cordial welcome. Although he had not been at the meeting, the priest seemed to know everything that had transpired in the shire hall that afternoon.

"You have given the people of Maldon some hope," he said affably. "That is a rare commodity in this town."

"We are here to dispense justice," said Ralph.

"That, too, has been in short supply of late." He waved them to the bench, which stood against the wall in the little vestry, then waited till they were seated. "How may I help you?" he offered.

"We are interested in this case of murder," said Ralph.

"So is the whole town, my lord. Guy FitzCorbucion was a forceful young man. He made his presence felt in every way. His death has set tongues wagging all over Maldon."

"With delight, from what I hear."

"That is not for me to say."

"Is the name of the murderer known?"

"Not for certain, my lord."

"Jocelyn FitzCorbucion seemed to think it was."

"He was referring to the boy."

"What boy?"

"Wistan, son of Algar." Oslac rested himself against the edge of the table and chose his words with care. "You will not need to be told that Blackwater Hall is the manor house of Hamo FitzCorbucion. He rules his demesne with firmness and his elder son, Guy, did likewise in his absence. One of the slaves on the estate was stricken with the ague. I myself was called to Algar and tried to arrest his fever with medicines but his condition was too serious. A sick man is unable to work. He was reported to Guy FitzCorbucion."

"Who punished him for laziness," guessed Ralph.

"Yes, my lord," said Oslac. "I was not there myself so I have only the word of eyewitnesses but they all vouch the same. The order was given to tie Algar up so that he could be whipped. His diseased old body would have been cut to shreds. He tried to fight back but Guy was far too strong for him. Algar died."

"Died—or was murdered?"

"The steward assured me that it was an accident."

"He would," said Ralph. "I believe I met the fellow at the shire hall and set him down for a liar on sight. How many other accidents have there been at Blackwater Hall?"

"This is not the first, my lord."

Ralph's ire was roused. "Guy FitzCorbucion intended to murder this wretch with the end of a whip but did it with his own hands instead. How does it sound to you, Gervase?"

"It could be argued that he killed in self-defence."

"A fit young man against a fever-ridden slave?" Ralph turned to Oslac again. "Was there no cure for his ague?"

"None, my lord. He would have died within a week."

"But Guy helped him on his way," he smacked his thigh in disgust. "This is brave work indeed! I have no sympathy for a slave who attacks a master. Underlings must know their place. But this is something of a different order. I would not treat a dog the way that Guy treated this poor man."

"You mentioned a son," recalled Gervase.

"Wistan. A boy of fifteen."

"Was he present?"

"Yes," said Oslac with a sigh. "Wistan was forced to witness it all. Such a tragedy was bound to etch itself deeply in his young mind and foster great bitterness. He was vengeful, that cannot be denied. I counselled acceptance of what had happened but he would not hear me. Wistan is a strong-willed boy. He vowed to kill Guy FitzCorbucion."

"And did he?" asked Gervase.

"I honestly cannot say."

"What does your instinct tell you?" said Ralph.

"No," decided the priest without hesitation. "Wistan is innocent."

"Guilty of the wish but innocent of the deed."

"Yes, my lord." He gave a shrug. "But I could be wrong."

Ralph leaned back and appraised the man. Oslac had been careful not to take sides. The death of Guy FitzCorbucion was being welcomed as a boon by almost every other Saxon in the town, but the priest had room in his heart both for the slave whom he had buried a week earlier and for the young Norman who had killed him and who now lay on the stone slab in his mortuary. There was nothing sanctimonious about Oslac the Priest. He was a practical Christian who served all his parishioners with undiscriminating care. Nor were his duties confined to the church itself. He not only conducted regular services in Latin and preached on occasion to his congregation, but he also tended the sick, relieved the poor, heard confession, arbitrated in disputes between neighbours, and acted as a reassuring wall against common fears of hell and damnation. Oslac was a friend, guide, and—until the Conquest robbed him of his land—a fellow farmer to the whole community. He refused to sit in judgement, even on such an incorrigible sinner as Guy FitzCorbucion.

"I have a favour to ask of you," said Ralph, getting to his feet. "May we view the body?"

"I fear not, my lord."

"It would take no more than a minute."

"It is not a favour I am in a position to grant," said Oslac. "You would need the permission of the family before you could be allowed into the mortuary."

"They would certainly refuse."

"Without question."

Ralph changed his tack. "This is important to us. It may have serious implications for our work here in Maldon. We would appreciate your help." He gave a confiding smile. "The family would not have to know about it."

"*I* would know, my lord," said Oslac firmly. "That is why I may not permit it. I guard that body as a sacred trust."

"We have no right whatsoever to trespass on that," conceded Gervase in a conciliatory tone. "But *you* have seen the body, Father Oslac, and that may be enough."

"In what way?"

"To begin with, you can tell us the cause of death."

"A knife wound through the heart."

"In his chest or in his back?"

"Both. There were fifteen stab wounds in all."

"A most thorough assassin," noted Ralph. "How long had Guy been dead when his body was found?"

"It is impossible to say with any accuracy."

"If you had to make a guess ..."

"Two, maybe three days," said Oslac. "My work here has made me closely acquainted with death and it has distinctive marks. When a body lies in water for any length of time, a number of things happen to it. First of all—"

"Omit the details," interrupted Ralph with a squeamish expression, not wishing to hear about the destructive properties of water. "A time is all we need. Two or three days?"

"That is what I would estimate."

"Who found the body?" said Gervase.

"Brunloc. A fisherman."

"Could we speak to him?"

"If you wish."

"Where could we find him?"

"Out in his boat, most of the time."

"This is work for you, Gervase," said Ralph quickly. "I will not venture near the sea except by compulsion. I have no love for surging waves."

"The sea is over ten miles away, my lord," said Oslac.

"Your gulls tell me otherwise."

"Meet Brunloc at the Hythe," suggested the priest. "I can arrange that for you."

"We accept that offer with gratitude," said Gervase. "A moment ago, you told us you did not think that Wistan was the killer of Guy FitzCorbucion."

"I also told you that I could be wrong."

"Is the boy capable of murder?"

"Indeed, he is. Wistan felt he had just cause. And he did run away once the corpse was discovered. That brought suspicion down on his head." Oslac gave it some more thought then reaffirmed his instinct. "But I still feel that this is not his doing."

"Why?"

"Because Wistan would strike in anger. A wild assault. And there is clear calculation in this attack."

"Calculation?" said Ralph.

"The body was mutilated."

"Fifteen stab wounds, you said.'"

"There was something else, my lord."

"Well?" Ralph saw the man's reluctance and tried to overcome it with a softer tone. "Something else?"

The priest threw a glance towards the mortuary. "I would not have this voiced abroad," he insisted.

"You have our word on that," promised Gervase.

"The truth has even been kept from Guy's own sister."

"We will not breathe it to a soul," vowed Ralph.

"That is vital." Oslac studied the two men closely until he was sure that he could trust them. They were royal commissioners who had been selected by the Conqueror himself for a complex mission and that said much about their character and their quality. There was also a sense of candour about them, which appealed to the priest. In a town where deceit and prevarication were found at every turn, it was refreshing to meet two people with such a clear-eyed commitment to truth. Oslac knew he could put his faith in them and he lowered his voice before continuing. "When the body was found," he explained, "it had been stripped of much of its clothing."

"What form did the mutilation take?" said Gervase.

"He was castrated."

There was a long and uneasy pause as the visitors absorbed this new intelligence and tried to wonder at its meaning. They plied Oslac with further questions but there was nothing more that he was able or prepared to add. When they pressed him for the names of other possible suspects, he refused to point a finger at anyone. His task was to bring some comfort to the bereaved family and not to indulge in speculation about the identity of the killer. They respected his position and thanked him for the help that he had been able to give. Oslac showed them out and walked through the little cemetery with them. The priory bell began to toll in the distance and it unlocked a memory.

"You were mentioned in prayers," he said. "Prioress Mindred and her sisters were intensely grateful for the protection you gave them on their journey. God's blessing was called down upon you."

Ralph grinned. "I can think of other ways in which the nuns could have shown their thanks but they may not fall within the rules of the Benedictine Order."

"I am certain of it," said Gervase crisply, then turned to the priest. "You visited the priory?"

"I do so on a regular basis to take Mass."

"Then you know its inner workings."

"I know only what they wish me to know," replied Oslac. "And that is as it should be. A convent of holy sisters is a community that looks inward and needs no interference from outside. They accept me at the priory but they administer it entirely by themselves."

"Prioress Mindred seems a capable woman," said Gervase.

"Extremely capable."

"I was more impressed by Sister Tecla," opined Ralph. "Even in her nun's attire, she struck me as a most attractive young woman and her voice was bewitching. What makes such a lovely creature as that turn her back on the world?"

"The call from God."
"I wish she had heard my call first."
"You must forgive Ralph," said Gervase quickly. "He is unaccustomed to the meaning of a spiritual life."
His colleague beamed. "Sister Tecla must instruct me."
"She has other preoccupations," said Oslac with a smile that showed he had taken no offence. "All ecclesiastical institutions have a special function to perform and the priory is no exception. It fulfills its purpose in the most striking way and I have nothing but praise for the holy sisters. They are all quite remarkable servants of God."
"Does that include Sister Gunnhild?" asked Gervase.
"Sister Gunnhild?"
"I met her when I arrived," he said. "The lady was less than friendly to me. Since I helped to escort her prioress and one of the sisters all the way back to Maldon, Sister Gunnhild might at least have shown a token of gratitude."
"She thanked you in her prayers," assured Oslac.
"That was not the impression I received."
"Do not worry about it, Gervase," said Ralph jovially. "You cannot expect your boyish appeal to win the heart of every woman. Sister Tecla fell in love with you—what more do you want? Forget this Sister Gunnhild."
"I simply wished to know more about her," said Gervase, unhappy at the teasing reference to Tecla. "The lady puzzled me, that is all. Her manner was peculiar." He turned to the priest. "Can you tell us anything about her?"
"Gunnhild is a true Christian," said Oslac.
"Of Danish stock, by the name."
"Indeed, she is, though born and brought up in Maldon."
"What did I do that upset her so much?"
"You share a grievous fault with me, I fear."
"With *you,* Father Oslac?"
The priest chuckled. "We are both men."
"Does she hate the sex so violently?" asked Ralph.
"No," said Oslac, "she just considers us irrelevant. A convent is by definition an exclusively female community and Sister Gunnhild sets great store by that." He put a hand on his chest. "In my case, I have to confess, she has a further cause for disapproval."
"What is that?" said Gervase.
"I am married."
Ralph Delchard laughed in surprise and warmed even more to the man. He despised the whole notion of celibacy and was delighted to find that the Church of All Souls' was served by a flesh-and-blood priest with the promptings common to normal human beings. Vows of chastity left a person with the bloodless pallor of a Brother Simon

or the porcine sheen of a Canon Hubert Oslac the Priest, by contrast, had a ruddy complexion and a twinkle in his eye, both of which Ralph ascribed to the presence of a woman in his bed at nights. Gervase Bret took even more interest in the news because it mirrored his own intent. It was love of Alys that had made him abandon his novitiate at Eltham Abbey and it was the prospect of marriage to her that gave his life such joy and direction. Gervase was touched by Oslac's readiness to confide in them.

"You are a bold man," he said. "Archbishop Lanfranc has attacked clerical marriage."

"Archbishop Lanfranc is a monk."

"He frowns upon relations with the fairer sex."

"The Archbishop of Canterbury is a great man who serves a great king," said Oslac, "and he has made substantial improvements to the Church since he was appointed. I am more than willing to accept his rulings on almost everything else but I will not divorce my wife because of his frown. My own father was a married priest and I inherited this benefice from him. I am hopeful that my son will take over here from me in due course."

"Your son?" said Ralph. "You have children?"

"Four."

"No wonder Sister Gunnhild dislikes you!" said Gervase.

They shared a communal laugh. It was time to leave Maldon and ride back to Champeney Hall but the two commissioners were glad that they had taken the trouble to meet Oslac the Priest. His help was invaluable. Their host had showered them with information about the town and its personalities while Gilbert Champeney dealt only in gossip and anecdote. Oslac's comments were at once more interesting and reliable. He lived at the very heart of the community in every sense and was thus more intimately acquainted with its nuances of behaviour. They liked him and resolved to call on him again before they finally departed from Maldon.

Ralph had been toying with the idea of asking about the origin of Humphrey's nickname but the nature of Guy FitzCorbucion's mutilation had somehow deprived him of that urge. A question that would in any case be improper to a priest had now become severely distasteful as well so Ralph mastered his curiosity. Instead, it was Gervase who sought elucidation.

"Do you know a man called Tovild?" he asked.

"I know three or four by that name," replied Oslac.

"This one is unusual."

"Then you are asking about Tovild the Haunted."

Gervase was pleased. "You *know* him?"

"Of course. We all know Tovild the Haunted."

"Who is he?"

"As harmless an old man as you could wish to meet."

"But where did he get his name?" asked Ralph. "Put Gervase out of his misery, I beg you, or I will have no respite from his ceaseless prattle about this Tovild the Haunted. Who is this fellow?"

"And what is it that haunts him?" said Gervase.

Oslac gazed in the direction of Northey Island.

"The Battle of Maldon."

* * *

Dusk encouraged him to move more freely about the island. Wistan had now got through the best part of a second day without detection and it bred even more confidence in him. He was learning to think like a fugitive and to see the folly of trusting in a single hiding place. He needed a variety of cover so that he could shift easily from one burrow to another, then on again to a third or fourth, when they finally came for him. Therefore, Wistan chose a series of locations where thick undergrowth or favourable contours could be used for concealment, and he practised scurrying between them at full pelt. The playful exercise cheered him. Time passed and drained even more colour out of the cloudless sky.

Two problems vexed him. The first was the possible use of animals to track him down. Like all Norman barons, Hamo FitzCorbucion was immensely fond of hunting and he kept a pack of hounds to help him pursue deer and wild boar. Those dogs could just as easily be turned on a human quarry and Wistan could never kill fifty baying dogs with a knife and a desire for revenge. A tree would give him a degree of safety if he climbed high enough, but the hounds might sniff him out and he would be trapped. His only salvation lay in the River Blackwater and it was to the muddy coastline that he now turned his interest. Water did not bear scent. Hiding places in the shallows or among the reeds would even defeat the delicate nostrils of hunting dogs.

Wistan's second problem was more serious. A fugitive could not himself be in pursuit of a prey. His lust for vengeance boiled inside him but it would not be satisfied as long as he stayed on Northey Island. Guy FitzCorbucion was dead but Hamo was the head of the family and Wistan had to execute him for his own father's sake. Jocelyn, too, deserved to die because he bore a reviled name and because he stood by and watched Algar being humiliated by Guy. In his swirling rage, Wistan even wanted to destroy Matilda as well so that the entire FitzCorbucion family were obliterated from Blackwater Hall.

But how was he to do it? He could hardly expect Hamo or Jocelyn to come obligingly onto the island with no soldiers at their back. When they hunted him, they would do so in force and Wistan would be lucky to see—let alone to get within striking distance—of the two men whose deaths he had sworn to bring about. If the ravens of Black-water would not come on their own to him, then he would have to go to them. He had no idea how he could possibly do this without taking unnecessary risks, but a vague plan began to form and it so filled his mind with its daring that it made him unwary. He strolled towards the margin of the water as unguardedly as if he owned the whole island.

The noise of the spear awoke him at once and he flung himself on his stomach in the reeds. Had he been seen? The soldier was clearly heading in his direction. Wistan cursed himself for being so careless. Two days of freedom had been thrown away in a second's inattention. His knife jumped into his hand but it would be no match for the spear that had been hurled with force into a fallen log. The sound still reverberated in his ears. That same spear could impale him to the ground if he lay there motionless. He had to escape somehow. Pulling his knees forward, he raised himself slowly and peered over the swaying tops of the reeds. It was difficult to see anything in the twilight but he knew the soldier was still there. He could hear the clash of a sword on a shield and a guttural battle cry. Was the man summoning the rest of the hunting party? When would they unleash their attack?

Wistan was about to take to his heels when he noticed something that stilled his fears. The man was old. He moved slowly. What he put his sword into his belt and tried to pull the spear from the log, he could not at first dislodge the weapon. It took him a couple of minutes of tugging and twisting before the head of the spear consented to part company with the timber and, in doing so, it threw him right off balance. Wistan saw something else. The soldier was not, as he had imagined, in the mailed hauberk of a Norman knight. He wore a long woollen coat, belted at the waist and reaching to mid-thigh. His legs were encased in tight trousers and his shoes were made of leather. The Norman helm that Wistan thought he had seen was, in fact, a conical helmet of iron with a thick nasal. Spear and sword were heavy implements of war and the long oval shield was embossed with a simple design at its centre. Wistan was utterly baffled.

The old man charged on unsteady limbs towards an invisible enemy and jabbed at the air with his spear. His war cry had been replaced by some kind of chant but the boy was too far away to pick out any of the words. Wistan's main concern was that he had not given himself away. He was safe. This strange creature who fought a nonexistent battle in the fading light on Northey Island had not come in search of him, and he was certainly not a member of the FitzCorbucion retinue. He was not a Norman knight at all. What Wistan was looking at was a Viking warrior in full battle dress.

Tovild the Haunted was on the rampage once again.

The cook excelled himself. The meal that was served at Champeney Hall that evening was so rich and appetising that even Brother Simon could not refuse it all. Meat, fish, and poultry of the highest quality were placed before the visitors and the aroma alone was enough to make Canon Hubert's mouth water with anticipation. Among a selection of fine dishes, he found the grilled quail most to his liking and he munched his way through four of them between frequent sips of wine. For those who preferred it, ale that had been spiced and honeyed was also available. A whole array of pies and puddings was brought in to complete what had been a virtual banquet.

Gilbert Champeney had even arranged for minstrels to play at the far end of the hall so that the frugal nibbling of Brother Simon was accompanied by the strains of an Irish ham and the noisy gormandising of Canon Hubert was sweetened by the plangent harmonies of the lyre. At his host's elbow, Ralph Delchard ate heartily and drank with enthusiasm while listening to Gilbert's amiable chatter. Gervase Bret dined with his usual moderation and took the opportunity, when the repast was almost over, to converse with Miles Champeney. The young man was pleasant and well mannered but unaccountably reserved, and Gervase was not sure if this was due to a natural shyness or if his companion was seeking to hide something. Miles was patently not at ease. From time to time, he seemed to wince involuntarily as he overheard some snatch of his father's banter. Gilbert Champeney clearly had the power to make his son squirm with embarrassment.

"We must congratulate your cook," said Gervase.

"Father brought him over from Normandy," said Miles. "He loves all things Saxon but he found their diet a little too plain and coarse."

"Do you share his admiration for the Saxons?"

"Not entirely."

Gervase waited for an explanation that did not come. The young man sipped his wine watchfully and waited for the next question. It was evident that he himself would not initiate any conversation.

"Essex is a strange county," observed Gervase. "Well over four hundred settlements were recorded by our predecessors yet you only have two of any size—Maldon and Colchester. Why is that, do you think?"

"I have no idea."

"Does it say something about the spirit of the people who live in this shire? Do they value their independence? Do they prefer life in a smaller community? Or is it to do with the geography of this part of the country?" He paused long enough to see that no answer was forthcoming and then he pressed on. "King William has not been kind to Essex."

"Kind?"

Gervase smiled. "Perhaps one should not look for kindness in a conqueror," he remarked, "but other shires have been treated with far less severity. Your father may love the Saxons but the King seems to have chosen Essex in order to show his hatred of them. Its history is one long tale of confiscation and loss. Did you know that less than one man in ten can now call himself free? Half the population of this county are mere bordars."

Miles was noncommittal. "It is not my doing."

"One is bound to be sympathetic, surely?"

But Gervase could still not draw him out. Whatever his views on the subject, Miles Champeney was not prepared to share them with him. The father could not be stopped from burbling about the cumulative indignities suffered by the Saxon community in Essex, but the son had nothing whatsoever to add. Gervase sensed deliberate evasion and so he switched to a topic he was fairly certain would elicit some kind of comment from the taciturn young man.

"We saw you in the shire hall this afternoon."

"Did you?"

"Why did you attend?"

"Father asked me to accompany him."

"What did you think of the proceedings?"

"They held my attention," said Miles levelly.

Gervase began to fish. "As you heard, Blackwater Hall is one of our main concerns. Hamo FitzCorbucion has increased his holdings quite appreciably in the past twenty years and not always by legal means." He looked artlessly at the other man. "How did he manage to get away with it?"

"That is for you to find out, Master Bret."

"Is there nobody in the town to stand up to him?"

"It appears not."

"Everyone seems to loathe the FitzCorbucions. They have annexed land on every side of them and behaved as if they are the royal family of Maldon." Gervase scrutinised the impassive face in front of him. "Is that why so few people mourn the death of Guy FitzCorbucion?"

Miles was enigmatic. "He was not popular."

"I gathered that," said Gervase. "In fact, when I read through all those names of dispossessed Saxons, I had the feeling that I was calling out a list of suspects."

"Suspects?"

"For his murder. They all had a motive to kill him."

"Hamo is the lord of the manor and not Guy."

"Of course," said Gervase, "but his elder son seems to have excited even greater hostility for some reason. We have not heard a good word said about Guy FitzCorbucion since we arrived in Maldon." He cast his line into the water again. "Can *you* say anything in the young man's favour?"

Miles was emphatic. "No," he said.

"That conforms to the general feeling."

"I had no time for Guy."

"Nor for Jocelyn, I noticed."

"Jocelyn?"

"You and he were highly displeased to see each other."

"I think you are mistaken about that."

"Your manner could hardly be called friendly," said Gervase. "In fact, it was downright—"

"Please excuse me," said Miles, rising to his feet to terminate the exchange. "It is late."

"Is there some particular animosity between you?"

"I am tired. I need my rest."

Miles Champeney spoke with politeness but there was no mistaking the glint of anger in his eyes. Gervase was deeply annoyed with himself. He had been too heavy-handed in his questioning and frightened the young man away. When Miles took his leave of the company and headed for the door, he shot a hurt look back at his interrogator. The father might be thrilled to have the royal commissioners under his roof but the son did not extend the same welcome. Gervase had definitely alienated him.

The departure of one person was the cue for others to struggle up from the table and find their way to their chambers. Gilbert Champeney, attentive host and indefatigable gossip, was left with only Ralph Delchard, Gervase Bret, and Canon Hubert for company. Emboldened by the wine, the prelate decided that this was the moment to take Ralph to task for his conduct of that afternoon's meeting.

"We shall proceed more briskly tomorrow," he said.

"Why?" joked Ralph. "Do you intend to stay away?"

"No, my lord. Since you did not control matters to my satisfaction, I intend to take a more active part. Watch me and you will learn what advocacy is."

"Gluttony, you mean." Ralph appealed to the others with outstretched hands. "Have you ever seen so much food eaten so fast? Ten quails went into that round belly."

"Four," said Hubert.

"Four, ten, twenty—what does it matter?" said Gilbert with a nervous laugh. "Food is one of the joys of life. When you sit at my table, take as much as you wish."

"Thank you, noble sir," said Hubert before swinging his purple cheeks around to face Ralph once more. "You are only trying to deflect me, my lord. My argument remains valid. I have the greater experience in legal matters so I should lead the way. I have no peer in the ecclesiastical courts."

"We are not in the ecclesiastical courts," reminded Gervase. "There is a world of difference between property disputes and the intricacies of canon law."

"I can master any charter of land," boasted Hubert.

Ralph grinned. "How many quails can you eat per acre?"

"Be serious!"

"I am in too merry a mood."

"We are here on urgent business."

"Granted," said Ralph, "but we must discharge our duties in the right place and at the right time. We must not bore our host with our petty squabbles." He emptied the wine in his cup. "If you want an argument to round off a splendid evening, then I have just the subject for you."

"What is it?" said Gilbert eagerly. "I adore argument."

"Marriage."

"Marriage?" echoed the canon.

"Clerical marriage."

"It is an abomination!"

"Yet there *are* married priests," said Gervase.

"A vice peculiar to the Saxons."

"That's why I find them so endearing," said Gilbert.

"Norman clerks have married," resumed Ralph, determined to get his colleague on the run. "Many have had mistresses. Some have had wives *and* mistresses."

"Archbishop Lanfranc has expressly forbidden it!"

"I know, Hubert. But the good archbishop cannot stand by the bed of every priest and monk in England to make sure that they get into it alone."

Gilbert sniggered. "Were you never tempted by female flesh, Canon Hubert?"

"Never, sir!"

"What about male flesh?" said Ralph, chuckling at the prelate's apoplectic reaction. "A pity!" he said. "You could otherwise have married Gilbert's wondrous cook and dined on grilled quail for the rest of your life."

"I'll not hear any more of this!" yelled Hubert.

"But you have not given us your view on marriage."

"I embody it!"

He manoeuvered his bulk into a vertical position and then lurched off towards the chamber, which he shared with Brother Simon. There, at least he could be assured of the total respect to which he felt his position entitled him and spend a chaste night in the company of an ascetic man who viewed the whole concept of marriage as anathema.

Gervase was conscious of the testing day ahead of them.

"Perhaps it is time we all retired," he suggested.

"I could sleep for a week," said Ralph, succumbing to fatigue. "That was a magnificent feast, Gilbert. If Hubert does not marry your cook, then *I* may!"

"He is already married."

"Do not tell that to our testy canon."

They got up from the table and walked towards the door in the flickering candlelight. Champeney Hall was unlike any Norman dwelling they had been in before and its atmosphere was curiously inviting. Ralph Delchard was drowsy but he was determined to ask one last question before he collapsed into his bed. He put an arm around Gilbert's shoulders.

"You must know every man in Maldon, dear friend."

"In person."

"So who is this Humphrey?"

"Humphrey?"

"*Aureis testiculi,*" said Gervase.

"Goldenbollocks," translated Ralph.

"Ah, *that* Humphrey!" Gilbert went off into a paroxysm of giggling, then he waved Ralph away. "I am sorry, sir. I cannot tell you how he acquired the nickname. It is a secret."

"But it torments me," said Ralph.

"How do you think Humphrey feels?"

Their host giggled afresh and leaned against a beam for support. Ralph pressed him for an explanation but in vain. On this topic, if on no other, Gilbert was discreet. Ralph gave up. After thanking him once more for his hospitality, he rolled off towards his chamber. Gervase was about to go with him when he was detained by a hand. Gilbert Champeney was not giggling now. His face was dark and his manner suddenly quite serious. Gervase thought that he had been caught up in the jollity of the occasion but his host had missed nothing of what went on around his table.

"You must forgive my son," he said.

"There is nothing to forgive."

"You touched a raw spot, I fear."

"I merely asked him about Jocelyn FitzCorbucion," said Gervase. "They obviously did not like each other."

"With good cause." Gilbert sighed. "A sad business."

"Why?"

"One of the perils of fatherhood."

"Perils?"

"Raising a son who does not take your advice."

"You lose me here," said Gervase.

"Miles is not to blame—*they* are."

"They?"

"Hamo and his monstrous brood." Gilbert sighed again. "Jocelyn has two reasons for hating my son. Miles fought with his brother, Guy."

"Fought? With weapons?"

"Hot words and fists, that is all. But I am told that my son got the better of it before the two of them were dragged apart." He became remorseful. "Miles was a fool! I warned him not to go there. I told him to stay away from Blackwater Hall. It was bound to lead to trouble."

"What was?"

"The situation, the situation. It's hopeless!"

Gilbert broke away and paced up and down in the narrow corridor. The bibulous host was now an anxious parent. His hands flapped about in gestures of despair. Gervase stepped in to confront him.

"Jocelyn had two reasons, you said ..."

"It was the other one that took him there."

"To Blackwater Hall?"

"Jocelyn has a sister. Matilda."

"I begin to understand."

"That is more than I do, Gervase," said the other. "It is a cruelty practised on a loving father. Why Matilda? Of all people—why *her*? My son could have any woman in the county, if he wanted, but he chooses a FitzCorbucion."

"Does the lady feel the same about him?"

"She does, alas!"

"You are obviously against the match."

"Everyone is," wailed Gilbert. "I am against it, Hamo is against it, Guy was against it—that is why he came to blows with my son—and Jocelyn is against it. Common sense is against it. Sanity is against it. Nature is against it."

"But Miles is still determined?"

"They have exchanged vows."

"How do they contrive to see each other?"

"They do not," said Gilbert. "Hamo has left orders that my son is not to be allowed near Blackwater Hall. But that does not deter him. He swears that he will wed Matilda."

Sorrow had finally taken its toll of Matilda FitzCorbucion. After another day of anger at her brother's death, its full impact hit her at last and she spent a sleepless night crying into her pillow or walking across the wooden floor of her bedchamber in her bare feet. The tears came less from love than from pity, because even a brother as disagreeable as Guy deserved that. As her grief deepened into a physical pain such as she had never known, Matilda came to see that she was mourning two brothers and not just one. Jocelyn was lost to her almost as much as Guy. When he was alive, Guy had either ignored or baited her and she had learned to avoid him whenever possible. Jocelyn had been her protector even when it landed him in trouble and she could always turn to him for help. That was all in the past. The moment the dead body of his brother had been found, Jocelyn changed irrevocably. He was no longer Matilda's friend but simply a more refined and calculating version of Guy.

In the long reaches of the night, other thoughts came to stick hot needles of doubt into her brain. They were vulnerable. The most powerful family in Maldon was not the impregnable force she had supposed. Blackwater Hall might have the sombre solidity of a castle but its defences had been breached. Guy FitzCorbucion, a virile soldier with great skill in arms, had been cruelly murdered and the alleged killer was a boy of fifteen. What surging hatred must have built up inside the lad for him to commit such a heinous crime? Would such blood-lust be satiated with one death or would he turn to strike at other members of the family? The name that she had carried with such pride now seemed like a badge of doom and fear for her own life sent her racing to the heavy door to make sure that it was bolted. Fresh tears moistened her haggard face. She was grieving over the loss of her safety. Matilda was terrified.

Searching for comfort, she found none within Blackwater Hall. Jocelyn was dead to her and Hamo would be so furious when he discovered what had happened that she would not even be able to speak to him. After her mother's death, the person who had consoled her least was her father. Hamo was a hard and ambitious man who took what he wanted by force of character and expressed affection only by means of gifts. Matilda's plight was helpless. A home that was already fraught with tensions would now become unbearable and there would be nobody to whom she could turn. Except perhaps one man. But even as she envisioned the kind face of Miles Champeney, she knew that he could not save her either. The murder of Guy FitzCorbucion had somehow put him forever beyond her reach. Miles was one more casualty of the killer's knife.

Prayer and rest. Oslac the Priest had advised her to pray for her dead brother's soul and to get as much sleep as she could in order to restore herself, but neither would come. Prayers died on her lips and sleep eluded her. She was instead held captive by grief and fear and gnawing doubt about the whole meaning of her life. What was the point of it all? Everything now seemed to have died with Guy. Even her hopes of escape.

When she eventually closed her eyes, it was in a slumber of sheer exhaustion and she did not have the strength to choose the comfort of her bed. She drifted off while sitting in the window of her chamber and her troubled head rested on hard stone without even feeling it.

Matilda was in a sleep of cold despair. How long she dozed she did not know, nor what it was that jerked her awake to face the pain once more. It may have been the insistent thud of the wind against the wall of the chamber, or the light slowly forcing its way in through the window with the stealth of a thief, or the dull ache in her bones from the awkwardness of her posture, or the cries of the gulls as they skimmed over water and marsh in search of their first meal of the morning.

As she opened her eyes, it was there. Matilda came out of her sleep and into a waking nightmare because the sight brought nothing but further apprehension. She rubbed at her eyes, then peered through the window once more to make sure that it was not an illusion. But it was still there. She had recognised it at once. The ship was long and narrow with a single, large sail that was filled by the gusting wind. Its prow was high, its draught shallow, and it was cutting through the dark water with eager purpose. The captain was navigating his way around Northey Island and setting a course for the harbour. They were still a long way from Blackwater Hall but Matilda knew whom the ship carried.

Hamo FitzCorbucion had come home.

Chapter Five

THE DAY BEGAN EARLY AT CHAMPENEY HALL. GUESTS OF SUCH STANDING AND IN such number imposed considerable extra burdens and the servants were up before dawn to clean the house, prepare the table, and serve the breakfast. The visitors, too, were soon out of their beds to wash themselves before sitting down to a meal of frumenty, enriched with egg yolks and a flavouring of dried saffron, and watered ale. Canon Hubert had recovered completely from his overindulgence the previous evening and attacked his food with his customary relish, but Brother Simon, stricken with guilt at his enjoyment of the banquet, and fearing that it was the first sign of moral decay, sat in his place like a repentant sinner and refused even to slake his thirst with water. The two of them went off for an hour of prayer and contemplation before they addressed their minds to the temporal commitments that lay ahead of them.

Gervase Bret returned to the chamber, which he shared with Ralph, so that he could once again study the documents around which all their deliberations in the shire hall would revolve. It was laborious but highly rewarding work. Under his expert scrutiny, simple facts about property ownership yielded a complex story of fraud, misappropriation, and violent seizure. A bewildering set of figures gave him a clear picture in his mind of the geography of the whole area. Bare names like Tovild the Haunted and Reginald the Gross helped to people the landscape and define the character of Maldon. The first commissioners had been regarded with the obedient derision that greeted all royal tax collectors but the returns that they had brought to the Treasury in Winchester, and that were set down in abbreviated Latin, were an ornate tapestry of English life to the discerning eye of a man like Gervase.

Ralph Delchard had never heard of Chapter Forty-eight of the Rule of St. Benedict and he would have been astounded to learn that one of his own beliefs had monastic authority, but he was convinced that idleness was bad for the body and soul of his knights. It was important to keep them alert and well disciplined at all times. If the threatened invasion of the Danes had, in fact, taken place, Ralph would have been called to lead his knights into battle and their military worth would have been put to the test. He was determined that his men would not be found wanting in any emergency. Ralph had planned to take them on an invigorating gallop before putting them through some training exercises with sword and lance. Gilbert Champeney's invitation to go hawking was thus particularly welcome because it enabled Ralph to combine a ride with his men and an hour's sport.

"What have we caught so far?" he asked.

"Duck, pigeon, and pheasant," said Gilbert, glancing at the game bag, which his servant carried. "They will make fine dishes during your stay with us. Canon Hubert tells me he is partial to hare as well."

"Hubert will eat anything that moves," said Ralph.

"My cook has a magical touch with hares."

"I prefer rabbit. I wish King William would bring more of them over from Normandy. They breed well and are easier to catch." Ralph winked at him. "Hubert gobbled them up by the dozen when he was serving the Lord in Bec."

"We must keep the Church happy."

They had ridden a few miles from the manor house and were on the edge of a small wood. Miles Champeney had joined them and his falcon was the most deadly of all the hunting birds. Ralph watched the young man as he un-hooded the creature yet again and flicked his arm so that the falcon left its leather perch and shot into the sky. It did not need to fly very far. Hovering above a clearing in the wood, it saw something that sharpened its instinct and concentrated all its fierce attention. The steady beat of its wings suddenly changed, its neck stretched forward, and it hurtled towards the ground with frantic speed. Through a cluster of trees, Ralph was just able to pick out a glimpse of its quarry as talons of steel sank into frenzied fur.

"I think you may have found your hare, Gilbert."

"Give the credit to my son."

"He has a rare talent for hawking."

"Hawking, hunting, and chasing women." Ralph sighed with nostalgia. "The bounty of youth!"

"And the consolation of old age."

Ralph chortled in appreciation. When the sport was over, the hunting party set off in the direction of Champeney Hall with a full game bag. Partridge and squirrel had also been killed, although the latter was discarded as unsuitable for the larder. Under their captain, the seven knights rode off hard and left the rest of the company to return at a more sedate pace. Ralph rode between father and son. Gervase had told him what he had learned about Miles Champeney and his friend was fascinated to know more. He tried to disguise his enquiries behind a chuckling jocularity.

"You are a true falconer, Miles," he observed.

"I like the sport."

"Every man should have a hawk and hounds," said Ralph. "If I were back on my estate in Hampshire, I would be out hunting right now. The King's business has robbed me of that delight. I am grateful that I have been able to snatch this hour of pleasure with you and your father."

"We mean to make you enjoy your stay," said the genial Gilbert. "Is that not so, Miles?"

"Yes, Father."

"Guests from the King are always welcome."

"We have been blessed by our host," said Ralph. "You keep a splendid house, Gilbert, and you know how to take the most out of this life of ours."

"I love Maldon. It is the next best thing to Heaven."

"Your son may not agree."

"Why?" asked Miles.

"Because the town has less to offer a sprightly young man like yourself," said Ralph. "Maldon is full of Saxon women and celibate nuns. They are like the squirrel that your falcon caught—pretty to look at but hardly fit for the larder. How can you practise the arts of dalliance without a supply of fair maids?"

"We do not lack beautiful women, my lord," said Miles with a defensive note. "They are here in plenty."

"I have not seen them," said Ralph. "They must be hiding behind their doors in the town or behind their veils at the priory." He paused for a moment then gave his companion a knowing nudge. "But you are right, Miles. There must be *some* ladies hereabouts who can make a man's blood race. *He* found them, after all."

"He?"

"Guy FitzCorbucion."

"Why do you say that?"

"Because it is what everybody else says," explained Ralph. "Your father among them. Guy was a ladies' man. He had a reputation for liberality and spread his love around."

"Guy was as lecherous as a monkey," agreed Gilbert.

"Then the town must be full of lovely ladies. Unless he was the kind of man to take his pleasures with servant-girls and other poor wretches who were afraid to disobey him." He looked across at Miles. "What do you think? I know we should not speak ill of the dead but then I do not hold carnal desire to be a sin, so it is no stain on his character. What was Guy really like, Miles?"

"You must ask of others, my lord."

"But I am told you knew him well."

"Too well."

Miles Champeney gave a nod of farewell then nudged his horse into a trot until he caught up to the servant who was carrying the wooden pole on which all of the hawks were perched and tethered. Ralph was disappointed. He had learned no more from him than Gervase. As before, it was Gilbert who tried to account for his son's behaviour.

"It is a difficult time for Miles," he explained. "He is not usually as uncivil as this. There is much on his mind and it has made him withdraw into himself. Guy's murder was bound to cause him anxiety."

"Anxiety?"

"Yes, Ralph. He may be called to give evidence."

"Called? By whom?"

"The sheriff and his officers."

"But Miles is not involved in the killing."

"They will want to make sure of that."

"The murderer has already been named," said Ralph. "A boy called Wistan whose father was struck down by Guy. They are combing the area now for the lad."

"Yes," said Gilbert, "and if they catch him and get a confession out of him, nobody will be more relieved than Miles. But I am not at all sure that this Wistan is the culprit. How could he get close enough to Guy to perpetrate such a foul crime? And what could a boy do against a man who was bigger, stronger, and properly armed?"

"Oslac the Priest thinks that Wistan is innocent."

"I agree with Oslac."

"Then let us assume he is right."

"If the boy did not do the deed ..."

"Someone else did."

"In which case, they will need to question Miles."

"But why?" said Ralph. "Your son is no killer. Why on earth should the sheriff wish to bother him in any way?"

"Because of a certain incident."

"Yes. Gervase told me about the fight."

"Did he tell you what caused it?"

"What often causes fights between young men," said Ralph with easy cynicism. "A young woman."

"Guy's sister. Matilda."

"Your son wishes to marry her."

"Madness!"

"And Matilda seems to requite his love."

"Chaos! It breaks my old heart, Ralph."

"But you have still not told me why the sheriff and his officers may come looking for Miles. What has he done?"

"When they came to blows," explained Gilbert, "there were witnesses. They heard what Guy said and they will be duty bound to report it. Miles did not go in search of trouble that day. He went—against my advice—to see Matilda but her brother caught them together. An argument started and a fight developed. They had to be pulled apart."

"What was it that Guy said?"

"He vowed that Miles would never marry his sister."

"Were those his exact words?"

"No," admitted Gilbert. "What he actually said to my son was 'As long as I live, you will never come near Matilda. I would die sooner than let you touch her.' Now do you see why Miles is so vexed? He had the best reason of all to kill Guy FitzCorbucion."

They were waiting for him at the quayside and he could read the disaster in their faces. As soon as the ship was sighted from the house, Jocelyn FitzCorbucion and the steward mounted their horses and rode to the harbour to meet it. They could see Hamo in the prow of the ship, waving happily to them and shouting something that was lost in the wind. When he got close enough to see their dour expressions, the waving stopped and the shouting was directed at the captain as Hamo vainly demanded greater speed from the craft. A successful visit to Coutances and a relatively calm voyage back across the channel had put him in a buoyant mood but it turned to black anger before he even set foot again on English soil. Bad tidings awaited him and Guy's absence alerted him. The favourite son should certainly have been there to meet the returning father. As the stout bulwark rubbed the quayside in greeting, Hamo jumped nimbly ashore before the first rope had even been tied to steady the ship.

There was no point in delaying the news until they were in a more private place. Hamo FitzCorbucion demanded to know the truth there and then. Jocelyn told him. His father was completely dazed. He refused to believe what he had heard. His elder son, who modelled himself so closely on Hamo, who had his energy, his ambition, and his ruthlessness, who shared his vision in every way, and who stood to inherit Blackwater Hall in the fullness of time, this son, Guy, who had been so strong and unquenchable, was now lying dead. Killed by the son of a slave. It was quite inconceivable. All his love and his hope had been placed on Guy. His wife was now dead, his other son less worthy, his daughter less important, so it was Guy who bore the blessing of his pride and affection.

Hamo FitzCorbucion was a stocky man of moderate height with the narrow, hook-nosed face of a predator and yellow eyes that glared from beneath a mop of black hair. As he fought to accept and understand the dreadful news, his head dropped, his shoulders hunched, and his whole body sagged, but he did not stay like that for long. As incredulity gave way to pain, it was in turn replaced by a cold rage that started deep inside him and slowly coursed through his entire being until he was simply pulsing with fury.

"Where is he?" Hamo asked.

"At the mortuary," said Jocelyn.

"Take me to him."

"You need time to prepare yourself first."

"Take me to him."

"Father, there's something I've not told you about—"

"I've heard enough!" howled Hamo, grabbing him by the throat and shaking him violently. "God's wounds, Jocelyn! You say that Guy is dead. You tell me my son has been murdered. Take me to him *now*!"

Jocelyn abandoned all hope of further explanation and led his father to the horse, which they had brought for him. All three of them were soon cantering towards the hill. They went past the priory, past the Church of St. Peter's, and up to the dark shape of the Church of All Souls'. Oslac was taking confession but Hamo's urgency brooked no delay and he raised his voice to such a pitch of anger inside the nave that the priest had to break off and calm him down. A sinful parishioner was sent on his way only half-shriven so that the lord of the manor of Blackwater could be conducted to the mortuary to view the remains of his son.

Oslac unlocked the heavy door and led the way into the dark, dank, little chamber, which was filled with the stench of decay. Herbs and fresh rushes had been placed around the slab to freshen the atmosphere but they were unable to compete with the reek of rotting flesh. Hamo retched.

"Dear God in heaven!" he exclaimed.

Oslac steadied him with an arm and Jocelyn moved in to support him as well but he soon shook them both away. He needed no help with a father's duty. The body lay on the cold slab beneath a thin shroud. Candles burned at its head and feet. Oslac had washed the corpse and tended its wounds but blood and filth still oozed out to stain the material. Hamo was overwhelmed with nausea and contempt. A son who had come into the world to such wealth and advantage was ending it in a fetid cavern that smelled of his own corruption. He reached forward to take the edge of the shroud and peeled it back to reveal the face. Guy FitzCorbucion did not rest in peace. His face was contorted with pain and his mouth twisted into an ugly snarl. Hamo let out a low moan and swayed to and fro.

When he steadied himself, he tried to pull back the shroud even further but Oslac the Priest stopped him with gentle firmness.

"You have seen enough, my lord," he suggested.

"Take your hand from me," hissed the other.

"Guy was most cruelly slain."

"I wish to see my son."

Oslac gave a little bow and stepped away. Hamo drew back the material and saw the worst. The two candles were throwing an uncertain light and much of the horror was lost in the shadows but Hamo saw enough to appall him even more. Deep gashes covered the muscular torso and the most hideous mutilation had been practised. With a cry of anguish, Hamo pulled the shroud back over the corpse to hide its shame and stormed out of the mortuary towards his horse.

Jocelyn and Fulk could hardly keep up with him.

"Has the murderer been caught yet!" he screamed.

"He soon will be, Father."

"Where is he?"

"The search continued at first light."

"Why haven't you found him, you idiot!"

"It is only a question of time."

"I want him!" growled Hamo.

"We have dozens of men out looking," said the steward.

"Yes," said Jocelyn. "The sheriff and his officers will be here to help in a couple of days."

"I need no sheriff," sneered Hamo. "I'll deal with the killer my way. I want him *now*. I'll find that boy if I have to search every corner of the shire for him myself. And when I get my hands on him, I'll show him what FitzCorbucion vengeance is like." He was leaping into the saddle now. "I'll pull off his ears. I'll gouge out his eyes. I'll stuff his pizzle down his throat." He looked back at the morgue. "Nobody does *that* to my son. I'll cut the devil into tiny strips and feed them to the ravens!"

Hamo FitzCorbucion galloped off to Blackwater Hall.

The commissioners arrived at the shire hall well before the appointed hour so that they could organise themselves properly for what promised to be a long and exacting day. They were due to hear a series of witnesses whose land had been taken away in a variety of ways by a grasping baron. Their predecessors had identified the abuse without being able to do anything about it and it was up to the second team of royal officers to rectify this situation. The town reeve had prepared everything for them and had even set out some jugs of wine and a plate of honey cakes in case they needed refreshment. Revived by their early-morning exercise, all eight knights were stationed at the rear of the hall. After discussing the broad lines of their approach, the commissioners took their places behind the table as before and set the documentary evidence in front of them. Jostling for position started immediately.

"Introduce me and stand aside," said Canon Hubert with an imperious flick of the hand. "I will take charge of the business of the day."

"You will wait your turn, Hubert," insisted Ralph. "*I* preside here."

"But I will speed up the whole process."

"Haste would be an injustice," said Gervase reasonably. "The people we have called deserve a full hearing and an impartial judgement. We can give neither if we are trying to hurry them along. Law is a tortoise and not a hare."

"That is very well put," said Brother Simon.

"Be quiet, man," said Hubert.

"Tortoise and hare."

"Who sought your opinion?"

"We are delighted to hear it, Simon," said Ralph. "And we are glad that you side with us for a change. Were we to take a vote on this matter, three of us would outweigh one of Hubert. Although if he eats his way through any more meals at Champeney Hall, he'll outweigh the whole household."

"I merely draw attention to my superior abilities," said Hubert with a supercilious air. "I bring the power of the Church to bear on the proceedings."

"That is my fear," said Ralph.

"God will hear your blasphemy."

"I am relieved to know that he still listens to me."

"My presence here is crucial."

"It is certainly welcome, Canon Hubert," said Gervase without irony. "You were rightly chosen for your legal acumen and you lend a gravity to this tribunal that is only proper, but I would remind you that we are engaged in a civil dispute and not an ecclesiastical one."

"I beg to differ."

"Not again!" groaned Ralph.

"We are about to move into a spiritual sphere."

"How can a civil action have spiritual connotations?" said Gervase with curiosity. "I have read all the relevant charters and I perceive no sign of them."

"Then you have not seen the wood for the trees."

"Please explain," said Gervase.

"In a single sentence," pleaded Ralph.

"I may do it in a single phrase, my lord, and it is one that you yourself used only yesterday in this very hall."

"What was it?"

"The Battle of Maldon."

"Yes," agreed Ralph. "Invaders versus Saxons."

"Look closer," said Hubert with booming condescension. "The bulk of our work involves annexations made by one particular person. We have set aside the whole of today to hear Saxon witnesses contesting with a Norman lord."

"The town of Maldon against Hamo FitzCorbucion."

"No!" said Hubert, clapping his hands suddenly together for effect and making Brother Simon sit up in alarm. "What *you* see is merely the civil action—Maldon against Hamo: What *I* see is the spiritual—good against evil."

"Stop playing with words, Hubert," said Ralph.

"Good against evil," he reiterated.

"They are abstracts," said Gervase.

"Wait until you meet him," warned Hubert. "We only saw the younger son in this hall yesterday but even he exuded a sense of natural wickedness. When his father appears before us, you will not think *him* an abstraction."

"Perhaps not," said Ralph with light sarcasm. "It is as well that we have you on hand to exorcise any demons."

"Do not mock, sir. You will need a force for goodness."

"We have one," argued Gervase. "It is called the rule of law."

Brother Simon piped up. 'It is named Canon Hubert."

"It is a combination of both," announced the prelate. "That is why I am your chief weapon in this trial of strength. No man here could question my goodness. When Hamo FitzCorbucion enters this hall, you will be in the presence of evil made manifest."

"Save your sermons for another day, Hubert," said Ralph dismissively. "The people of Maldon need practical help, not windy moralising from you. Let us get on with our work."

He gave a signal to one of the soldiers at the rear of the hall and the man went smartly out through the door. The commissioners readied themselves. Ralph Delchard sat bolt upright in his chair, Gervase Bret looked through the list of names, Canon Hubert inflated himself to his full pomposity, and Brother Simon lifted his quill pen in anticipation. But nothing happened. They were expecting over twenty witnesses to come flooding into the hall with their claims but not one appeared. Minutes elapsed and there was still no surge. Ralph grew impatient. His command had the power of royal warrant behind it and he had ordered a prompt start. He was about to dispatch a second man in search of the witnesses when the first came back rather shamefacedly.

"Where are they?" demanded Ralph.

"They are not here, my lord."

"Twenty-four were summoned for ten o'clock."

"They have not come."

"None of them?"

"One or two only," said the man, "and even they are hesitating to appear before you. They are fearful."

"They have no need to fear us," affirmed Ralph. "We are here to help them regain their land."

"It is not you that they fear, my lord."

"Then who is it?"
"Hamo FitzCorbucion. He is back in Maldon."
"I warned you," said Hubert in self-righteous tones. "Evil stalks the town. We must fight it with goodness."
"We will fight it with the King's writ," said an irate Ralph, rising to his feet before addressing his full complement of knights. "Go outside and bring them in here. Then fetch the town reeve so that he can conduct you to the homes of those who have dared to resist our summons. I want every one of them inside this hall within the hour. Do not stand on ceremony." He stamped a foot. "Drag them here!"
The soldiers went out at speed and Ralph Delchard sat down. Gervase Bret was disappointed at the setback and Brother Simon was deeply disturbed. Canon Hubert, however, was quietly congratulating himself on his correct assessment of the problem that confronted them.
"You will need the power of my goodness now," he said with a complacent sniff. "True evil has returned."

Matilda waited on the fringe of her father's displeasure and felt a pang of sympathy for her brother. Jocelyn was bearing the full brunt of his father's wrath.
"You are to blame for all this!" roared Hamo.
"I do not accept that, Father."
"When Guy was missing, you should have searched."
"I am not my brother's keeper."
"You might have saved him."
"That is highly unlikely."
"Yet you did nothing!" Hamo was livid. "You turned your back on him. When Guy was away for that first night, you should have wanted to know the reason why."
"I thought that I already did, Father."
"You let your brother down!"
"That is not true."
"You betrayed him!"
"No," said Jocelyn without flinching. "Guy often spent a night or two away from here when it suited him and we both know where he went. He would not have thanked me for going after him each time and disturbing his latest rendezvous." He gestured towards his sister. "Matilda will vouch for me. I assumed that Guy was taking his pleasure somewhere and I said as much when she pressed me to go in pursuit of him. It was not my place to organise a search party to find out which bed my brother was in."
"You should have *cared*!"
Hamo FitzCorbucion was still shaking but his anger had abated

slightly. There was reason in Jocelyn's argument and he was defending himself with controlled vigour that was impressive. In the past, the younger son would have buckled in front of his father's tirade but he was standing up to it well and showing something of Guy's spirit. It made Hamo pause to consider. He had lost one fine son but another seemed to be emerging. It was a small consolation.

Jocelyn was anxious to prove his mettle to the full.

"We have another problem, Father."

"All else pales beside this."

"Royal commissioners are in town," said Jocelyn. "They have come to vex us. Blackwater Hall is the main subject of their enquiries and they mean to prosecute their case against us with zeal."

"Ignore them!"

"They will not easily be ignored."

"Then defy them."

"I have already taken action," said Jocelyn coolly. "Fulk and I appeared before them yesterday at the shire hall and let them know who we are. They were left in no doubt about the power of the FitzCorbucion name."

"Good," said Hamo.

"Several witnesses were due to be called against us this morning," continued Jocelyn. "Yesterday evening, I sent Fulk out with a dozen men at his back to visit these same witnesses. He did not even have to speak to most of them."

Hamo smiled for the first time since his return. His son had done exactly what he himself would have done. He gave him a pat of appreciation on the shoulder. Jocelyn chose the moment to advance his claims.

"Take me with you, Father," he asked. "When you are called before these commissioners, let me be your advocate. I know that I can confound them. Guy was the stronger of us but I am the more cunning. I have studied hard. My brain is agile enough to fend off these royal officers and to send them on their way. Have me beside you, Father."

Fatigue began to clutch at Hamo and he looked drawn. The voyage from Normandy had tired him and the news about Guy was like a physical blow that left him bruised. His initial rage had spent itself and weariness set in.

"I will think about it, Jocelyn," he promised.

"You will not regret it. If you let me—"

"No more," interrupted Hamo. "I will think."

Jocelyn was satisfied. He had survived the tempest of his father's anger and gained a purchase on his attention. It was progress. Since nothing more could be achieved, he backed his way out with the excuse that he was going to join the search for the killer who was still at large. Hamo waved him off. He was about to climb the stairs to the gallery when Matilda glided across the hall towards him. Her father blinked in astonishment. He had hardly noticed that she was there.

"We have given you a poor welcome home," she said.

"Leave me be, Matilda."

"But I wish to speak with you, Father."

"I need to be alone with my thoughts."

"This will not take a moment."

"Talk to me later."

"It will not keep."

"I have no time for you now," he said, walking towards the stairs. "Hold off a day or two at least."

"No, Father!"

She got to the steps first and blocked his path. His eye kindled with irritation but she did not move aside. Hamo was not used to such a display of temper from her.

"Out of my way, Matilda."

"I share your worries," she said. "I grieve with you over Guy's death. I am as concerned as you must be about what these royal commissioners may do. You are bound to be oppressed and I feel that same oppression." She touched him lightly on the arm. "But I have worries of my own."

"This is not the time," he whispered.

"I know why you went to Coutances. I heard the jokes. I heard them laughing at me behind my back." She took her hand away and drew herself up. "Your visit concerned me."

"Among other things."

"Am I not to be told what transpired?"

"Yes," he said. "When I am ready to tell you."

"This is important to me, Father. I have a *right*."

"The only right you have is to obey me."

"You went to Coutances to find me a husband."

"Matilda ..."

"But I have already found one for myself."

"That's enough!" he said.

"There is only one man I wish to marry."

"Your wishes do not come into it."

"Miles Champeney is my—"

"Silence!" His bellow sent her cowering away. "Guy has been murdered. Some slave has dared to hit out at Black-water Hall. Royal commissioners are in the town to harry me with their questions. And I have to listen to *your* bleating!"

"All I wish to ask is—"

"It is settled," he said peremptorily. "The marriage has been arranged. You will sail for Coutances in six weeks. No father more willingly parted with his daughter."

Matilda stepped forward again but he brushed her aside and went up the stairs. Her cries of protest followed him but he was deaf to all entreaty. He walked along the gallery and in through a door before closing it behind him to keep out the sound of her complaint. Hamo was in Guy's chamber. He seemed to sense his son's presence. Jocelyn's apartment was full of books but Guy was a true soldier. Swords and shields decorated the walls. The bed was covered with the skins of animals he had killed in the hunt. Jocelyn had carved himself a chess set out of wood but Guy had fashioned knives and arrowheads out of a stag's antlers. Guy had lived in his father's image. As Hamo looked sadly around, a first tear began to form.

He crossed to kneel beside the oak chest where Guy kept his most treasured belongings. The key was in the lock. It did not need to be hidden away. Nobody would steal from Guy FitzCorbucion. Servants would not even dare to enter the chamber without his permission. Turning the key and lifting the lid, Hamo sorted his way gently through the contents. He took out fine apparel and a whole assortment of weapons. He found brooches, handkerchiefs, and other keepsakes from the ladies in his son's life. There were rings and bracelets and a large drinking horn. Hamo saw everything he had expected to find except the object he most wished to see. It was not there. He searched again more thoroughly and lay everything on the floor beside him until the chest was empty. But it was still missing.

Jumping to his feet, he scoured the room to see if it was kept somewhere else but there was no sign of it. He went over to the ransacked chest again and picked through the objects on the floor with increasing frenzy. The one that he wanted had gone. The precious heirloom, which his wife had left in her will to her eldest son, was missing. Hamo's fatigue had lifted. Fresh anger seized him. He grabbed the lid and slammed it down with such force that the sound echoed throughout the whole house. The most valuable item in the chest had been taken. It was like a further mutilation of the body of Guy FitzCorbucion.

* * *

Prioress Mindred polished the cup with loving care then set it beside the crucifix on the tiny altar in her quarters. The silver chalice sparkled afresh and she allowed herself a few minutes to admire its quality. The workmanship was truly superb. Tall and elegant, the chalice had the most intricate designs etched into its gleaming surface and they were thrown into sharp relief by the four rubies that had been set into the silver with equidistant care. Mindred could only guess at its cost but she was more concerned with its value to her little community. Poverty was enjoined upon the holy sisters but Mass deserved to be celebrated with the finest chalice and paten. Anything less was an insult to the Almighty. The prioress glanced at the crucifix and then genuflected before crossing herself in gratitude.

There was a gentle tap on her door. She opened it.

"Come in, Sister Tecla," she invited.

"You sent for me, Reverend Mother?"

"Indeed I did. Please sit down."

Mindred closed the door while Tecla lowered herself onto a stool so that her back was to the altar. The prioress gave a sweet smile and sat opposite her.

"It is good to be back in Maldon, is it not?" she said.

"Yes, Reverend Mother."

"God watched over us on our journey."

"God and St. Oswald."

"We must never forget the blessed saint," agreed the older woman. "Shall I make a confession to you?"

"You are the one to receive confession."

"I have sins of my own, Sister Tecla," said Mindred with a wry expression. "Although I cannot believe that this thought is in any way sinful except that it shows too much ambition."

"Ambition?"

"I wish I had taken the veil at your age."

Sister Tecla was not quite sure how to react to this disclosure. It aroused somewhat mixed feelings in her own breast but she was in no mood to discuss those at that moment and so she opted for an obedient nod and a modest enquiry.

"Is that your only confession, Reverend Mother?"

"It is but the beginning," explained the other. "If I had entered a religious house when I was young and strong enough, I would have prayed to God to put my youth and my strength to some real purpose. I could have fulfilled my ambition and kept the memory of St. Oswald alive in his own part of the country."

"Northumbria?"

"That name has perished along with so much else. But I would have tried to revive some of its former glory. When Christianity first came to England, it took the firmest root in Northumbria." She took Sister Tecla's hands in her own. "Do you remember what Abbess Aelfgiva was saying to us about houses of nuns?"

"There are but nine in all—and this small priory."

"Each and every one of them serve the Lord truly but they all do so in the south of the country. There is no nunnery to the north of the River Trent." Mindred squeezed her hands. "Can you not see why I was fired with ambition? I would like to have founded this priory where it could rekindle a flame of hope. Maldon may need us but Yorkshire would need us even more. We would have been missionaries."

"St. Oswald would have blessed the enterprise."

"I am too old and weak to pursue it now."

"The wish is a noble one," said Tecla, "and I am honoured that you have shared this secret with me."

Prioress Mindred released her hands and sat back to appraise her. There was a serenity about the young nun, which was altogether pleasing, but she still found herself unsure about the depth of Sister Tecla's belief and commitment.

"Are you happy with us?" she said.

"A bride of Christ enjoys the greatest happiness."

"That is not what I asked, Sister Tecla."

"I have no cause whatsoever for complaint."

"Sister Gunnhild is still concerned."

A long pause. "Sister Gunnhild is most kind," she resumed, "but her concern is quite unfounded. Everything I want is within these walls."

"That is as it should be."

"I am at peace with the world."

"It gladdens my heart to hear that."

"I have seen the face of Jesus," said Sister Tecla.

Prioress Mindred reached forward to squeeze her hands again then stood up and walked around behind her. She took a moment to find the right words.

"Sister Gunnhild has voiced some worries."

"Worries?"

"About your spiritual needs. I have asked her to ... look after you."

"Is that your wish, Reverend Mother?"

"It is, Sister Tecla."

"Then I abide by it."

Her voice was as soft and submissive as ever but the prioress could see that her body was tense. Mindred felt the need to reassure her.

"Sister Gunnhild is a woman of rare qualities," she said.

"I know it well."

"Nobody in our convent has her insight and holiness. Such things only come from long years of devotion. I am the prioress here but I tell you this. There are times when I feel inadequate in that role if I compare my humble gifts with those of Sister Gunnhild."

"All this I accept," said Tecla quietly.

"Then take her as your mentor."

"I will."

"Good."

The prioress felt relieved that she had passed on her directive. She knew that it would not be entirely welcome to the nun, and she herself had vestigial reservations about it, but her word had been given to Sister Gunnhild and she had to honour it. Mindred was more relaxed when she came back round to face the other woman, able to relate to her more easily now that her decision had been announced. They discussed the books that they had brought back from Barking Abbey, and they shared a smile at Sister Lewinna's propensity for laughing at Aesop's *Fables* at the most inappropriate times.

"I heard her giggle in the chapter house today."

"Why?"

"She said that she was thinking about the fable of the fox and the grapes." The prioress gave a fond sigh. "I suppose we should be grateful that dear Sister Lewinna was at least thinking."

"There is no harm in her, Reverend Mother."

"Indeed, no. But she must learn to curb her giggling."

"Thank heaven that Sister Gunnhild was not there!"

Sister Tecla blurted out the comment before she could stop herself and it brought the conversation to a halt. Sister Lewinna was a devout nun with a girlish exuberance, which had not yet been suffocated beneath the demands of convent life. The prioress and the others treated her with an affectionate indulgence while trying to correct her by means of persuasion. Sister Gunnhild merely admonished her and tried to frighten the last sparks of vitality out of her. Sister Tecla obviously feared that the Danish nun would do the same to her.

After a strained silence, she rose to go. The prioress conducted her to the door and put her hand on the latch.

"You have been working in the garden, I see," she said.

"It needs constant attention."

"Weeds grow much faster than flowers and vegetables."

"I love the garden here."

"It has profited from that love."

"I am always happy to work there," said Sister Tecla. "There is no part of the priory I would rather be."

There was another taut silence then Mindred opened the door for her to leave. When the nun had gone, the prioress shut the door once more and turned back to the altar. The sight of the chalice restored her at first; then it began to dampen her spirits. She moved quickly across to it and removed it from the altar, putting it away temporarily in the leather pouch that had borne it on the journey from Barking Abbey. It was out of sight but not out of mind. Prioress Mindred kneeled in front of the crucifix and offered a prayer for forgiveness.

Ralph Delchard did not believe that his dignity could only be preserved if he sat behind a table in judicial pose. He was a leader of men who talked best in the language of soldiers and that is what he chose now. Strapping on his sword and adopting a military swagger, he came out into the body of the hall and berated the skulking burgesses who had just been rounded up like sheep by his soldiers. He tried to shame them into a semblance of valour.

"Do you call yourselves men?" he demanded. "You have lost your land and you will not raise a finger to get it back. Do you not have wives? Do you not have children? Do you not care if you behave as cowards and weaklings in front of them? Hell and damnation! What is wrong with you?"

"They came to talk to us, my lord," said a spokesman.

"Who did?"

"Fulk the Steward with a dozen knights."

"If he had brought a hundred, he would not frighten me out of my rightful claim!" asserted Ralph. "What has happened to the red blood of Maldon? Has it been thinned down over the years? The warriors of this town fought a famous battle against the Vikings and gave their lives sooner than yield up their land. Yet twelve knights and a donkey-faced steward ride out to show off their armour and you surrender all."

Canon Hubert was highly critical of his colleague's method of argument and he grimaced repeatedly but Brother Simon was mesmerised by the performance. It was left to Gervase Bret to appreciate the irony of a situation in which a Norman soldier who had spent his formative years fighting Saxon housecarls was now reminding a Saxon audience of their warrior heritage and their famed encounter on the banks of the River Blackwater with the Vikings. Moreover, Ralph was doing it in order to stir up their passions against a fellow-Norman. The burgesses first began to whine, then to protest, and then to challenge. When he had them thoroughly roused, Ralph had achieved his objective and he took his place behind the table.

Gervase took command and called the men one by one to make sworn statements and to produce whatever contractual evidence they had. The burgesses were subtenants, holding their small amounts of land either directly from the King or from the tenant-in-chief who owned it. Hamo FitzCorbucion had systematically hived off part of their property for his own use so that they were in the invidious position of having to pay rent for land that they could not farm and that was adding more money to the coffers of the lord of the manor of Blackwater. Hamo was no crude landgrabber. He acquired his extra property in all manner of ways. Bemused subtenants had awakened one day to learn that their most productive acreages had been bought, borrowed, or repossessed by Hamo even though he produced no written evidence of these transactions.

Other abuses appeared. One man had lost twelve cattle when they strayed onto Hamo's land and another lost forty sheep by the same means. In both cases, dogs had been used to drive the animals away from their pastures and onto the Norman's property. A third man was exercising his rights of pannage in the wood when sixty of his pigs were rounded up by Guy and taken off to stock the kitchens at Blackwater Hall. During a hard winter, a fourth had gone to cut down some trees on his land for firewood and found that they no longer existed. He traced the logs to Hamo, made vociferous complaints, and returned home to discover that half his land had been annexed by way of punishment. And so it went. Stories that had been missed by the first commissioners now came thick and fast. People who had been too intimidated even to appear at the shire hall on the previous occasion now spoke angrily and—for the most part—honestly.

There were a few exceptions, men who had a personal grudge to work off and who overreached themselves by making claims and accusations that arose more from malice than from fact. Canon Hubert exposed such falsehood at once and was scathing in his condemnation of the perpetrators. He was anxious to uphold any legitimate charges against Hamo FitzCorbucion, but he would not tolerate any random Saxon venom against a Norman lord. Sententious to a fault, Hubert was also merciless in cross-examination and he uncovered a series of disputes between the burgesses themselves. They might be united in their hatred of a local tyrant, but they were bitterly divided in other ways. As the full facts were exposed, a more rounded portrait of life in Maldon came to light.

Ralph Delchard unblocked the dam to allow the river of allegations to surge through, Gervase Bret used the water to turn the mill wheel of legal process, while Canon Hubert was simultaneously filtering out any impurities. It was a most productive session in the shire hall and Brother Simon's hand was aching from hour upon hour of neat calligraphy. When the material had all been amassed, Ralph told them they should not be intimidated by threats from Black-water Hall when there was a higher authority in the town. Hubert added his own rider to this advice.

"Today," he said, "we have heard the testimony of Saxon subtenants. Tomorrow, we shall call Norman witnesses before us, some of whom will be your own landlords with evidence that may contradict or countermand your own. Only when we have decided where the real truth lies will we summon the lord of the manor of Blackwater to marshal his defence."

The session was over and the burgesses began to rise from their benches to leave, considerably more pleased than when they arrived, although still afraid of repercussions from Blackwater. Ralph went after them to detain them briefly at the door with a confidential question. Hilarious laughter broke out and knowing looks were exchanged all around. He repeated his enquiry but they shook their heads in denial and left the hall in mirthful moods. Ralph turned to Gervase with a gesture of despair.

"Will *nobody* tell me where Humphrey got his name?"

Blackwater Hall was trembling with fear by the time that Hamo FitzCorbucion rode off with his men. All the servants were hauled into Guy's chamber to be challenged about the missing heirloom. None could help him. Even when cuffed and kicked by him, they denied any guilt and suggested that the object might be in another part of the house. A complete search failed to uncover something that Guy would never have parted with and that meant that it had to have been stolen, but an even more rigorous interrogation could not identify the thief. When their master finally left, the household was in a state of utter panic.

Hamo let his horse feel the sting of his rage as he led a detachment of his men across his estate. His fortnight in Normandy had proved to be a ruinous expedition. He came back to find his elder son murdered, his demesne besieged by royal commissioners, his daughter recalcitrant, and a prize family heirloom stolen. What new afflictions awaited him?

"That was the house, my lord," said the steward.

"Where?"

"That pile of ashes. Jocelyn ordered us to burn it."

"Good!"

"Algar lived there alone with the boy."

"A slave and his miserable whelp!" Hamo reined in his horse and the whole company came to a halt. "Ride to the next dwelling. Bring me Algar's neighbour."

"We have already questioned him."

"*I* will speak to him now."

Fulk rode off with two of his men while Hamo dismounted and walked into the middle of what had once been a hovel. He kicked the ashes viciously then looked up towards the town.

"Did they bury him up there?" he yelled. "I'll dig his foul body up and bring it down here to roast it!"

The steward soon returned with the prisoner. The man was another slave on the estate and he was being dragged along by the two soldiers with ropes. He could barely keep his feet and fell headlong to the ground when he reached Hamo. A kick made him moan and writhe. The soldiers jerked their ropes and the man was hauled upright. He already bore the marks of a beating but Hamo did not even notice them. He took out his sword and used the flat of the blade to strike the prisoner across his chest. The man doubled up in agony.

"Where is the boy?" demanded Hamo.

"I do not know, my lord ..."

"Where is Wistan!"

The sword hit his thighs this time and brought him to his knees. He swore that he knew nothing but Hamo did not relent for a second. The pain was excruciating and the man gabbled for mercy. Wistan had fled in the night and nobody had any idea where. Hamo kept striking him until a stray remark finally brought the savage assault to an end.

"Wistan was a strong swimmer, my lord ..."

"Swimmer?"

Hamo turned to look at the estuary with brooding ire.

"Fulk ..."

"Yes, my lord?"

"Have you searched Northey?"

"No, my lord."

"Why not?"

"Jocelyn did not think the boy could have—"

"He may be wrong."

Hamo snapped his fingers and the two soldiers released their ropes. The prisoner collapsed to the ground and lay there in a twitching heap. Unaware of the truth, he had unwittingly given them a clue, which might lead them to Wistan. His pain was now mixed with remorse. Hamo put a foot in the stirrup and mounted his horse.

"When is the next low tide?" he said.

Oslac the Priest was a reliable friend. When Gervase Bret walked across to the Church of All Souls' to remind him of his promise, the man went off with him at once to the Hythe. The fishermen had been back hours ago to unload the day's catch but many loitered throughout the afternoon to talk with the crews of any trading vessels or to make running repairs to their own boats. There was a chance that Brunloc was among them. Since it was Brunloc who had found the body of Guy FitzCorbucion in the water, Ralph Delchard had declined the opportunity of making his acquaintance. Fishermen and sailors made him queasy. Therefore, when Gervase went off, he stayed at the shire hall to question the town reeve more about the problems of collecting taxes in the community. Canon Hubert had been separated from food for far too long and was riding back to Champeney Hall on his donkey with Brother Simon and an escort They felt it had been a profitable day. While Hubert revolved on a spit of self-congratulation, Simon basted him with flattery.

Gervase was in luck. Among the boats that crowded into the harbour was the one that belonged to Brunloc. It did not take the priest long to find the man and to introduce him to Gervase, but he was an unwilling witness. Authority of any kind unsettled him and the sight of a royal officer made him doubly wary. Brunloc, a dark, wiry man in his thirties, possessed the ruddy face of his occupation as well as its unambiguous stink. He was a simple soul who made a simple calculation. Gervase was only in town for a short while. When the young man left, Hamo FitzCorbucion would still be there and the father of the murder victim might not be pleased if Brunloc had passed on too much information to this stranger.

"I have my work," he grunted.

"We will not keep you long, Brunloc," said the priest. "We just wish to know how and where you found the body."

"I've already told you."

"Tell me again, please."

"It could help," said Gervase.

The man looked at him with suspicion, then gave a very brief account of what had happened. Even when Oslac tried to coax more out of him, the fisherman remained laconic. Gervase tried his own form of persuasion and seemed to be winning the man's confidence, but he extracted no more information. He thanked Brunloc and walked away with the priest towards the place where the body was actually found. The fisherman's directions had been exact but it still took them some time to locate the correct part of the marshes. Oslac watched with amazement while Gervase hitched up his gown and plunged into the filthy water, squelching along the muddy bottom of the river and pushing his way through the reeds. It was a bold and dangerous method of research but it told him precisely what he wished to know.

When Gervase had examined the area carefully, he came back to the bank to be hauled ashore by Oslac's outstretched hand. He squeezed the worst of the water out of the hem of his gown and rubbed the mud off his shoes in the long grass. He was cold and sodden but he felt that the experiment had been worthwhile. Gervase was still trying to tidy himself up a little when a figure suddenly jumped out of the bushes. A wizened, white-haired man had been watching him from cover and now hopped up to him with a vacuous grin on his face. At the sight of the sword and shield, Gervase backed away but the newcomer clearly intended him no harm. He simply came in close so that he could whisper a secret that was giving him an intense pleasure.

"I saw who killed him!" he said with a cackle.

Before Gervase could reply, the old man let out a whoop and scuttled off quickly before vanishing into the bushes. His mad laughter could be heard mingling with the cries of the birds.

"Who on earth was that?" asked Gervase.

"Ignore him," said Oslac. "He talks in riddles."

"But he said he witnessed the murder."

"He says lots of things, I fear. Pay no heed."

"Why not?"

"Because the poor man has lost his wits."

"Who is he?"

Oslac smiled. "The friend you sought."

"Friend?"

"That was Tovild the Haunted."

Chapter Six

As soon as he heard the noise, he knew that they had come for him. They were still half a mile away but the distant baying of the hounds sent a hideous message echoing across Northey Island. Wistan flew into a panic and took to his heels. He ran the fifty yards to his next lair and dived into it like an animal going to ground. Even there he did not feel safe and he soon abandoned the first burrow for another that he had picked out. Keeping low as he raced across a field, he flung himself down with panting gratitude as he reached his new hiding place. It was beneath the roots of a huge old elm. Nature had capriciously gouged a massive handful of earth out of the ground beside the tree and created an inviting refuge for someone who was prepared to crawl in under the exposed roots. Wistan caught his breath. He began to think clearly for the first time.

Know your enemy. Algar had taught him that. Before he dropped back to his next burrow, he ought to assess the strength of the pursuit. Only when he knew exactly what he was dodging could he best decide on his tactics. Wistan came slowly out of his cave beneath the tree and climbed up the side of the pit, putting his hands on the rim before raising his head with furtive care. When he got his first glimpse of them, his heart nearly stopped. There were dozens of them and they seemed impossibly closer. Their horses cantered gently at the heels of the hounds who were sniffing and yelping their way along in high excitement. Wistan was not looking at a solitary old man in Viking battle dress this time. These were Norman soldiers in full armour and he could even identify the FitzCorbucion crest of a raven. The might of Blackwater Hall had been unleashed against him.

Blind fear took over once more and he completely forgot about the little bundle that he had carried with him into the hollow beneath the elm. Instead, he crawled out of the pit and into the undergrowth before he dared to stand up again. Ignoring the other hiding places that he had found and made ready, he sprinted the few hundred yards towards the coastline. Wistan was now on the little promontory to the northwest of the island and water was on three sides of him. The thought gave him confidence. Even a pack of hounds could not find his scent in the sluggish movement of the river. He ran into the shallows then swam to a thick clump of reeds, which were diverting the current with their obstinate tenancy. Wistan went in amongst them, his body still submerged by water and his head concealed by the spikey reeds.

He did not have to wait long. The frisky dogs grew louder and he caught the jingle of harness for the first time. Spread out in a long line, the search party had combed the island thoroughly and their hounds had scattered sheep, cattle, and any other livestock that got in their way. The barking became more agitated and men's voices were raised in a shout of triumph. They had found his burrow under the elm tree. Wrapped in some old rags were the few things that he had taken with him when he fled from the house. Worthless to anyone else, the belongings had a sentimental value to Wistan. A club, a carved snake, and a necklace of oyster shells, which his father had made, had now betrayed him. One voice rose high above the others and Wistan shivered. Hamo FitzCorbucion was there.

The hounds set off again and searched the promontory with moist noses and wagging tails while the soldiers hacked at the undergrowth with swords and lances to make sure it did not conceal their quarry. When figures appeared on the bank opposite him, Wistan held his breath and sank below the water, staying there for as long as he could while praying that they would not see him. His fear had been tempered by the spirit of revenge and he wanted to fight back. Hamo had returned from Normandy. Another target for his hatred was now standing on the bank no more than twenty yards away.

His mind was bursting and his lungs were on fire when he finally dared to come up for air. They were still there but the reeds hid him from their gaze. He was about to sink below the water again when Hamo FitzCorbucion gave an order and they all moved off to continue their search elsewhere. Wistan stayed there for an hour before he felt safe enough to return to the bank. Days of freedom had ended dramatically. They had tracked him to his lair and made a decision for him. When darkness fell, Wistan would have to get back to the mainland.

"Domesday Book is indeed an apt name for it," said Gilbert Champeney. "It spells doom for so many people."

"It is a survey," corrected Canon Hubert pedantically. "King William ordered it to be undertaken chiefly for financial and military purposes."

"It is essentially a tax inquest," argued their host. "And it is made so much easier, as I have always claimed, by the efficiency of the Saxons."

Ralph Delchard grinned. "If they were so efficient, why did we beat them at Hastings?"

"That is another matter." Gilbert was into his stride now. "This survey of yours, this Domesday Book, or whatever you choose to call it, provides the King with an exact record of contributions to Danegeld or Heregeld—the one great Anglo-Saxon tax that was levied uniformly on the country. We Normans inherited their system and that makes your job so much the easier."

"Easier!" snorted Ralph. "If only it were, Gilbert!"

"Do not forget the legal implications," said Gervase Bret. "Part of the function of the survey is to legalise the changes in land ownership that occurred after the Conquest and to root out the irregularities that have taken place since. It is indeed a kind of Domesday Book."

Hubert snuffled. "That notion is sacrilegious!"

"I wondered why I liked it so much," said Ralph.

"The Last Judgement does embody a legal concept," said Gervase. "And we do seek to uncover sin. It was you, Canon Hubert, who told us we were engaged in a spiritual battle between good and evil."

"He drags religion into everything!" said Ralph. "So why do you object to this nickname, Hubert? If we are engaged in compiling a Domesday Book, then you are the bold St. Peter who is standing at the gates of Heaven to prevent the unworthy from sneaking in. I should have thought that role would suit you admirably."

Gervase smiled and Gilbert laughed breathily but the canon inhaled deeply through his nose and chose to maintain a dignified silence until he suffered an inconvenient outbreak of flatulence and had to disguise it beneath a flurry of protests. It was a lively debate. The four of them were sitting over the remains of another fine meal and watching the last hour of a long day slowly expiring. Apart from a few servants waiting to clear the table, everyone else had taken to their beds. Ralph and Hubert were sipping from cups of French wine, Gervase was sampling some home-brewed ale, and the Saxon-loving Gilbert was drinking mead.

"What lies ahead for your tomorrow?" asked Gilbert.

"Further deliberations in the shire hall," said Hubert.

"We will not begin until ten," Ralph reminded him, "and that will give us ample time for other things. I will take my men out for exercise shortly after dawn."

"I may join you," volunteered Gilbert. "Gervase?"

"I will stay here."

"Come with us. A gallop will invigorate you."

"I will be too busy trotting through more documents," said Gervase. "Besides, if I can find an hour, I need to spend it with one of your neighbours."

"Which one?"

"Tovild the Haunted."

Gilbert chuckled. "Better you than me!"

"Why do you say that?"

"The fellow is crack-brained. He has been fighting the Battle of Maldon these past forty years and he still cannot decide whether he is Saxon or Viking." Gilbert gave a compassionate shrug of the shoulders. "Tovild will not harm a fly but his company can be troublesome."

"Where might I find him?"

"On the battlefield," said Gilbert. "Where else?" He turned to Canon Hubert. "Which will you choose? An hour in the saddle with us or an hour of amiable madness from Tovild the Haunted?"

"Neither," said Hubert. "Horsemanship does not interest me and I already have enough fools and madmen to deal with. When I have worked and prayed, I will visit the convent. Prioress Mindred invited Brother Simon and me to call on her and her little community."

"Take me with you," offered Ralph with enthusiasm.

"The invitation was for two of us only."

"Then two of us only will go. Brother Simon goes weak at the knees when he gets within a hundred yards of a woman. To take him into the priory would be an ordeal both for him and for the holy sisters. Just think how unhappy he was in Barking Abbey." Ralph tapped his chest. "I will take Simon's place. I'll even wear his cowl, if you wish."

"I wish that you would reconsider, my lord," said Hubert.

"I do. I'll omit the cowl but I'll still come."

"Prioress Mindred may be a trifle disturbed."

"Then you will be on hand to comfort her." Ralph warmed to the prospect. "It will be good to see her and Sister Tecla again. I'll give both of them your love, Gervase."

"My regards will be sufficient."

"Shall I pass them on to Sister Gunnhild as well?"

"Who is Sister Gunnhild?" asked Hubert.

"A Danish nun," explained Gilbert, "and a lady of some distinction. She takes a leading part in the running of the priory and has only one flaw."

"Flaw?"

"She disapproves of men."

"There you are, Hubert," said Ralph jovially. "Sister Gunnhild is ripe for conversion. She does not sound like my ideal of womanhood so I will leave you to introduce her to the delights of male companionship. I will reserve my attentions for dear Sister Tecla."

Time had been both kind and cruel to Sister Gunnhild. At an age when most nuns were vexed by failing eyesight and brittle bones, she remained in robust health and shirked none of the manual labour that fell to her. While the years had dealt lightly with her body, however, they had been altogether rougher with her mind and heart.

Sister Gunnhild felt that her qualities had never truly been appreciated and that this had militated against her on a number of occasions. She studied hard to make herself devout and cultured but others still persisted in the belief that her education was somehow suspect, and that the very fact of her Danish ancestry disabled her from becoming a true Saxon nun. Abbess Aelfgiva had valued her as a reliable workhorse rather than as the worthy successor that Gunnhild had hoped to be. She was coming around to the dispiriting view that the abbess had released her to join the priory as much to get rid of her as to provide Mindred with a wholly dependable helpmeet. It was a sobering reflection.

Sister Gunnhild was a martyr to her own unpopularity and it gave her a sometimes abrasive streak. There were compensations and she thanked God daily for them. If she could not rule her own house, she would exert a degree of control through Prioress Mindred. It was a slow process, which could not be hurried, but her position was increasingly influential and it enabled her to correct the recurring mistakes that the prioress made out of sheer inexperience. In a small community, too, relationships were more intense and she derived much pleasure from some of these. Sister Lewinna might exasperate her but the others were friendly and respectful. Then there was Sister Tecla.

Thoughts of Tecla lifted Sister Gunnhild out of her bed that morning. It was her self-appointed duty to ring the bell for Matins and start each day of the spiritual life. Other nuns found it difficult to wake at such an early hour but she could do so without apparent effort or discomfort. St. Benedict was no remote and insensitive dictator who imposed his Rule without making provision for human frailty. The order might be strict but it was shot through with an understanding of the limitations common to all. Instead of decreeing that the brothers should be torn rudely from their sleep by the clanging of the Matins bell, Benedict advised that they should first be brought from their slumbers with a gentle shake so that they were properly awake when they were summoned to the first service of the day.

Holy sisters were no less deserving than holy brothers of this act of consideration, and Sister Gunnhild shuffled out to perform it. Each of the nuns had a small, bare room off a narrow passageway and it was along this that Gunnhild now crept in the darkness. There was a set order to her morning ritual. Sister Lewinna had to be roused first because she took longest to wake and a vigorous pummelling of the shoulder had to be substituted for the soft touch of an arm, which could rouse the others. Last to be awakened was Sister Tecla. This gave her an extra minute of precious sleep and enabled Gunnhild to show her favouritism in yet another way.

Padding down the passageway, she slipped first into one room and then into another until all five nuns had been brought back to the realities of the world. Prioress Mindred slept behind a locked door and a sharp knock was used to intrude into her dreams. With duty over, Gunnhild could now turn to pleasure and she found her way to the last room.

"Wake up, Sister Tecla," she whispered. "It is time."

There was no groan of acknowledgement and no shifting of the blanket under which she slept. Tecla often woke as soon as Gunnhild entered the room and the excuse to touch her was taken away. Gunnhild approached the bed.

"Wake up, Tecla," cooed Gunnhild. "It's me."

But her hand met no warm body and no smooth skin. As her eyes grew accustomed to the gloom, she saw that Sister Tecla was not in her cell. Wherever could she be at that time? It was unimaginable that she was sharing a bed with one of her holy sisters, but Gunnhild nevertheless went quickly back into the passageway and checked each room more carefully. She then went to the front door of the priory but it was still bolted from the inside and locked by the key that was kept in Mindred's quarters. Gunnhild flitted around in mild alarm until she remembered the one place where Sister Tecla might be and headed straight for it.

The garden reposed in deep shadow. A crescent moon was shedding only the most grudging tight. A distant owl joined a choir of nightingales to sing an occasional solo. Sister Gunnhild hurried out onto the grass and peered around intently, trying to make sense of the dark shapes all around her. At first she could find nothing, but a closer inspection yielded success. Sister Tecla was lying on the grass, tucked away in the far corner of the garden. Evidently, she had been there for some time and was fast asleep. Relief at having found her jostled with concern for her health and Gunnhild knelt down to bend right over her and take her by the shoulders. She rocked the supine figure with a tender hand.

"Wake up, Sister Tecla. You cannot sleep here."

She began to stir. "What ... ?" she mumbled.

"You are in the garden. Open your eyes."

"Who is it?" said Tecla, struggling to awake.

"It's me, Sister Gunnhild."

"Tired ..."

"You can't lie on the grass like that."

"Fell asleep ..."

"Let me help you up."

"So tired ..."

Sister Tecla allowed herself to be lifted up into a sitting position and became aware of where she actually was. She rubbed her eyes and gave an involuntary shudder. It was enough to make Gunnhild throw protective arms around her.

"Oh, my poor child!" she said. "What ails you?"

Before Sister Tecla could answer, another figure stepped across the grass in the darkness and stood beside them. There was a slight note of reprimand in Prioress Mindred's voice.

"Thank you, Sister Gunnhild," she said. "You may ring the bell now. I will take over here."

It was a moving service. Guy FitzCorbucion was universally disliked outside Blackwater Hall yet everyone who passed the Church of All Souls' that morning had paid him the tribute of a passing sigh. Few wished him to be alive but the manner of his death aroused a spark of sympathy in most of the people of Maldon and they accepted his right to be buried with all due respect. In front of a full congregation, Mass was sung for the soul of the departed, then Oslac the Priest gave a short address, which struck exactly the right note. He praised Guy's few good qualities while carefully sliding over his many bad ones, and he tried to draw positive lessons out of the searing tragedy. When the mourners followed the cortege out into the churchyard, most were weeping and some had to be steadied or even carried along.

Matilda found it totally harrowing and she clung to Jocelyn's arm throughout, near to collapse at times and bursting into tears at the point where Guy's body was lowered into the grave. Guy had been a destructive presence in her life but he was still her brother and the blood tie could not be denied. Part of Matilda herself was being sent into that gaping hole in the ground. Jocelyn bore up well. He was visibly shaken during the service but sensed that others would need to rely on him and that it was vital to show strength and control. Beneath the expressionless face was also a stirring of the ambition that had been ground down for so long. Guy was finally out of his way.

Hamo FitzCorbucion behaved with a restraint which few expected. He shed no tears and required no supportive hands. He subdued his anger beneath his grief and watched in mute torment as his elder son took his leave of the world. Fears that he might explode during the service were not realised and Oslac was especially relieved that the grave of Algar was neither attacked nor even reviled. The ravens looked like family members around this corpse and they were not cawing nor pecking.

When the service was over, the priest spoke first to the distraught Matilda and then to the dignified Hamo. His offer of help was well intentioned and sincere but neither would be able to take it. The daughter was too enmeshed in her own ambivalence and the father was too keen to take the edge off his sorrow by capturing his son's killer. Most of the congregation would be returning to Blackwater Hall for the funeral bake-meats but the master of the house would not be with them. No sooner did he step off consecrated ground than he became a coarse apostate.

"Bring the men and ride to Northey Island."

"Again, my lord?" said the steward.

"He's still there! I smelled his stink!"

"Will you be at the hall, my lord?"

"No! I will lead the search."

"*Now?*" said Fulk in surprise.

"Now!" confirmed Hamo. "Guy is in his grave. We must find the slave who put him there." He raised his voice to a bellow as his knights milled around him. "Catch him alive and fetch him before me. I'll make him eat his own offal before I tear him to pieces with my bare hands! Away!"

Tovild the Haunted lifted his shield up on one arm and held his spear poised in the other hand. He was ready for battle. The tide was ebbing fast and the causeway, which reached out the island, rose briefly above the water before being washed under again. A stiff breeze tore at the white hair that streamed out from below his helmet. In the armour of a Saxon warrior of old, Tovild took his brave stance and declaimed his speech to the gulls.

"The tide went out, the pirates stood ready, many Vikings eager for battle. Then the protector of heroes commanded a warrior, stern in fight, to hold the bridge; he was called Wulfstan, bold among his race ..."

Gervase Bret recognised him at once and he also knew the poem whose words were being thrown up into the sky with such challenge. Tovild was not just quoting from "The Battle of Maldon," he was re-enacting it with weapon and gesture. Gervase watched as a phantom Viking was speared to death, then he stepped forward to interrupt the carnage.

"You are Tovild, I believe?" he said.

"My name is Wulfstan," said the other. "Leave me be."

"I must speak with you, Tovild."

"We are fighting a battle."

"The Vikings will win."

"Not if I hold the bridge!" He killed another imaginary attacker then warded off a third with his shield. "Fight beside me, young man. Our leader commands it."

"Rest yourself from the fray, sir. You deserve it."

Gervase stood right in front of him and the spear was raised to strike him. He got a much closer look into the gnarled face this time. Tovild was ancient. The scrawny body looked ridiculous in the armour and the weight of shield and lance was already making him breathe stertorously, but he did not desist. He was animated by a spirit that drove him on to fight a battle that had been won and lost almost a century earlier on that same bank of the estuary. His eyes flared with anger and his arm drew back. When the spear was hurled, however, it sank harmlessly into the ground beside Gervase.

"Thank you, Tovild. I will not keep you long."

"Who are you?" croaked the old man.

"My name is Gervase Bret."

"Saxon or Viking?"

"Saxon, like you. We have met before."

"You fought at the battle?"

"We met yesterday. I searched among the reeds. You came out of the bushes to speak to me. Do you not remember?"

Tovild narrowed his eyes to squint at Gervase but there was no hint of recognition in his gaze. He put his shield down beside the spear then beckoned his companion over.

"Question me with wise words, young man," he said.

"It concerns a murder."

"Let not thy thought be hidden."

"You said you were a witness."

"I will not tell thee my secret if thou concealest thy wisdom and the thoughts of thy heart."

"We need your help, Tovild."

"Wise men must needs exchange proverbs."

"You *know* something."

But the old man clearly did not trust him and he shook his head slowly from side to side. The eyes now had a cunning glint to them as if Tovild was enjoying a game with his questioner. He began to hum quietly to himself.

"Listen to me," said Gervase, enunciating his words carefully. "There was a murder. A young man was stabbed to death in the marshes. You saw it, Tovild."

"Yes, yes," he admitted with a cackle.

"Tell me what happened."

"A raven was killed."

"How?"

"I hate all ravens."

"What happened?"

"The knife cut his wings off."

"Who did it?"

Gervase put a hand on his arm but he jumped back as if he had been scalded and rubbed the place where he had been touched. The Saxon warrior now looked like a beaten child.

"Keep away!" he begged. "You're a friend of the ravens. You've come to peck at me. I won't help them. Keep away."

"I'm a friend of Oslac the Priest," said Gervase, trying to soothe him. "You saw me with him. Yesterday."

"Oslac?"

"He will vouch for me. I am a visitor here."

Tovild grew faint. "I saw nothing, young sir."

"You did. You told me."

"The ravens will come for me."

"I have nothing to do with Blackwater Hall."

"They'll eat me alive with their beaks."

"You saw me with Oslac."

Gervase was up against a powerful blend of madness and apprehension. The old man was an impossible witness. All he wanted was to be left alone to fight his battle once more. Tovild the Haunted patently knew something about the murder of Guy FitzCorbucion but he was too confused to remember much about it and too frightened to admit the little he did recall. Gervase made a vain attempt to pluck a few details out of him but his efforts were short-lived. There was a rumble of thunder behind him and he turned to see what it was.

The sight was daunting. Hamo FitzCorbucion had shaken off all the restraints of mourning. He was riding towards them at full pelt with his sword in his hand and forty armed men at his back. It was a veritable cavalry charge and there was no doubt where it was heading. Gervase was forced to jump back as Hamo pounded past him onto the causeway. Fulk and the leading riders went after him in clamorous pursuit and urgent hooves sent up a thick spray that obliterated them as they splashed their way to the island. Gervase dodged as best he could but they came at him too fast from too many angles. The flank of one horse eventually caught him a glancing blow and knocked him to the ground, leaving him stunned. The hooves of another drummed past his ears. He lay there awhile until the entire troop was safely past him and churning up the water on the surface of the causeway. Hamo and his men were thirsting for blood.

When Gervase felt able to get up, he looked after them as they fanned out across Northey Island. There was no pack of hounds this time. Hamo had the scent of his quarry in his nostrils. It had been a perilous place to be standing and Gervase was grateful that he had survived with no more than a few bruises. He hoped that Tovild had not been hurt by the furious passage of the knights. But the old man was no longer there. The Battle of Maldon had been suspended for the day. Tovild had vanished into thin air like the ghosts who haunted him.

Ralph Delchard was on his best behaviour as they made their way to Maldon Priory with an escort of four men. Canon Hubert had grave reservations about his companion but he also had a profound respect for his abilities as a soldier. Like the canon, Ralph had been chosen by King William himself and no recommendation was higher than that. Other teams of commissioners had been sent out to correct the multiple illegalities unearthed by their predecessors, but few had their reputation for effectiveness. Hubert liked to believe that this was largely due to his presence in the quartet, but he was honest enough to admit to himself that Ralph Delchard's zestful leadership and Gervase Bret's penetrating intelligence were the key factors in the commission's success. It reconciled him to Ralph. When the latter was not making irreverent observations about the Church or about the appetite of one of its luminaries, Canon Hubert could easily tolerate him.

By the same token, Ralph had a sneaking admiration for the prelate and for his undoubted skills both as a lawyer and as an administrator. Although there was much to mock, there was even more to praise. Canon Hubert was a man of some renown at Winchester, possessing all the political shrewdness that was needed for advancement in the Church. There were times when Ralph discovered that he had a bluff affection for his colleague and he enjoyed the ride into Maldon with him.

"What do you expect to find, Hubert?" he asked.

"Find?"

"At the priory."

Hubert was guarded. "Do I detect sarcasm here?"

"No," said Ralph seriously. "I ask in all humility. You are more well versed in the ways of holy women than I. Until we stopped at Barking Abbey, I had never been inside a nunnery. I was most impressed with Abbess Aelfgiva."

"We all were and rightly so."

"In what way will Maldon Priory differ?"

"It will be much smaller," said Hubert, slipping into homiletic vein. "And it will share the faults of all new foundations. A religious house takes time to achieve the requisite tone and spiritual resonance. Prioress Mindred is a devout lady but she has come late into claustral life and may not as yet fully appreciate its intricacies. On the other hand," he continued, "I judge her to be a true Benedictine who will not allow the laxity that used to bedevil so many of the English nunneries."

"Laxity?"

"Women do not always enforce the Rule with appropriate vigour," he said. "Vanity is their downfall. They wish to wear fine dresses, expose their hair, cover themselves with adornments, and even to dance within the enclave! It is reprehensible. When they take the veil, they should turn their back on all worldly things." He rolled his eyes in disapproval. "Some nuns have even kept pets."

"Pets?"

"Dogs, cats, caged birds."

"They are showing Christian love to God's creatures."

"No," reproved Hubert. "They are flouting Chapter Thirty-three."

"What is that?"

"St. Benedict is quite specific. Chapter Thirty-three of the Rule leaves no room for misinterpretation." He quoted it in Latin then translated the first line for Ralph's benefit. "'The sin of personal possesion, above all others, should be cut out by its roots ...' St. Benedict calls it a most pernicious vice. I am sure that Prioress Mindred abhors it."

"So that is what awaits us," observed Ralph. "No fine dresses, no long hair, no adornments, no dancing, and no pets. They have to deny their womanhood in every way." He glanced at the hill, which loomed ahead of them. "There is one thing that has always puzzled me. Why are there so few nunneries and so many monastic foundations?"

Canon Hubert's detailed explanation lasted all the way to Maldon and they were soon dismounting at the priory gate. Their escort remained outside but they were admitted by Sister Gunnhild and conducted to the prioress's quarters. Mindred received them warmly and motioned them to seats before turning to Gunnhild with a gracious request.

"Will you ask Sister Lewinna to serve refreshment?"

"Yes, Reverend Mother."

"Thank you, Sister Gunnhild."

When he heard her name, Ralph Delchard took a closer look at the departing nun. Gervase had complained of her inhospitable manner but she had been perfectly polite to her two visitors. What Ralph did notice was how little of the woman's face was visible and how thick and calloused her bunched hands were. There was no whiff of laxity about Sister Gunnhild. Her hair was completely hidden by her wimple. Given a beautiful dress, he mused, she would probably take it straight into the garden to bury it.

Canon Hubert made polite enquiries about the running of the convent and Prioress Mindred's answers seemed, for the most part, to satisfy him. She was very much at ease in her surroundings and told them that she had dedicated the remaining years of her life, without a backwards glance, to the service of God. Ralph said little but showed a touch of gallantry when the nervous Sister Lewinna brought in wine and cakes on a wooden tray. He rose to take the tray from her to place it on the table and thanked her with such a kindly smile that she blushed the colour of beetroot. When she had served the refreshments to the prioress and to the guests, she dropped a hesitant curtsey then went out. Ralph nibbled a cake and found it still warm.

"How is Sister Tecla?" he asked solicitously.

"She is well, my lord."

"I was hoping that we might see her."

"Sister Tecla is too busy, I fear," said the prioress sweetly, "but she wished me to give you her regards. They are sent to you as well, Canon Hubert."

"Thank you," he said.

"Are you both fully recovered?" asked Ralph.

"Recovered?"

"From that ambush on the journey home."

"We have prayed to St. Oswald for our rescue." She folded her hands in her lap and looked down at them as she spoke. "It was a frightening experience, my lord, but one that we must endeavour to put behind us. These are dangerous times and the countryside is full of such outlaws."

"That may be, my lady prioress," said Ralph, "but this was no ordinary band of outlaws. How did they know that you were coming?"

"I do not understand, my lord."

"That ambush was well laid," argued Ralph. "When they chose that copse, they picked the best possible place along the way to make their surprise attack."

"They were lurking in wait for anyone who passed," said Canon Hubert.

"No," said Ralph. "They might have waited for days before anyone rode by. Those men knew what they wanted and when it would be coming towards them. How?"

Prioress Mindred shook her head. "I really cannot say."

"Perhaps they had a confederate."

"A confederate, my lord?"

"Someone who gave them forewarning of your journey," said Ralph, "and who described the valuables you carried."

"A holy relic and some sacred books. That is all."

"In that case, they may have wanted something else."

"What was that?"

"Sister Tecla."

The prioress shook her head. "I do not think so," she said firmly. "Desperate men will attack any travellers and we were unfortunate to be their victims." Ralph was about to speak again but she moved swiftly to quash any further comment on the subject. "As I told you, my lord, we are making every effort to erase that ugly memory from our minds. It is unhealthy to dwell on such things. Sister Tecla and I are back here, safe and sound, among the holy sisters. That is all that matters."

"I agree," said Canon Hubert. "Thank God for your deliverance and continue steadfastly in His service."

When they finished their wine and their cakes, she took them on a brief tour of the building. Hubert was fascinated by every aspect of the priory but Ralph was more interested in somehow making contact with Sister Tecla. He had the feeling that she would not so easily have swept the ambush out of her mind. His hopes were dashed. Although he saw four of the nuns working in the garden, they had their backs to him and thus looked virtually identical. All that he recognised was the stouter frame of Sister Gunnhild. She was using a spade to dig a patch of earth and working with a rhythm and zeal that her sister nuns could not match. Ralph Delchard had never seen a noblewoman doing manual work of this kind before and he found the sight oddly chastening.

The tour ended in the tiny chapel where the nuns sang their offices each day. Ralph thought the place was chill and forbidding but Canon Hubert nodded his approval. Both men noticed the chalice at once. It stood in a small recess to the right of the altar and its quality was evident from the most cursory glance. Hubert was so taken with it that he asked if he could examine the object. With obvious misgivings, the prioress handed it over.

"Norman craftsmanship," noted the canon. "This chalice would grace a cathedral. Was it a gift to the priory?"

"No, Canon Hubert."

"You donated it yourself?"

"It was part of a dowry;" she explained. "One of the nuns included this in her payment to us."

"Which one?" asked Ralph.

"That is a confidential matter, my lord."

"Of course," he apologised.

It was a question that he did not need to ask because he felt he already knew the answer. The chalice provided a second possible answer as well. Canon Hubert was holding it up to the light to appraise its engraving but Ralph wondered if he might be looking at a reason for an ambush. An object of such value would be worth stealing if it had been carried by two nuns travelling from Barking Abbey. Yet why would it be in their possession on the journey? If it belonged to the priory, it would have stayed there during their absence. He could see no just cause for removing it from its home. Ralph was bemused.

Their short visit was over. The chapel was now needed for the next service of the day and they themselves had to adjourn to the shire hall to continue their work. Canon Hubert knelt ostentatiously in prayer and Ralph felt obliged to bend his own knee. While they were thus preoccupied, the prioress took the chalice across to the altar and reached up to place it beside the crucifix. The folds of her sleeve fell back for a moment and Ralph opened his eyes to catch a fleeting glimpse of a thick gold bangle halfway up her arm. The prioress tugged the sleeve quickly back into position so that the arm vanished.

Ralph Delchard was astonished at himself. When he had first met the two nuns on the road, he had been moved by abstract desire to speculate on what exactly lay beneath the habit of Sister Tecla. Yet now, incredibly, he was far more curious about what the prioress would look like without her cloak and her wimple. He remembered what Canon Hubert had told him about Chapter Thirty-three of the Rule of St. Benedict. Personal possessions were strictly forbidden inside a religious house. The piece of jewelry he had seen was elaborate and costly. It certainly had no place in a convent where simplicity of attire was enforced. Prioress Mindred insisted that she took the veil without a single regret, but the adornment clearly belonged to her earlier life. The stately figure assumed a new interest for Ralph. He wondered what else she was hiding beneath her apparel.

Miles Champeney took his horse from the groom and mounted it in one fluent movement. He was trotting away from the stables when his father came out from the house to intercept him.

"Hold there!" said Gilbert. "Where are you going?"

"I will be away for most of the day."

"Why?"

"I have business to attend to, Father."

"Of what nature?"

"Private matters."

"There should be no privacy between father and son," said Gilbert in hurt tones. "We used to be so close at one time yet now you have become detached and secretive. This is not good, Miles. It is not fair."

"I am sorry."

"Do you still blame me?"

Miles bit back the reply he was going to make and tried to stay calm. "You are entitled to your point of view, Father."

"I have never stopped you doing anything before."

"That is true," conceded his son, "but I wish you were not determined to get in my way now. It's disheartening. There are enough obstacles to overcome without having another one on my own doorstep."

"I am not an obstacle!" rebuked his father sharply.

"Then why are you obstructing me?"

"I'm your father, Miles! I have a right."

"To advise me, yes. But not to coerce me."

"To do whatever I choose!"

"I, too, have rights, Father."

"Not in this instance," said Gilbert with rising anger. "You've thrown them away. If you will not listen to sense, I have to impose my wishes in another way. God save us! I'm *helping* you! One day, you will thank me for it."

"I doubt it."

"Forget her, Miles! Find someone else."

"There can be nobody else for me."

Gilbert was scornful. "Then you must resign yourself to bachelorhood for you will never marry her," he said. "Even if I died tomorrow—even if one obstacle were removed—they would still not let you anywhere near Matilda."

"We will see." He glanced away. "I have to go, Father."

"Give her up now! Stop torturing yourself!"

Miles Champeney saw the futility of further argument. They had been over the same ground a hundred times and it always produced the same barren harvest. He tugged on the reins to pull the horse's head around, then set off across the yard. Gilbert took a few steps after him.

"Will you be at table with us this evening?" he called.

"No, Father."

"But we have guests. They expect entertainment."

His son did not even answer. The duty of playing host to the visitors from Winchester was irksome to him when his mind was elsewhere. Gilbert watched him ride away for a few minutes, then went disconsolately back into the house. The rift with Miles was like an open wound that festered. What troubled him most was that he could see no means of healing it. He was in an impossible dilemma. Gilbert Champeney was a doting father who would do anything to help his son except the one thing that was being requested of him. An affable and gregarious man was being asked to ally himself with the only family in Maldon whom he loathed.

Miles rode on. His father had many endearing virtues but they counted for nothing now. The son had priorities that had turned the man he most loved and respected into a stubborn opponent. Miles had reasoned with his father and even pleaded with him, but all to no avail. At a time when he most needed moral support and practical help, he was totally isolated. His mother echoed her husband in all things and was far too weak and vague to make up her own mind. She hated to see the dissent between the two men but there was nothing she could do to alleviate it, let alone to bring about any kind of reconciliation. Miles was on his own and that put him into the exact position that Matilda herself occupied. It was a further bond between them. Both were imprisoned within the hostile attitudes of their respective families. Matilda's predicament seemed to be the worse of the two, because her father had never loved her enough to take a serious interest in her, but the mild and doting Gilbert Champeney could be just as uncompromising as Hamo FitzCorbucion.

After riding towards the town, he kept his horse at a steady canter and swung off towards a wooded embankment. He twisted in the saddle to make sure that nobody was following, then scanned the landscape on both sides. Distant figures were scything yellow corn. Children were engaged in scaring birds with yells and missiles. Animals grazed. When Miles was convinced that he was unobserved, he went into the trees and brought his horse to a halt. Dismounting at once, he tethered the animal to a hawthorn bush and walked on foot to the top of the embankment. Foliage was thicker here and concealment total. He leaned against an ash and waited.

Miles was patient but, when the first hour had passed by, he began to get restive. He went back to check his horse, which was still happily chomping the grass in the shade of the trees. He climbed up the gradient again to resume his vigil beside the ash, but another half hour brought him no relief and anxiety set in, deepened, as more time passed, by a profound sense of helplessness. There was simply nothing that he could do. It was infuriating. Another half hour drifted away. He was about to abandon his long wait when he heard the thud of approaching hooves. Miles took out his sword and prepared to defend himself. Hoping for a friend, he could just as easily get an enemy from the same source. Only when he saw the man's face did he relax. It was the servant who had been used as an emissary before and he was riding the same roan. Furtive and scared, the man brought the horse towards him at walking pace.

Miles rushed eagerly up to him and held out a hand. The servant pulled a letter from inside his tunic and passed it to him. Breaking the seal, Miles opened the missive and read it with a mixture of excitement and fear. Matilda's love for him was unchanged but a more immediate shadow now hung over their romance. A marriage had been arranged by her father. Having buried a dead son in Maldon that morning, Hamo was now planning to bury a daughter alive in Coutances. Her letter ended with a plea to her beloved and his reply needed no consideration. He looked up at the man and nodded firmly. The servant pulled the roan in a half circle and picked a way swiftly through the trees. He had no wish to linger and run the risk of being seen with Miles Champeney. Loyal to his mistress, he was all too aware of what might happen to him if his role as an intermediary were discovered. All he was now carrying back to Black-water Hall was an oral message and that put him in less danger.

Miles ran back to his horse and leapt into the saddle. The words of the letter had burned themselves into his brain like a hot brand. Matilda was to be married to a man in Coutances. If that were allowed to happen, he would never see her again and he was prepared to go to any lengths to prevent it. As his horse took him off in the direction of the town, his mind sizzled with pain and confusion. He was so caught up in his thoughts that he did not see the man who arose from his hiding place in the undergrowth to stretch his aching limbs and curse the amount of time he had been forced to lie there. It had been an ordeal but it had brought its reward and the soldier would earn the gratitude of his master. He crept away to the brake where he had concealed his own horse and mounted.

Another message made its way back to Blackwater Hall.

The shire hall had a much smaller number of witnesses that morning but they brought much louder complaints. Norman landholders had not been spared by Hamo FitzCorbucion out of any sense of comradeship. He stole property and livestock from them with the same easy contempt that he showed to the Saxon subtenants. His main technique was to seize the outliers or berewics, those outlying portions of land that were separate from a manor but taxed with it rather than as a detached holding. Bordars, cottars and other peasants who served one lord had suddenly been given a more demanding master. Slaves who had gone to sleep under the aegis of one Norman baron awoke to find that they were now under the heel of another. Slowly but inexorably, Hamo FitzCorbucion had completely redrawn the map of Maldon and its environs. Those now in the hall had protested strongly to him but he was powerful enough to ignore them and they were now in the humiliating position of paying taxes on land that someone else had annexed for his own advantage.

"Was this land granted to you by King William?"

"Yes, my lord."

"Were you given a charter?"

"Yes, my lord."

"Did it bear the royal seal?"

"It did, my lord."

"And can you produce that same charter now?"

"No, my lord."

"It has been mislaid?"

"Destroyed," said the man ruefully. "When I took it to Blackwater Hall to wave under his nose, he grabbed the charter from my hand and held it over a flame. I could do nothing to stop him."

"Were there witnesses to this alleged crime?"

"My two sons, who sit with me here."

Ralph Delchard called both of the young men to substantiate their father's claim under oath and they did so. It was only one of a number of documents that Hamo FitzCorbucion had burned, stolen, torn into pieces, thrown into the river or—in one case—scrunched up into a ball to force down the throat of the minor baron who had dared to show it to him. Ralph was much more attuned to the minds and hearts of the witnesses. They were Norman soldiers of his own ilk—two from his native Lisieux—and they had earned their property in Essex and elsewhere by service in the army of the Conqueror, only to have it taken from them in slices by the avaricious Hamo.

Gervase Bret examined what documentary evidence could be produced and attested to its authenticity. Canon Hubert put more searching questions to the witnesses and disentangled the legitimate claims of pillaged landholders from the deep envy that they were bound to feel towards someone who was more powerful and wealthy than they. More than one of them was using the occasion to pay off old scores against Hamo, which had nothing to do with any annexation of property. They were treated to some wordy vituperation from Hubert for wasting the time of the commissioners with matters that did not come within their jurisdiction.

What did emerge was precisely what they expected when they first studied the returns for Essex in the Treasury at Winchester. There had been massive theft of property over a lengthy period. Disguised in all manner of ingenious ways, it had finally been brought into the light of day in its full horror. The rapacious Hamo FitzCorbucion was the undoubted victor in the Battle of Maldon.

"As I predicted," boomed Hubert "Good against evil."

"It is not quite as clear-cut as that," said Gervase.

"No," added Ralph. "Hamo may be evil but these barons we have just examined are by no means entirely good. Some of them would have done what he did if they could have got away with it. As it is, we have uncovered a few abuses of which they themselves were guilty."

"Seventeen," said Brother Simon, leafing through the parchments on which he had set down the details. "Seventeen clear instances of illegal seizure of land. These men were not all saints."

Canon Hubert sniffed. "Compared to the lord of the manor of Blackwater, they were holy angels. We must keep everything in proportion."

The witnesses had departed and the four men were alone in the shire hall. It had been another gruelling session but they had worked well together to extract all the detail they needed. The complexities of land tenure in and around Maldon were now clearly established. They could prosecute their case against Hamo FitzCorbucion.

Canon Hubert looked forward to the encounter.

"Call him before us tomorrow," he said. "We will give him an opportunity to answer these charges before we bring him face to face with his accusers."

"What if he will not come?" asked Brother Simon.

"We will compel him," said Ralph.

"But he has scores of knights at his command."

"A royal warrant gives us power over any subject."

"Perhaps we should delay," said Simon meekly. "It may be untender of us to call him so soon. Blackwater Hall is a house of mourning."

Ralph was scornful. "Thanks to Hamo, this town is full of houses of mourning. He has killed off property rights in every part of the borough. Summon him before us. We will only be trespassing upon the grief of a man who has caused widespread anguish himself."

"I agree," said Canon Hubert. "Your anxiety is wholly misplaced, Brother Simon."

"It is not anxiety," said Gervase. "It is respect for the dead and Brother Simon is right to remind us of our duty here. Hamo FitzCorbucion buried his son this morning and you wish to haul him before us tomorrow. Give him another day at least to come to terms with his loss."

"What about the losses he inflicted on others?" said Ralph. "He paid them no respect."

"Indeed, not," replied Gervase, "and we must call him to account. But we cannot do that until we have fully mastered all the new evidence we have collected and I would value another day to prepare our case. There is much to study here. If we spare him tomorrow, we show him an indulgence that he may appreciate and give ourselves time to become so familiar with the fine detail of our argument that it will be quite unanswerable."

"That is sound reasoning," conceded Hubert.

"I endorse every word," said Brother Simon.

Ralph was still keen to press ahead on the following day but he caught Gervase's eye and read the message in it. The delay was not principally for the benefit of a bereaved father at all, nor was it being suggested because it would create valuable time in which the commissioners could assimilate the mass of evidence which had been gathered. Gervase wanted an opportunity to pursue the investigation into the death of Guy FitzCorbucion because he felt it was in some way intertwined with their visit to Maldon. Only when they solved a murder would they be in a position to deal properly with the lord of the manor of Blackwater.

"Gervase counsels well," said Ralph. "We will resume the day after tomorrow. That will content Simon and I daresay that Hubert will not object to an extra day in the tender care of the cook at Champeney Hall. He will think it the best possible reason for staying our hand."

"The thought never entered my mind!" said Hubert.

The meeting broke up good-humouredly. Canon Hubert and Brother Simon left with part of the escort while Ralph Delchard and Gervase Bret compared their experiences that morning. Gervase told him about his encounter with Tovild the Haunted and how certain he was that the man had some vital information locked away in his distracted mind if only they could find a way to release it. Ralph talked about the visit to the priory and his feeling that the silver chalice might in some way have provoked the ambush.

"There is only one problem," he admitted.

"What is that, Ralph?"

"Why should Prioress Mindred have been carrying it in one of her leather pouches? When she went to Barking Abbey, the chalice would have stayed at the priory."

"There is a certain way to find out."

"How?"

"I will ask Oslac the Priest," said Gervase. "He celebrates Mass at the priory and will know what chalice he used during the absence of the two travellers. I need to speak with him about Tovild again and I will raise this other matter with him as well."

"Do so straightway," urged Ralph. "In the meantime, I will acquaint myself with the sheriff of this blighted county. The town reeve tells me that Peter de Valognes was due to ride in with his men this afternoon. The sheriff may be able to solve this mystery."

"The murder of Guy FitzCorbucion?"

"The name of Humphrey *Aureis testiculi.*" Ralph led the way to the door. "If I lived in Maldon, I would fear for my manhood," he said. "It is a town of extremes. Humphrey may have goldenbollocks but poor Guy has none at all. Ask the priest if he can explain *that* as well."

There were six of them. When Gervase Bret walked through the churchyard, they gave him a raucous welcome. The most recent occupant of the consecrated ground had already acquired some feathered tenants. Six ravens stood on the grave of Guy FitzCorbucion and kept vigil. They were not there to peck or scavenge but simply to honour one of their own. Three more flew in to join them on the mound of fresh earth and others circled in the air. Gervase was reminded of his last glimpse of the Tower of London. Like the birds he had seen on that occasion, these ravens were disturbingly at home.

The church was open but it seemed to be empty. A smell of incense hung in the air. He closed the door behind him and genuflected towards the altar before walking down the nave and into the chancel. He tapped on the door to the vestry but there was no reply and the door was locked. The priest was evidently not in the little Saxon church and Gervase decided he might well have returned to Blackwater Hall with the mourners to offer what consolation he could. After a last glance around, he went back down the narrow aisle towards the exit and was about to leave when he heard the noise from the mortuary. It was the shuffle of leather on the stone paving. Oslac the Priest was there, after all.

The door to the mortuary was at the rear of the nave and Gervase knocked politely. When there was no answer, he used a bunched fist instead of his knuckles but there was still no invitation to enter. Gervase tried the door and it swung back to reveal the dank chamber where the dead of Maldon were laid out to await burial. The candles had been extinguished and the window slits admitted such meagre light that the place was in almost complete shadow. The mortuary seemed empty, but Gervase was certain that he had heard movement so he went down the steps and into the tiny chapel. Guy FitzCorbucion had quit his lodging that morning but his odour still lingered to offend the nostrils.

There were four stone slabs on which to lay out the dead of Maldon and three were bare. But the slab that Guy had briefly occupied now had a new corpse. The body was covered by a shroud. He walked around it in reverential silence until he noticed something that made the cadaver highly unusual. Its feet were poking out an inch or two from beneath the linen and they had rough leather shoes on them. Gervase recalled the noise he had heard. Moving to the other end of the slab, he took the edge of the shroud between his fingers and peeled it gingerly back.

The result was startling. As soon as the tousled head came into view, the body came back to life and leapt at him. A knife flashed in the gloom but he was ready for it and seized the wrist in a firm grip, twisting the blade away from him, then forced the arm down so that it struck the side of the slab. There was a yell of pain and the knife dropped to the floor. Gervase grappled with him but his adversary had a surge of power and threw him off. Snatching his weapon, he was about to lunge at Gervase once more but the latter had realised who he must be and held up his palms in a conciliatory gesture.

"Calm down, Wistan," he said gently. "I am a friend."

The boy was unappeased. "Out of my way," he grunted.

"If you wish," said Gervase, standing aside to let him leave. "But you will only be running back into danger out there. Sanctuary lies here. Oslac the Priest will help."

Wistan edged his way towards the door with his knife brandished and Gervase made no effort to stop him. The boy had second thoughts. He was bedraggled. The torn woollen tunic had been soaked during Wistan's second nocturnal swim in the River Blackwater and it had still not dried out. He had made his way to the Church of All Souls' under cover of darkness and hid among the churchyard yews while the burial service took place, waiting until they had all left before he gained the relative safety of the mortuary. His hair was unkempt, his arms and legs scuffed, his face hunted.

"Who are you?" he said.

"I told you, I am a friend. My name is Gervase."

"You know me?"

"Oslac the Priest spoke of you," said Gervase, trying to soothe him. "You are Wistan, son of Algar. Your father was most cruelly treated. He lies in the cemetery outside. I know little beyond that, Wistan, but I know the most important thing about you."

"What is that?"

"Put the knife away and I will tell you."

"Keep off!" said Wistan, holding the weapon up as Gervase took a step forward. "You are lying."

"Take your chance to run, then," offered Gervase. "I will not stop you. But ask yourself this. How long will you last out there?" The boy hesitated. "Go and they will catch you. Lower the knife and you will hear what a good friend I am. What do you have to lose?"

Wistan studied him with beetle-browed intensity. Gervase had an honest face and an unthreatening manner. The boy was so unused to kindness from anyone that he was highly suspicious of it. When he left Northey Island, he decided that Oslac was the only person who might help him, yet this stranger was now offering his assistance as well. Wistan slowly lowered his arm until the knife hung by his side.

"What can you tell me?" he said.

"I know that you did not kill Guy FitzCorbucion."

"I *wanted* to!" retorted the boy.

"You were not alone in that desire," said Gervase. "It was a common feeling in Maldon. But his death was not your work, Wistan. I would swear to it. You are innocent."

The boy was so taken aback by this unexpected support that he wanted to burst into tears. Days on the run had made him fear everyone and he was prepared to kill in order to retain his freedom, yet this young man believed in him. Gervase had never met him before, but he somehow had enough faith in the boy to want to save him. Wistan did not know what to do. Gervase made the decision for him.

"Give me the knife," he said. "Show that you trust me."

He held out his hand and waited. Wistan realised that a bargain was being struck. Gervase would help him but only if the boy surrendered his weapon. It was a big risk and he needed a long time to think about it, but he finally came around to the view that he had no alternative. Flight from the church in broad daylight would be madness. He was bound to be seen. If he stayed at the Church of All Souls' the priest would not betray him, nor would this new-found friend. Wistan had to choose between being an eternal fugitive and placing his trust in this stranger.

"Come, Wistan," said Gervase quietly. "Let me help."

Wistan lifted his arm and handed over the knife.

Chapter Seven

BLACKWATER HALL WAS LESS LIKE A HOUSE OF MOURNING THAN A CASTLE UNDER siege and it was striking back hard at its attackers. Hamo FitzCorbucion was furious when his charge across Northey Island failed to capture the fugitive, but that fury turned to manic violence when he was told that Peter de Valognes, the Sheriff of Essex, had arrived in town to take over the investigation. The servant who passed on the news was beaten savagely, the soldier who tried to help him was kicked senseless, and the rest of the men around him were put to flight when Hamo began to break furniture and throw the pieces at them. It was left to Fulk the Steward to calm Hamo down but there was only a temporary lull. The sheriff rode into the courtyard with his men. Expecting to be welcomed as an officer of the law, he was instead repulsed by such a torrent of abuse that he felt as if he were having boiling oil poured over him.

Matilda's anger was self-inflicted. The man whom she had sent with a message for Miles Champeney had been followed and reported. What horrified her most was that it was Jocelyn who betrayed her. While her father was tearing madly across Northey with his knights, she thought that it would be safe to dispatch her servant with the letter for her beloved, but her brother had been expecting such a move and he had put a watch on Miles Champeney. When the meeting took place on the wooded embankment, the spy witnessed it from his hiding place, then brought word back to Blackwater. Jocelyn promptly incarcerated her servant in the dungeon and then took the outrageous step of locking his own sister in her room. When his father's temper cooled, he would earn his gratitude by telling him how he had foiled his sister's attempt to defy paternal wishes and escape from the marriage that had been arranged for her.

She was beside herself. Not only had she committed the servant to certain punishment, she had also put Miles in danger. Blackwater would be waiting for him now and he would be quite unaware of it. Matilda paced her room in a frenzy, fearful of what might happen to her and desperate to warn her beloved. She blamed herself for her carelessness. Guy had been a constant trial to her but at least he had been a visible enemy. His hatred of Miles Champeney had been as open as it was virulent. Jocelyn worked more slyly to achieve his goals and she had not taken him seriously enough. Because of that, an innocent servant would take a dreadful beating and a hopeful lover would ride into a trap. She was so annoyed with herself that she hammered on the stone wall with her clenched fists until she drew blood, then she fell to the floor and wept bitterly.

With his brother not yet cold in his grave, Jocelyn did not brood or grieve. Like his father, he was taking action to repel an attack, but it was of a legal nature in his case. Royal commissioners had gathered evidence against Black-water Hall and it was only a matter of time before the family had to defend itself against charges of spectacular theft and misappropriation. While Hamo ranted in the hall below, his son sat quietly in his chamber and went through the manorial charters and accounts once more. He wanted to beat the newcomers with their own weapons and that necessitated the most detailed preparation. Jocelyn stalked the battlements of the law with growing confidence, believing that they might outwit the commissioners with an amalgam of his father's overbearing character and his own acumen.

It was Fulk the Steward who interrupted him.

"Your father wishes to see you," he said.

"Has he quietened down yet?"

"He has stopped throwing the chairs around."

"Good," said Jocelyn. "What of Peter de Valognes?"

"The sheriff has been sent on his way with a flea in his ear. Your father asked him why it had taken him so long to begin a murder inquiry. His language was hot. The sheriff wisely withdrew to town to begin his investigation there and to wait until your father was more amenable." A bellow rose up from below. "He is calling for you."

"I will come at once."

Fulk led the way downstairs and was dismissed with a glare by Hamo FitzCorbucion, who wanted a private conference with his son. Jocelyn saw that his father was marginally calmer but still capable of exploding. Hamo was also drinking heavily and that introduced a maudlin note into his voice. He waved his son to a seat with his cup of wine and spilled some on the floor. Jocelyn picked up one of the few chairs that had not been dismembered and righted it so that he could sit down. His father strutted over to him.

"I am surrounded by fools!"

"Yes, Father."

"We buried Guy this morning," said Hamo blankly. "My son went into his grave. That surely entitles me to respect. That surely earns me some sympathy. But what do I get? Eh?" He lurched a few steps and swayed over Jocelyn. "I get fools and idiots upsetting me! I get people daring to argue with me. I get that buffoon of a sheriff riding in here as if he is doing me a favour, trying to pick up a trail that is already three days' old." He emptied his cup then dashed it to the floor. "Why does nobody actually *help* me!"

"I'm helping you, Father."

"How?"

"Sit down and I'll explain."

Jocelyn stood up and guided his father into his chair. Then he picked up a stool so that he could sit in front of him. Hamo was swaying slightly but quiescent at last.

"I have tried to share some of the load," said Jocelyn. "You went all the way to Coutances to negotiate something and I did not want it to be thrown back in your face."

"Thrown back?"

"I speak of Matilda."

"Why? What has she done?"

"Sent word to Miles Champeney."

"Hell-fire! She was forbidden!"

"That is why I kept him under surveillance," said Jocelyn quickly, before his father's anger was ignited beyond control again. "Matilda is cunning and resourceful. If I watched her too closely, she would have known. So I set a man to spy on Miles Champeney and the fellow's vigilance may yet redeem your voyage to Coutances."

"Why, Jocelyn? Tell me. What happened?"

"A messenger was sent today ..."

When he described the sequence of events, it was all he could do to stop his father from storming up to Matilda's chamber to take a whip to her. Hamo's ire shifted to the servant who was now locked in the dungeon below.

"I'll leave him there to rot!" he vowed. "I'll starve him to death then send in the dogs to eat the bones!"

"Forget him, Father," advised his son. "He is nothing."

"He was part of a plot against me. I want revenge!"

"Then take it out on the right person."

"On Matilda?"

"On Miles Champeney. She sent for him. He will come."

A slow grin spread over Hamo's face. "He will come and I will prepare a welcome for him!" He nodded eagerly. "You are right, Jocelyn. *He* is the culprit here. It was he who led my daughter astray and I've not forgotten his fight with Guy. Yes, that is the way to take revenge." He patted Jocelyn. "You have done well here. You have done very well."

His son basked in the praise for a few minutes then turned to what he considered a much more important topic. Matilda's happiness was of no real concern to him now. When Jocelyn had been at the mercy of his brother, she had been a useful ally against Guy, but the balance of power within the family had now shifted. To advance himself, he was quite willing to sacrifice her. In six weeks, she would be packed off to Coutances for the wedding and Jocelyn would not have to see her after that. Matilda had no place in the new dispensation at Blackwater Hall. She would only get in his way.

The royal commissioners were the serious problem.

"They will call us soon, Father," he cautioned.

"Who?"

"Ralph Delchard and his cohorts."

"Let them call. I will defy them."

"There is a better way," said Jocelyn. "I have studied all the charters and the accounts. If we are astute, we can pull the wool over their eyes. Follow my advice and we can pick up the law and hit them over the head with it."

Hamo pondered. "Will we get away with it?"

"I think so, Father."

"Thinking is not enough against royal commissioners."

"Then I *know*," vouched Jocelyn. "We have to face them in argument sooner or later. They have documents to hold over us but we have even more of our own. While they have been getting fat on the meals at Champeney Hall, I have been eating nothing but grants, leases, renewals, agreements, and purchases. They came to Maldon to talk about our crimes and forfeitures. Let *me* contest the issue, and I'll have them out of the town within a couple of days and we'll not be an acre of land worse off." Jocelyn beamed with self-esteem. "What do you say, Father? May I speak for us?"

Hamo FitzCorbucion was no longer listening. One phrase had been enough to alter his whole strategy. Jocelyn might lust for the chance to prove himself as an advocate but that would involve long hours of litigation in a murky shire hall. His father believed in the simplest and most direct solution to a problem. He began to laugh.

"Do you agree, Father?" said Jocelyn hopefully, but Hamo shook his head and laughed even louder. "Why *not*?"

"They are eating their heads off at Champeney Hall!"

"What is so funny about that?" asked the son as his irritation showed. "They have a fine cook. He will fill their bellies until they are fit to burst. Gilbert Champeney is a generous host."

"I know," said his father. "I intend to partake of his hospitality myself. That is what makes it so funny!"

Cruel laughter brought the conversation to an end.

Oslac the Priest was not easily surprised. His vocation gave him an insight into the very worst aspects of life in Maldon and he had learned to take even the most jolting shocks in his stride. Experience hardened him. However, when he returned to the Church of All Souls' that evening, he was met by a situation that even he had not encountered before and it astonished him. Gervase Bret was lurking inside the door of the mortuary to protect the hapless Wistan from discovery. Oslac recovered quickly. He took both of them into his vestry and locked the door behind them. A slightly greater degree of safety had been attained and Wistan was relieved. He now had two friends who were on his side.

The vestry was hardly big enough for the three of them together. It was the place where the priest hung his vestments, stored the candles, and kept his few books. It had never before contained a royal commissioner from Winchester and a runaway slave who was being hunted for murder. In the hours he spent with the boy, Gervase had won his trust enough to coax the truth out of him. Wistan was certainly innocent Accused of murder, he had no option but to flee. The pursuing pack would not even bother to listen to his alibi, still less believe it. Certain death was all he could expect.

Oslac the Priest was full of compassion.

"You did right to come here, Wistan."

"It was all I could think to do."

"It was a sensible decision." He ran a hand across his chin. "The question is, what do we do with you now?"

"Keep him away from my lord, Hamo," said Gervase. "And there is one sure way to do that."

"What?" grunted the boy.

"Surrender to the sheriff."

"No! No! I'm innocent!"

"That's exactly why you should go to him," said Gervase softly. "To clear your name. Peter de Valognes is an honest man. He will hear you out. He will also look after you."

"I am not so certain of that," opined Oslac.

"But he is the Sheriff of Essex."

"I know his position and I respect the man who holds it but he does not have much influence over Blackwater Hall. He and my lord, Hamo, have had many battles in the past and the sheriff has yet to win." He put a consoling arm around Wistan. "If we deliver the boy, the sheriff will lock him in the town prison while he questions him."

"No prison," begged Wistan. "No prison. *Please.*"

"At least, you would be safe there," argued Gervase.

Oslac shook his head. "I fear not. My lord, Hamo, has great sway here. He will bribe or bully his way into the prison. He will not rest until Wistan is in his hands."

"Save me," wailed the boy. "Please save me."

The priest calmed him down and mulled over the matter.

"You will come home with me," he said at length.

"With *you*?' Gervase was uneasy. "That would put you in danger as well, Father Oslac. Consider well. Hamo holds the advowson of this church. You are vicar here with his approval. Were he to find that—"

"He will not," said Oslac crisply. "In any case, I refuse to put myself before a child in need. Wistan will stay in here until it grows dark. Then I will take him back to my house. It is close by. They will not search there."

Gervase was contrite. "You are a brave man," he said, "and you are right to chide me for reminding you of your self-interest. Wistan has suffered enough. He needs refuge until the real murderer is caught and then his life will be safe." He turned to the boy and patted his shoulder. "This is the best way. Are you content?"

Wistan gave a lacklustre nod. Oslac might hide him for a short while but that would not solve a long-term problem. Even if the real culprit were apprehended and his own innocence proved, Wistan could not imagine returning to the demesne of Hamo FitzCorbucion. It was his son, Guy, who had slain Algar and further vengeance had to be taken for that. The priest might hide the boy in the belief that he was not a killer, but Wistan still had murder in his heart.

Oslac could see how fatigued and hungry he was. He sat him on a stool and found some bread and water to sustain him until the priest's wife could cook him proper food. There was a service to be taken soon in the church. Oslac locked the boy alone in the vestry and came out into the nave with Gervase.

"We have much to thank you for," he said. "Wistan is fortunate that it was you who walked into the mortuary. Anybody else would have raised the alarm and the boy would now be lying dead somewhere in Blackwater Hall."

"Call on me if I can be of further assistance."

"I will."

"The town reeve will know where to find me."

"God bless you for your kindness!" He looked back towards the vestry. "The only way to rescue Wistan is to find the person who killed Guy FitzCorbucion. Let us pray that Peter de Valognes does that."

"He may need our help."

"Why?"

"The sheriff comes too late on the scene," said Gervase. "He will waste time trying to track down Wistan instead of hunting the man whom Tovild saw."

"Tovild the Haunted?"

"He was an eyewitness."

"Is that what he told you?"

"He was about to," insisted Gervase, "but he was frightened away by the knights from Blackwater Hall. I am certain that Tovild is our best ally."

"A dubious asset. Where did you find him?"
"In the middle of the Battle of Maldon."
"What did he say?"
"He spoke in gnomic utterances."
Oslac sighed. "Yes, that is Tovild the Haunted."
"But he *knows*. He was there in the marshes at the time. Tovild holds the vital clue that will lead us to the murderer."
"Then we will never find him, I fear. Tovild's mind is full of shapes and phantoms. He has witnessed so many imaginary deaths in his dairy Battle of Maldon that he could never separate them from any real one." Oslac was fatalistic. "Look elsewhere for your vital clue. Tovild will not help."
"He will, he will," declared Gervase. "I sensed it."
"His wits have turned. You merely sensed madness."
"I must see him again. Tell me where he lives."
"On the shore. In the battle."
"Does he not have a home?"
"Yes," said Oslac, "but he is rarely there. He only visits the house to get weapons and change into different armour. I'll tell you where it is, and how to get there, but you will be very lucky to catch him at home."
Gervase took the directions and thanked him. The priest showed him out of the church. He was about to walk away when he remembered the request from Ralph Delchard.
"You celebrate Mass at the priory, I believe?"
"I am one of three priests in the town who do so."
"Does the chapel possess a wonderful silver chalice?"
"Why, yes, Master Bret. How did you know?"
"Is that always used during Mass?" asked Gervase.
"Whenever it is available."
"Available?"
"It disappeared for a week while the prioress was away in Barking Abbey," said Oslac. "She is inordinately fond of that chalice and probably locked it away for safety. I used another in her absence, far less ornate but it served the same function." He smiled quizzically. "Does that answer your question?"
"Extremely well."
"May I know what it concerns?"
"An ambush," said Gervase. "I would like to see this silver chalice. It has been much praised."
"Rightly so. It is a true symbol of Maldon."
"Symbol?"
"Yes," said the priest. "You have been here long enough to get the measure of us. What are the main features that you have noticed since you have been here?"

"Your kindness and Gilbert Champeney's hospitality."

Oslac laughed. "Those are only minor blemishes on the face of Maldon. What is the major wart that you see?"

"Hamo FitzCorbucion."

"And is there any hint of beauty here?"

"Spiritual beauty, yes. The priory."

"Put them both together, Master Bret."

"Together?"

"Come, come," said Oslac, almost teasing him. "You are a highly intelligent man. If you cannot spy *my* meaning, you will never solve any of Tovild's riddles. Priory and Hamo. Or put it another way, if you wish. Priory and Hamo. Mass and FitzCorbucion. What else am I saying to you?"

"Chalice and raven."

"Excellent! And what do you have now?"

"Chalice and raven," repeated Gervase. "The emblem of St. Benedict was a broken cup, which held poison, and a raven that removes it at his bidding. Chalice and raven. Maldon is truly Benedictine." They shared a smile and Gervase let his mind play with the image of an emblem that had been conjured up. "Chalice and raven. The mark of a saint sits upon the town. What an extraordinary coincidence!"

"Yes," said Oslac, growing serious. "Except that this cup holds the blood of Christ and the raven will do nobody's bidding but his own."

Gilbert Champeney was at his most genial that evening. He presided over the feast with loquacious cordiality, passing on items of local gossip, extolling the virtues of the Saxon community, and pressing his guests to try each new, enticing dish which was brought in from the kitchen. There was no hint in his effusive manner of any domestic anxieties, and his cheerful boasts about his son completely hid the deep divisions that existed between Miles Champeney and his father. Such was his love of disseminating happiness that Gilbert could even believe he enjoyed some himself.

Canon Hubert was in his element. Rich wine, delectable food, congenial company, and the fawning attentions of Brother Simon allowed him to pontificate on his favourite themes.

"The Church has effected the real conquest of England," he said, reaching for another girdle bread. "Archbishop Lanfranc is bringing about a revolution. No other word is strong enough to describe the fundamental changes he has wrought. A veritable revolution in matters spiritual. I have discussed it with him."

"Canon Hubert has the archbishop's ear," said Simon.

"Who has the rest of his body?" joked Ralph.

"You remind me of poor St. Oswald," said Gilbert with a nervous laugh. "When he was killed in battle by King Penda of Mercia, his body was sacrificially mutilated to Woden. The head, arms, and hands of St. Oswald were hung up on stakes. They were later recovered and venerated in different places. The head was buried in Lindisfarne but moved elsewhere in time. The arms were deposited at Bamborough, although one was later stolen by a monk of Peterborough and taken to Ely. The body was buried at Oswestry, then translated to Bardney, then on again to Gloucester. Holy men in Durham claim to have seen his uncorrupted hands." He gave a reverent giggle. "St. Oswald has been all over the country to spread his cult."

"Wait till Humphrey dies!" said Ralph. "Every red-blooded man in England will want *his* relics."

"Who is this Humphrey?" asked Brother Simon.

"May I continue?" said Canon Hubert, stepping up into the pulpit once more. "I was speaking with the Archbishop of Canterbury ..." He omitted to mention that over fifty other leading churchmen were present at the synod. "... and he told me of his conviction that canon law must be our watchword. That is why he has created so many separate ecclesiastical courts in England. He is laying the foundations. Archbishop Lanfranc is making the free operation of canon law possible." He almost choked on his girdle bread and swilled it down with some wine. "Look at the corruption and inefficiency of the Saxon church and you will see what a revolution this is. We are imposing real definition on the spiritual life of this land. We are cleansing it. We are saving it."

"That 'we' being you and Lanfranc's ear," said Ralph.

Hubert snorted. "Is *nothing* sacred to you, my lord?"

"Of course. Sister Tecla."

"I must protest, Canon Hubert," said Gilbert. "You are too harsh on the Saxon church. In my opinion ..."

He and the prelate argued contentedly for an hour.

The food kept coming, the wine flowed, and their host's benevolence reached new heights, but Gervase Bret was more interested in the one person who was absent from the table. When the feast was over and the guests rolled off to their respective bedchambers, he remarked on it to Ralph Delchard.

"Where was Miles Champeney?" he said.

"Where every virile young man ought to be," replied the other. "Warming the bed of his latest mistress."

"He has pledged himself to Matilda FitzCorbucion and he is faithful to her," said Gervase. "Only true love could survive all the obstacles that they must have met. But why was he not at the table with us? He is the son of the house."

"Perhaps he is away on business again."

"His horse was in the stable when I returned."

"In that case, Miles may be unwell."

"He was healthy enough first thing this morning."

"Then perhaps he and Gilbert have fallen out?"

"Why then did his father talk so fondly of him during the meal?" Gervase sat on his bed and pondered. "Miles is less than welcoming to us. He has obligations to fulfill when there are guests of such distinction here, yet he keeps out of our way. He must have a reason."

"And what might it be?"

"Guilt."

Ralph was incredulous. "Miles, a killer? Never!"

"We have, at least, to consider the possibility."

"What was his motive?"

"Hatred of Guy FitzCorbucion."

"Everyone had that."

"They did not all fight with Guy. They did not all see him as a barrier between them and the woman they loved. We have been scouring the town for suspects when one might lie right here at Champeney Hall."

"No, Gervase. You are wrong. Miles is a fine young man."

"He is a fine young man in love."

"Would he try to *kill* his way to the altar?"

"If there were sufficient provocation."

"The brawl with Guy?"

"And the taunts that must have gone with it." Gervase went over the sequence of events. "When we arrived, Miles had been away for a few days. During that time, Guy was stabbed to death. Could not Miles simply have pretended to leave the area so that he had an alibi?"

"Yes, he could. But I would doubt it very strongly."

"Why?"

"Damnation! He is Gilbert Champeney's *son*!"

"That does not guarantee his innocence."

"He would not kill merely because he hated someone."

"I think he did it because he loved someone."

"What proof do you have?"

"None," admitted Gervase, "beyond the fact that he has been acting so strangely since we came. But as you say, he is Gilbert's son and a Champeney is always single-minded. Look at this manor house, Ralph. Think what an effort of will it must have taken to create it in the teeth of opposition and mockery. Fired by his love for Saxon culture, Gilbert has stuck to his mission." He stood up again. "Miles would stick to *his* mission as well—fired by love of Matilda."

"You are forgetting one thing, Gervase."

"What is that?"

"The mutilation," said Ralph. "It is possible, I grant you, that Miles just *could* have stuck a knife into the loathsome Guy. But why would he castrate him?"

"An accidental injury in a frenzied attack."

"No, Gervase. The killer knew what he was doing."

"Then Guy must have goaded him about his manhood."

"You're guessing here," said Ralph sceptically. "You will tell me next that Guy was castrated as part of a ritual mutilation to some pagan deity. After all, they dismembered St. Oswald. That must be it! Miles Champeney worships Woden!"

Gervase smiled. "I think you will find that Woden looks remarkably like this Matilda of Blackwater Hall." He gave a shrug. "The evidence is slight, I know, but somebody killed Guy FitzCorbucion and Miles has to be a leading suspect. If *he* did not commit the murder, then who did?"

"An irate husband. Maldon must be full of them."

"Irate husband?"

"Yes," said Ralph. "We know that Guy was a demon lover who rode far and wide in search of pleasure. Such men are catholic in their taste. Wives, widows, or spinsters, it does not matter to them. They are all grist to the mill." He walked to the window and peered out into the courtyard. "Somewhere out there is a cuckolded husband who decided to put an end to Guy's romping. *That's* why he lost his bollocks, Gervase. They became golden with overuse. He stole one wife too many."

"That, too, is a possibility," said Gervase.

"It is more than that. It is the only explanation."

Ralph turned away from the window and crossed to his bed. It was getting late. There was no session at the shire hall on the following day but he and Gervase had more than enough to keep them occupied. When they had set out from Winchester, the assignment in Maldon had seemed perfectly straightforward. The murder had complicated everything. Until that was solved, they would never be able to complete their work. Ralph lay down on his mattress.

"What will you do tomorrow?" he asked. "Arrest Miles?"

"Gather more evidence."

"From where?"

"Tovild the Haunted. He is still our best witness."

"A raving madman fighting a long-dead battle?"

"He saw *something* in the marshes, Ralph."

"The Viking invaders!"

"I still have faith in him," said Gervase. "It may take time to separate the wheat from the chaff of his mind, but it will be worth it. Even madmen can make a sane comment."

"Yes," agreed Ralph. "Look at Hubert. To be serious for a moment, what about the boy?"

"Wistan? He is safe with Oslac the Priest. I will call on both of them as well. A night's sleep in a real bed will refresh the lad's memory. He has much more to tell us yet."

"About what?"

"Life on the Blackwater demesne," said Gervase. "He has endured it for fifteen years and will have his own stories about Hamo and his two sons." He lowered himself onto his mattress and put his hands behind his head. "Yes, I will be kept busy tomorrow. I need to see if I can draw anything more out of Brunloc the Fisherman and take another look at the place where he found the dead body." He reached over to the candle and snuffed out the flame between moistened finger and thumb. "What about you, Ralph?"

"I will devote the day to searching for Humphrey."

"We have a case of brutal murder on our hands."

"Yes," said Ralph with mock annoyance. "And I have the feeling that it will be easier to solve than the mystery of Humphrey's shining spheres. I need to spend more time with Peter de Valognes. He was in a vile mood today because Hamo had spurned his offer of help, but our sheriff is a man to be cultivated. He knows what has been going on at Blackwater and any information on that score may advantage us." He stifled a yawn. "What I would really like is an excuse to return to the priory."

"Why?"

"Cakes and wine with Sister Tecla."

"You told me that you did not even see her there."

"That is why I wish to return, Gervase. To meet the beauteous Tecla and ask her about her prioress. Why does Lady Mindred wear jewelry under her habit? What really took her to Barking Abbey and why did that chalice go with her? There are many things I would love to ask her."

"Let me add one more," said Gervase. "Why did the prioress use a Saxon charm when she prayed with Sister Tecla in that church at Mountnessing?"

"Then we come to the biggest question of all."

"Biggest?"

"Sister Gunnhild."

"What about her?"

"Is she really a woman—or a man?"

Prioress Mindred stood in front of the mirror in her chamber and brushed her long hair before plaiting it with care and letting it hang forward over one shoulder. She wore a plain white shift and a pair of slippers, which had been embroidered with gold thread. Both arms were adorned with gold clasps and there was a necklace of mixed stones around her neck. She tilted her head to admire the noble profile then fingered the jewelry at her neck. She might have repudiated her former life when she entered a religious house, but she could not disown all the gifts that her husband had bought for her.

On the table before her were several gold and silver rings. One had a large ruby in a setting of tiny pearls, another bore a sapphire, a third had a fierce agate, which sparkled in the flames of the candles. Mindred put the rings on her fingers and held them up to admire them. After another day behind the veil, she now felt a sense of release and elation.

Pleasure was soon replaced by remorse. The prioress was there to lead an exemplary life and not to indulge in the vanities of feminine behaviour. Pulling off the various pieces of jewelry, she put them into a box and shut the lid tight, then she turned away from the mirror and began to undo her hair before reaching for her wimple to hide it completely. Mindred then slipped on her gown and tied the drawstrings. She was about to leave the chamber when she remembered her footwear. Kicking off the embroidered slippers, she went barefoot to the door and let herself out. It was no new struggle in which she was engaged, but one that claimed her at regular intervals. Temptation was very strong and she sometimes yielded to it. But there was a perverse pleasure in repentance as well.

She went silently along the passage way and let herself into the chapel, intending to spend some time on her knees in contrition before returning to her virtuous couch. But there was someone already there. Even in the darkness, she knew it was Sister Tecla. Seen in dim outline, the young nun was lying prostrate on the steps in front of the altar, raising her head from time to time to gaze in longing before lowering it again to the hard stone. It was not the first occasion when the prioress had disturbed her nocturnal prayers. Mindred genuflected, then stepped slowly forward. Taking the nun by the shoulders, she helped her up from the ground and wrapped an arm around her.

Sister Tecla made no protest. She permitted herself to be led out of the chapel and back to her little room where she was lowered onto the bed and covered with a blanket. Mindred bent down to kiss her on the forehead and the nun began to sing quietly to herself and to rock very gently to and fro. The prioress used tender force to still her movement, then she put a finger on Tecla's lips to silence the song. The nun turned over and drifted off to sleep. Mindred was happy. She felt that her good deed would help to atone for her bad impulse of vanity. After a last look at the slumbering Tecla, she tiptoed out and went back towards the chapel to offer her own prayers.

The splashing noise was clearly audible. As she went past the bathhouse, she heard the unmistakable sound. It was now past midnight and all the sisters should be in their beds. Who could possibly want to take a bath at that hour? There was not even a flicker of light under the door. She groped her way to her chamber and brought one of the lighted candles back with her. The splashing continued. Bath times were strictly regulated and each nun bathed alone. Heating the water was a communal effort. Whoever was in the bath now had not only filled it herself, she must be lying in water that was stone cold. Prioress Mindred hesitated to burst in, but her duty was clear. Someone was breaking the rules in the most flagrant way and would have to be punished.

Lifting the latch, she held up the candle and entered.

"Prioress Mindred!" exclaimed Sister Gunnhild.

"Dear God!"

The prioress was completely unprepared for what she saw. Sister Gunnhild was reclining naked in the bathtub and rubbing her body all over with some rough twigs. Huge breasts bobbed in the water, a fat stomach protruded, thick white thighs were braced against the side of the tub. But it was something else that alarmed Mindred so much that she emitted a soundless scream and dropped the candle. The flame went out and she was left in total darkness with the Danish nun.

Sister Gunnhild was the first to recover. Her voice was calm and reassuring as she hauled herself out of the water.

"Go to the chapel," she said. "I will get dressed and join you there. We must pray together."

Miles Champeney waited until the whole household was asleep before he let himself out by a door at the back of the building. Moonlight guided his steps to the stables where he found the two horses he had saddled earlier. He led them a hundred yards away from the house before he mounted, and the soft thud of the hooves went unheard as he cantered away towards the hill, pulling the second animal behind him with a lead rein. It was a fine night with only the lightest of breezes to disturb his mantle and his cap. Miles rode steadily on and rehearsed the details in his mind. Months of planning had gone into an operation that would last no more than a few minutes, if all went well, and it was important to adhere to what had been agreed. By the time the daunting outline of Blackwater Hall rose before him, he had been through it all a dozen times.

He approached the property from the rear so that he did not disturb the dogs who were kennelled in the courtyard at the front. Close to the perimeter wall, he tethered the two horses and proceeded on foot. The coil of rope he brought now came into its own. A high stone wall was easy enough for a fit young man to scale, but Matilda would need assistance to get back over it. So he tied the rope securely to an abutment and let the end fall down to the ground. He tested it with a hard pull, then lowered himself down. Miles was now inside Blackwater Hall. The first hurdle had been cleared. Keeping low, he moved stealthily towards the house.

The ground floor was used for storage and the main entrance was at the front. Steps led up to the first floor so that provisions could be taken to the kitchens, but the occupants only used the external flight of steps to go into the house. Matilda would now use the rickety kitchen staircase to come down to him, but not before she had first signalled that everything was in order. Miles hugged the shadows and fixed his eyes on a window at the very top of the house. It was in darkness at the moment but his faith in her did not waver. She would come. If necessary, he was ready to wait for Matilda all night.

Ten minutes was all that she took. A light moved twice across the upstairs window and then vanished again. Miles came out of his hiding place and scurried across to the stout oak door of the storeroom. He was rescuing her at last from the home that she despised. They did not know exactly what would happen once they got over the wall together but they did not care. Escape was an end in itself. All else would follow naturally. They would be together and nothing else mattered besides that fact. Miles was on edge as he waited. It was weeks since he had seen her, months since they had been able to talk properly and exchange their vows. Matilda was coming to him and he shivered with anticipatory delight.

When he heard the bolt being drawn, he stepped forward with his arms out wide. The door shuddered, then swung back on creaking hinges to reveal Matilda. She wore a cloak with a hood that was pulled over her head and she came willingly into his embrace. When Miles tried to kiss her, however, she grabbed him by his tunic and swung him so violently against the wall that he could hardly stand. A kick from his beloved sent him to the ground and a blow from her club made him groggy. He tried to protest and reach out for her but the club descended again with greater force and Miles Champeney pitched forward into oblivion.

Hamo FitzCorbucion stepped out of the storeroom with four more of his men. The fifth now pulled back the hood and enjoyed the crude ribbing of his colleagues. The trap had been set and their quarry had strolled right into it.

"Take him away!" ordered Hamo, giving the prone figure a gratuitous kick. "Throw him in the dungeon!"

Two men grabbed Miles by the legs and dragged him unceremoniously into the building. They bumped him down a flight of stone steps into a passageway that was lit with guttering torches. They came to a massive door into which an iron grille had been set. A key went into the lock and the door was opened. Miles Champeney was flung headfirst into the dungeon. The servant who was curled up on the ground in the pitch darkness yelled in pain as the body landed right on top of him, and the two guards roared with laughter.

"Howl as loud as you can," said one. "Nobody can hear you."

The door clanged shut and freedom became a memory.

Clouds drifted in not long after dawn and Maldon was soon washed by a heavy drizzle. The breeze had stiffened into a gusting wind. Those who could, stayed indoors, those who could not, braved the elements and cursed their luck. Farmers saw their harvest soaked and their livestock drenched. Sailors and fishermen felt the worst of the weather, wet through from the downpour and blown around on the normally placid waters of the River Blackwater. When the drizzle eased, they were the first to be aware of the slight improvement.

The figure on the shore was untroubled by the damp. His armour was bubbled and his mantle sodden but he still fought on in slow motion, his words blown across to Northey Island on the wind. Tovild was haunted.

Then came the clash of shields. The seamen strode up, angered by war. Often a spear went through a doomed man's body. Wistan then went forward, the son of Thurstan, and fought against the foe. He was the slayer of three of them in the throng before Wigelm's kinsman lay among the slain. It was a fierce encounter there. They stood fast, those warriors in the strife. Fighting men fell weary from their wounds. Blood fell to the ground ...

His sword-arm flashed and more Viking blood stained the battle-field of Maldon. Tovild the Haunted was fighting well that morning. The rain seemed to refresh him. He was proud to stand alongside the other hearth-warriors to defend the town. Nobody had told him that the Vikings would eventually drive them all back and exact tribute. Tovild was haunted by the wild idea that the Saxon army could win this time.

Gervase Bret had been to Tovild's cottage and found it deserted. Riding down to the shore, he saw the lonely figure engaged in his daily ritual and paused to admire him. The demons that drove him did not relent when foul weather came. Tovild would go on fighting in a snowstorm.

Wrapped in a cloak, Gervase rode right up to him.

"Good morrow, Tovild!" he called.

The old man pointed his sword. "Friend or foeman?"

"Friend. We spoke near here only yesterday."

"You fought in the battle beside me?"

"Yes," said Gervase. "You slew three Vikings."

"I will slay more if they keep coming at me."

He flailed away with his sword and quoted more of the poem. Gervase dismounted. He caught Tovild's sword-arm with gentle firmness and took his weapon from him. The old man began to whine piteously.

"I cannot fight without my sword," he wailed. "They will cut me down. These fierce warlords will murder me."

"Let us talk of another murder first."

Tovild peered at him. "You came to me before."

"Because we need your help. You saw a man killed in the marshes. A young man, stabbed to death by his assailant. Or maybe he was attacked by more than one." He pulled Tovild to him so that the horse screened the two of them from the sudden punches of the wind. "Four or five days ago," said Gervase. "Not far from here. I met you at the spot."

There was a long pause as Tovild scrutinised him. His manner was more friendly but there was still distrust and caution. He gave a little whoop and turned in a circle.

"Do you like riddles, young man?"

"That is why I am here. The riddle of the murder."

"Who am I? Who am I?"

"Tovild the Haunted."

"No, listen to me. Listen. And tell me who I am." The riddle was accompanied by a graphic mime. "The sea fed me, the water covering enveloped me, and waves covered me, footless, close to earth. Often I open my mouth to the flood; now some man will eat my flesh; he cares not for my covering, when with the point of his knife he tears off the skin from my side and afterwards quickly eats me uncooked." Tovild danced up and down like a child. "Who am I?"

Gervase knew the answer because he had heard the riddle before but he also knew the importance of entering into the spirit of the game. Tovild was testing him. Only if he talked in the roundabout language of the old man would he get any help out of him. He scratched his head and pretended to be having difficulty working out the answer.

"Who am I? Who am I?"

"A fish?"

"No, no. I'm not a fish!"

"A crab?"

"No, not a crab either. Who am I? Guess!"

Gervase clicked his fingers as if it had just dawned on him. "I know who you are—an oyster!"

"Yes, yes. That's right."

"Try me again, Tovild."

"Another riddle?" asked the old man excitedly.

"As many as you like."

"They are very cunning."

"I will have to think hard, then."

"Who am I? Who am I?"

Gervase played with him for fifteen minutes to secure his trust and win his friendship. Always taking time to work out something he soon guessed, he identified Tovild as a whole range of things—fire, swan, badger, weathercock, key, and even battering ram. The old warrior chortled with glee. Someone was actually playing with him on his own terms. He threw a final challenge at Gervase.

"Who am I? Who am I?"

"Tell me the riddle."

"It is the most difficult of all."

"Who are you, Tovild? Who are you?"

"I've heard of a bright ring interceding well before men, although tongueless, although it cried not with a loud voice in strong words. The precious thing spoke before men, although holding its peace: 'Save me, Helper of souls!' May men understand the mysterious saying of the red gold, the magic speech; may wise men entrust their salvation to God, as the ring said." Tovild clapped his hands. "Who am I? Who am I?"

Gervase really did need time to consider because he had not heard this riddle before. He repeated snatches of it to himself as he wrestled with its meaning. Tovild sensed victory and cackled happily. He taunted Gervase by throwing some of the phrases at him again.

"Who am I? Who am I?"

"A chalice."

Tovild was deflated. "How did you *know*?"

"The bright ring is the sacred vessel that brings thoughts of Christ to the minds of men during the celebration of Mass. In short—a chalice." He put a congratulatory hand on the other's shoulder. "It was the most cunning riddle of all. You are very clever."

The old man took his sword from Gervase and ran twenty paces away before turning to face him again. He beckoned him to follow. Gervase had at last established his credentials. As Tovild scampered across the wet grass, Gervase led his horse and walked after him. The drizzle had all but stopped now and the sky was lightening. Tovild was skipping as if he had just won the Battle of Maldon single-handed.

They eventually came to the place in the marshes where Brunloc the Fisherman had first found the dead body. It was a convenient venue for murder. Trees and bushes were in full bloom on the bank and the river was dotted with clumps of reeds and masses of water lilies. A corpse that was hurled in at a well-chosen point might lie undetected for weeks in the slime. Guy FitzCorbucion had been lucky to be discovered so soon by a fisherman making his way home.

"Think carefully," said Gervase. "What did you see?"

"A raven from Blackwater Hall."

"He was killed and thrown into the water right here."

"The war-knife shed his blood."

"How many people attacked him, Tovild. One, two, more?"

"One only plucked his black feathers."

"What happened? Tell me?"

"Who am I? Who am I?"

"We've had enough riddles, Tovild."

The old man banged his chest. "Who am I?" He used his sword like a knife to stab at the air. "Who am I?" He jabbed a finger at the reeds. "Who am I?"

Gervase was to get his answer in the form of a riddle.

"You are a killer, Tovild. Tell me your name."

"I am a wondrous creature" sang the old man. "I vary my voice; sometimes I bark like a dog; sometimes I bleat like a goat; sometimes I cry like a goose; sometimes I scream like a hawk; sometimes I mimic the grey eagle, the laugh of the warbird; sometimes with a kite's voice I speak with my mouth; sometimes the song of the gull where I sit in my gladness. They call me G, also A and R; O gives aid, and H, and I. Now I am named—who am I?"

Gervase was baffled and he was given no time to solve the riddle. Instead of waiting to urge him on, Tovild ran to the water's edge and fell forward. Gervase thought at first that he was diving in but he was merely hanging over the bank to fish in the muddy water with a long arm. He brought something up in triumph and ran across to give it to his new friend. Gervase was so hypnotised by the object that he simply stared at it for minutes on end. When Gervase finally broke out of his trance, Tovild the Haunted had gone and taken his riddles with him. He had, however, left behind an invaluable item. Gervase Bret knew exactly what it was. He wiped the knife in the grass to get the worst of the slime off it.

He was holding the murder weapon.

Ralph Delchard was deeply dissatisfied with his day so far. It began badly when the lusty-throated cockerel at Champeney Hall brought him rudely out of his dream at the very moment when Sister Tecla was about to tear off her habit and submit her body to his passionate embraces. It was not helped by the general consternation that seized the house when it was learned that Miles had been missing all night along with two of the horses. The loss of a nun was compounded by the loss of a son. There was worse to come. Having waited until the rain had stopped, he set off for Maldon in the sunshine with four of his men, only to be caught in a sudden shower when he was too far away from the demesne to turn back and not close enough to the town to seek immediate shelter. It was a wet and decidedly jaded Ralph Delchard who finally met with the man he had come to see.

Peter de Valognes did little to raise his spirits. The sheriff was still smarting from his brush with the prickly Hamo FitzCorbucion on the previous day. Having ridden all the way to Maldon from some distance away, he had expected at least a welcome and a show of gratitude. Instead, he had been given a reprimand for his tardiness and a total lack of cooperation at Blackwater Hall. Peter de Valognes, a tall and dignified man in his thirties, was Sheriff of Essex and Hertfordshire. He was also a nephew of the Conqueror and brother-in-law to Eudo *dapifer*, one of the King's stewards. A powerful member of the Norman aristocracy, he did not appreciate the brusque treatment he had so far received in Maldon.

"What have you discovered, my lord, Sheriff?" said Ralph.

"That I wish I had stayed in Hertfordshire."

"You caught Hamo on a bad day."

"Does he ever have a good one?"

"He has had far too many," said Ralph with feeling. "That is why we are here. To call this raven to account."

"I came to solve a murder," said Peter irritably. "When I left Blackwater, I was in a mood to commit one."

They were in the shire hall where the town reeve had provided some refreshment for them. Ralph had the chance to dry out slightly and Peter de Valognes was able to work off some of his frustration by parading his complaints. Under Edward the Confessor, the sheriff was merely a landowner of second rank whose status depended on being the agent of the King. The office was now held by more senior nobles whose position resembled that of a *vicomte* in Normandy. Peter de Valognes was thus a high-ranking royal officer with a wide field of jurisdiction and he was not being accorded the immense respect due to him.

"Where are your men?" asked Ralph.

"Most have joined the search for this boy, Wistan," said Peter, "even though I am not convinced that he is the culprit. We must catch him before Hamo does or the lad will be slain on the spot at once."

"What if you do not find him, my lord Sheriff?"

"Then we will impose the usual fine on the hundred."

"Maldon is assessed as a half-hundred."

"Do not quibble with me, my lord," said Peter. "You know the law as well as I. When we came to England, the King had to protect his followers from random attack. He decreed that whenever a Norman is killed by an assassin who escapes, the hundred has to suffer a fine. Guy FitzCorbucion's death will be paid for by everyone."

"That will not content his father."

"I have lost interest in his contentment!"

"Have you called witnesses?" said Ralph.

"Dozens."

"What has emerged from your enquiries?"

"That is our business, my lord," said Peter with a touch of haughtiness. "It can have no interest for you."

"It has every interest. Hamo is the chief subject of our investigation. Anything that pertains to him and his egregious family has interest for us." He sat back in his chair. "What exactly did the stricken father say when you rode out to Blackwater Hall?"

Peter de Valognes was quite prepared to describe the encounter in detail and Ralph gleaned a lot of information about their adversary. Hamo's grief at the death of his son had been sharpened by the theft of an object from Guy's chamber, which had great significance for both men. Ralph's ears pricked up when he heard that it was a silver chalice that was missing. The sheriff had nothing useful to add about the murder investigation and it became clear that he would need at least a week to get anywhere near the point that Ralph and Gervase had already reached. It was up to them to solve the crime. A man of Peter's eminence only frightened the townspeople and his bustling officers were all too reminiscent of members of the conquering army that had first moved into Essex twenty years ago. An official enquiry imposed from above would accomplish little. Two men like Ralph and Gervase, working from below, might be able to insinuate themselves into the places where the truth lay.

"How long do you expect to stay, my lord, Sheriff?"

"It already feels like a year!"

"Maldon is a pleasant enough town."

"I will think twice before *I* come here again."

"What if Hamo presses an invitation upon you?"

Ralph was tactful enough to withdraw before the sheriff could answer the question. The storm had passed and the sun was out again but his attire was still damp. Ralph dismissed his men and gave them the freedom of the town for a couple of hours while he rode back to Champeney Hall to change out of his wet tunic and mantle. He needed no escort on such a short journey and valued the opportunity to be alone. He could speculate on whether the silver chalice at the priory might actually be the one taken from Blackwater Hall, and think luscious, highly irreligious thoughts about the divine Sister Tecla.

They were a hundred yards or more away when he first sighted them and he reined his horse in behind the cover of some bushes. Three men were cantering towards Champeney Hall and they soon passed close enough to him for Ralph to recognise their leader. It was Fulk the Steward, the man who had accompanied Jocelyn FitzCorbucion to the shire hall on that first afternoon. He rode with the air of a man on an important errand and Ralph wondered what it might be. Gilbert Champeney loved the whole world but even his spacious affection could not accommodate Black-water Hall. The very sight of these emissaries would make the mild-mannered Gilbert froth with rage.

Ralph followed at a discreet distance and watched them ride into the courtyard. By the time that he had stabled his horse, the three men had disappeared into the house. Ralph let himself in quietly and went up to his chamber. Raised voices could be heard from below and then a door banged. When he crossed to the window, he saw Fulk and the two men walking towards their mounts. The steward seemed to be in high humour as he rode off the premises. Ralph slipped out of his wet apparel and found a clean tunic. He was about to put it on when he heard a soft creak on the stairs outside. Somebody was approaching the chamber with a furtive step and he reached instinctively for his sword, moving into an alcove to conceal himself.

There was a tap on the door to make sure that the room was unoccupied and then someone entered. Ralph drew himself right back into the alcove and listened. The intruder went straight to the satchel in which Gervase Bret carried all of his writs and charters. Ralph heard the leather strap being undone and the rustle of parchment. The thief was trying to steal their documentary evidence. Without that, the commissioners would be severely handicapped in their forthcoming tussle with Hamo. Ralph was furious. Hurling himself out of the alcove, he threw his back against the door so that it slammed shut, then held his sword at the throat of the man who was taking their property.

Gilbert Champeney turned white with guilt then fell to his knees in supplication and burst in tears.

"Ralph!" he exclaimed. "Thank God! Please help me!"

They were together at last and yet kept cruelly apart. She knew that he was there. From her chamber window, Matilda could see the two horses down in the courtyard of Blackwater Hall. Miles Champeney had come for her during the night and been taken prisoner by her father. The two horses on which they would have ridden away were now drinking contentedly from the water trough. She was trembling with impotent rage. Matilda blamed her father for his ruthlessness and her brother for his duplicity, but she reserved the greatest scorn for herself. It was her fault that Miles had been captured. The man she loved had been delivered into the hands of those who hated him and she had to take the responsibility for that. Atonement could only be made if she rescued him but the chances of that were slim. Locked in her chamber, with an armed guard outside her door, she was not even sure where Miles was being kept.

Noises from the courtyard took her to the window once again and she saw Fulk riding in with his two men. Hamo and Jocelyn came out to greet them and the steward gave them his news. Hamo burst into laughter and clapped the man on the arm in appreciation before striding back into the house. Jocelyn was also delighted at the turn of events but he wanted the pleasure of gloating. He gazed at her window with a sly grin and gave her a mocking wave. Guy had been killed but another brother exercised power over her now. Matilda drew back in cold horror. She had the terrible feeling that she might never see Miles Champeney again.

The dungeon was small and airless. A thin sliver of light came through an aperture high in the rough stone wall but an oppressive darkness filled most of the chamber. The straw that half-covered the uneven floor had been there for weeks and was ripe with souvenirs of former occupants. The stench of human excrement was almost unbearable. Insects crawled up the walls and across the low ceiling. Spiders were spinning their patient webs. A rat nestled in the darkest corner. Miles Champeney was outraged that he had been cast into such a foul cell, but his cries of indignation went unheard and his pounding on the door went unregarded. He soon came to understand the seriousness of his plight and the sheer irrelevance of any protest.

His companion in the grim dungeon was the servant who acted as an intermediary between him and Matilda, and the man had no hope of ever leaving the place alive. Miles felt a stab of guilt. Indirectly, he had helped to put the man in the fetid prison. The servant's only crime had been loyalty to his mistress but he would be forced to pay a dreadful penalty for it. Compassion touched Miles. Even though he was concerned for himself and distracted by fears for Matilda, he could still spare a thought for an incidental casualty of their love. The man did not deserve his fate.

Miles shuffled about and hurled a kick at the door.

"We must get out of this hole!" he urged.

"It is impossible, my lord."

"There *has* to be a way!"

"Nobody has ever found it before."

"I still have my dagger," said Miles, pulling it from its scabbard. "They did not take that away from me."

"What use is one dagger against a dozen swords?"

"I will attack the guard when he brings food."

"He will not even come, my lord," said the servant. "We get no food. Starvation is part of our punishment."

"They can't treat us like this!" yelled Miles.

"My lord, Hamo, can do whatever he wishes."

Miles Champeney railed aloud but he knew that his cries were futile. He was an enemy of Blackwater Hall who had dared to trespass on it. Hamo FitzCorbucion would show no mercy. Matilda was trapped as helplessly as her beloved so there was no possibility of rescue from her. Only one person could save him now but he had estranged himself from that same person by his flight from Champeney Hall. Gilbert had threatened to disown him if he persisted in the folly of trying to wed Matilda. Why should a father come to the aid of a son who so blatantly defied his wishes? Miles began to resign himself to the inevitable. He was doomed.

Ralph Delchard listened to Gilbert Champeney with gathering impatience, then smashed his fist down on to the oak table. They were in Gilbert's chamber and the latest example of Hamo's perfidy had been exposed to view. Ralph demanded action.

"Take your men and ride to Blackwater Hall!" he said.

"What good would that do?" asked Gilbert sadly. "Hamo has four times my number of knights and he will mock me."

"Let me go in your stead!" volunteered Ralph.

"That would serve no purpose."

"I will insist that he hand your son over."

"Hamo would not receive you," said Gilbert. "He would simply close his gates upon you and keep you outside. Even your writ does not extend to Blackwater."

"Then we must call on Peter de Valognes."

"No, Ralph!"

"He is the sheriff."

"Then he has business enough to keep him occupied."

"Peter de Valognes has the authority to compel Hamo."

"Not in this instance, Ralph."

"Send in the sheriff. Demand the release of your son."

"How do we know that Miles is held at the house?" said Gilbert balefully. "Fulk was far too wily to tell me more than is needful. They may have him hidden anywhere on the demesne. We cannot ask the sheriff to go searching for a missing son when he is already hunting for a murderer." He bit his lip and shook his head. "Besides, this is a domestic matter. It must be sorted out between Hamo and me."

"Then what do you propose to do?"

"Offer him money. Try to buy him off."

"Money!" Ralph was fuming. "Danegeld!"

"What other way is there?"

"Brute force," said Ralph. "He may have his army of knights but most of them are still out searching for Wistan. Add my men to yours and we have a sizeable troop. Join them with the sheriff and his officers and even Hamo will have to pay attention to what we say."

"It is not that simple, Ralph."

"Miles is your son. Fight to get him back."

"I would," said Gilbert in despair, "but Hamo holds all the weapons. He sent his steward here to strike a bargain. Miles will be set free if I hand over the documents that accuse Blackwater Hall."

"That would disarm us completely. When we meet him at the shire hall, we would have no case to offer against him." He flashed an admonitory glance at his host. "Would you really have betrayed us in that way, Gilbert?"

"I was sorely tempted, I know that."

"To steal from your own guests!"

"My son's life is at stake here."

"Then take your case to the sheriff!"

"No!" shouted Gilbert vehemently, rising to his feet. "What am I to tell him? That my son ran off against my wishes and was caught in a snare by Hamo? What proof do I have? You saw Fulk enter this house but you did not hear what he told me. He has only to deny every word that passed between us and my case crumbles." He walked up to Ralph with his hands spread in a plea. "There is no help for me here. Peter de Valognes is a power in the shire but he will not thank me for trying to drag him into a dispute of this kind. Where is the crime in his eyes? A sheriff must stay above the petty squabbles of barons." More tears formed. "And besides, I have my pride, Ralph. I would be too ashamed to admit what has befallen me and how I was even driven to steal from worthy friends like you. People may laugh at Champeney Hall but it has a reputation to uphold."

Ralph Delchard could hear what the other man was saying and he had profound sympathy. The son may have inadvertently plunged them into the mess but the father was not entirely free from blame. His attitude had been one of the pressures that forced Miles to follow such a reckless course of action. Ralph was angry that a host would dare even to think of stealing from his guests, but his real venom was directed solely at Hamo FitzCorbucion. The master of Blackwater Hall was entirely without scruple. To disable the commissioners who could threaten his position, he had turned a generous man like Gilbert Champeney into a common thief. He would have no compunction about starving the son to death if the father did not meet the terms of the corrupt bargain.

After lengthy brooding, Ralph spied a possible solution.

"I would like to meet this Matilda," he said.

"Matilda?"

"If she can inspire such love in your son, she must be a remarkable young lady." He gave a reassuring smile. "Miles risked his life to get to her. He may be foolhardy but I like his courage. It must not go to waste. Take heart, my friend. We will save him."

"How?"

"By turning Brother Simon loose on Hamo."

"Brother Simon?"

"Yes," said Ralph with a grin. "He may seem a timid creature who is afraid of his own shadow, but he is the strongest weapon in our armoury. Let us find him. Two lovers may yet be rescued by a Benedictine monk."

Chapter Eight

BRIGHT SUNSHINE HAD FOLLOWED THE UNCERTAIN START TO THE DAY AND THE earlier squall was a receding memory. The wind had now dropped to a token puff. Maldon was warm, dry, and positively throbbing with activity. It was market day and stallholders who had set out their wares during the last of the rain were now wiping the sweat from their brows and complaining about the heat. People streamed into the town for the occasion, some by horse or on foot from outlying areas, some by boat from Goldhanger or West Mersea and beyond. Fish was fresh, oysters were cheap, and vegetables were plentiful. The local cheese was much in demand. Live poultry, leather goods, basketware, dyed cloth, and pottery were also on sale with dozens of other items. There was even a man who simultaneously told fortunes and pulled teeth with an alarming pair of pincers. One glance at the blood-stained molars that lay in his earthenware bowl was enough to cure most species of toothache.

Gervase Bret was searching the market for a cutler. Having tethered his horse nearby, he made his way through the seething mass of people who had converged on the junction of High Street and Silver Street. The noise and bustle could not compare with the pandemonium that London had to offer but it still took him some minutes to find what he wanted. The cutler was a short, tubby man with a ragged beard. He wore a rough woollen tunic, which was making him perspire, and kept taking a swig out of a cup of water near his hand. When Gervase came up to the stall, the man was sharpening a blade on a whetstone, which he revolved by pressing his foot on a treadle. Sparks flew up into his pudgy face but they did not seem to bother him at all.

The cutler glanced at Gervase and scented a potential customer. He broke off from his task and gave a lopsided grin.

"Can I help you, young sir?" he asked.

"I hope so," said Gervase. "I found a knife and I wondered if you could tell me anything about it."

"Found one?" He was disappointed. "Is that all?"

"Your help could be important."

"Not to me, sir. I only sell or sharpen knives."

"I'll pay you for your time," volunteered Gervase, and the cutler's manner changed at once. "Here's the knife."

The murder weapon was tucked in his belt and he pulled it out to pass it across. It was a long-bladed implement with a stout bone handle, which had been worn to the shape of someone's palm by constant use. The cutler took one look and gave a satisfied chuckle.

"What can you tell me?" asked Gervase.

"Anything you want to know, sir. I made this."

"You made it?"

"A kitchen knife. For slicing food of any kind."

"Are you certain that it is yours?"

The man looked offended. "My mark is upon it!"

"Of course." Gervase thrust a hand into his purse and gave him a few coins. "Tell me all you can."

"There's not much more to say," admitted the man, "but this is my workmanship. Look, sir. I have the twin to your knife lying here on my stall." He picked up one of the knives on display and placed it beside the other. They were virtually identical. "I have made and sold a hundred or more like this."

"And who buys them?" said Gervase.

"Everybody with an eye for quality."

"So you cannot tell me who bought this particular one?"

"Your guess is as good as mine." The cutler waved a stubby hand at the crowd. "There is my market, sir. I work for all and sundry. This knife of yours might have been sold to a baker to slice his bread, a butcher to cut up his meat, or a fisherman to gut his catch. Any wife might have bought it to use in her kitchen." He gave a dark laugh. "Or on her husband! For it will go through live flesh just as easily as dead."

Gervase could vouch for that. He took the implement back and turned it over in his hand as he examined it.

"How long ago did you make this?" he said.

"A year at most. Maybe as little as six months ago."

"Could it get so worn in such a short time?"

The man gave his lopsided grin. "I can see you do not work in a kitchen, sir. If you hold anything in your hand for ten hours a day, you will leave your imprint on it. This knife has been well used but it has been looked after. The blade is as sharp as any razor and the point is like a needle. My guess is that it belonged to a cook."

"Someone from Maldon?"

"Who can say?" He started the whetstone. "You'll find my knives in Barking and Brightlingsea, in Colchester and Coggeshall. Why, sir, I daresay that knives just like the one you hold are being used by the monks of Waltham Abbey at this very moment to cut their venison."

Gervase smiled. "Forest law forbids them to hunt deer and the Rule of St. Benedict prevents them from eating rich meat."

"Laws and rules don't bother them," said the man as he sharpened his blade again. "Most of the brothers I've met are fatter than me and they didn't get bellies like that from eating gruel and fish." He glanced at the knife that Gervase was putting back in his belt. "Give it to me, sir."

"Why?"

"So that I can sell it again. It's no use to you."

"But it is, my friend."

"In a Kitchen?"

"No," said Gervase. "In a court of law."

He thanked the man and moved off through the crowd. The stroll to the Church of All Souls' took no more than a minute and he was pleased to find Oslac inside. The priest was kneeling in prayer before the altar and he remained there for some time. Gervase waited quietly at the rear of the nave then stepped forward. Oslac was pleased to see him and hustled his visitor straight into the vestry.

"I have a message for you."

"For me?"

"You are to return to Champeney Hall as soon as possible," said the priest. "One of the soldiers from your escort called in at the church even now. He knew that you would be coming here at some point."

Gervase frowned. "Did he say why I was summoned?"

"No, but he was anxious to reach you. That suggests the matter is of some importance."

"I will go at once," said Gervase, turning away.

"Wait!" said Oslac, with a restraining hand on his arm. "I must hear your news first. And you must hear mine. You can stay in Maldon two minutes longer, surely?"

Gervase relaxed slightly. "At least."

"Tell me what you have found."

"I tracked down Tovild the Haunted once more."

"Was he still fighting?"

"Furiously."

"Which army was he in this time?"

"The Saxon," said Gervase. "I found him killing Vikings and quoting his poem."

"They say that the Battle of Maldon lasted for fourteen days, but Tovild has been fighting it for fourteen years and more." He smiled sadly. "Did you draw anything out of him?"

"A stream of riddles."

"That is his way, I fear."

"I proved one thing for certain," said Gervase. "He did witness the murder. Of that there can be no doubt."

"Why?"

"He gave me this." He took out the knife. "It was used to kill Guy FitzCorbucion then tossed into the water."

Oslac looked at the weapon with horrid fascination as if wanting to take it but fearing its taint if he did so.

"Can you be sure that this is the murder weapon?"

"I would swear it, Father Oslac."

"And Tovild found it for you?"

"At the scene of the crime."

The priest grew wary. "Did he tell you who the killer was?" he asked. "Did he give you a name?"

"No name, only another riddle."

"What was it?"

"I cannot remember it all," confessed Gervase, "and I am nowhere near solving it yet. There were some letters in it but I would need to rack my brain to tease each one out again. Tovild gabbled away at me, gave me the knife, and then vanished into thin air."

"He gave you the knife?"

"From the place where it had been thrown. He had to lie on his chest and grope about in the mud."

"But he knew exactly where to look, it seems."

"What do you mean?"

Oslac stared at him with a level gaze and Gervase realised what he was suggesting. It was a notion that had never crossed his mind and he was shocked that the priest would even consider it. Gervase dismissed it out of hand.

"No, no," he said. "Tovild is quite innocent."

"Then how could he lead you straight to the knife?"

"He saw where it was tossed."

"Could he not have put it there himself?" said Oslac. "If a man wanted to get rid of a murder weapon, would he not cast it right out into the marshes? Yet you tell me that Tovild lay down on the ground and reached for it."

"That is true."

"It was in its hiding place."

"Then why give it to me at all?" asked Gervase. "If he was the killer, he would do everything to conceal the crime and not assist me in solving it. You said yourself that the man is completely harmless. Can you *see* that gnarled old warrior committing a murder?"

"Frankly—no."

"Then put the whole idea aside."

"I fear that I cannot," said Oslac tenaciously. "I love Tovild as much as I pity him. He is in the grip of some benign madness that makes him play the soldier. Tovild could never commit a murder because that needs sanity and a degree of premeditation." He pointed to the knife. "But he could kill a man by accident in the heat of battle."

"By accident?"

"You have seen the way he hacks the air with his sword and jabs at his unseen enemy with his spear." Oslac shook his head slowly. "His very harmlessness may be the key to it all here. Guy would not have been troubled by his approach."

"But why should Tovild approach him?"

"Because Guy came to laugh at him. Because Guy was there to taunt a ridiculous old man in rusty armour." He developed the idea with a growing belief in its virtues. "That must have been it, Master Bret! Do you not see? Guy FitzCorbucion was trespassing. He was treading on the sacred battlefield where Tovild worships each day. It was sheer sacrilege. A young Norman Knight was goading a decrepit old Saxon. Is it not conceivable that Tovild lashed out at him? He has been killing imaginary invaders all these years, why should he not cut down a real one? Guy did not have time to defend himself because he was taken unawares." Oslac was talking with great intensity now. "I viewed the body and it had been cruelly disfigured. Such mutilation happens in combat. We may smile at Tovild the Haunted because of his strange antics, but there is a lot of wanton violence in a man who fights a bitter foe every day of his life."

Gervase had to concede that it was within the bounds of possibility. He also saw that a murder committed in such a way would not be recognised by Tovild as a crime. It would be one more brave action in the eternal battle that he waged. Handing over the knife to Gervase was a circuitous way of boasting about his triumph. Somewhere in that final riddle Tovild might even have hidden a form of confession. It was all possible and yet Gervase could not somehow accept it. What really puzzled him was why Oslac was so ready to incriminate the old man. From the moment he saw the murder weapon, the priest had been speaking with a defensive urgency that Gervase had never heard before. He slipped the knife back into his belt and nodded.

"I will think on it," he said, "but now I must go."

"One second more, please."

"They have sent for me. I am needed at Champeney Hall."

"You have not heard my tidings yet," said Oslac. "You have at least made progress. I have only found setback."

"Setback?"

"Wistan. He spent the night in my house."

"Was he discovered?"

"Worse than that."

"What has happened?"

"He has run away."

"When they are still out searching for him?" said Gervase in disbelief. "He might just as well give himself up to Hamo. What chance has an unarmed boy against all those soldiers?"

"He is not unarmed," said Oslac solemnly. "There was a sword at my house. Wistan took it along with a supply of food. The boy has plans." He pointed to the knife thrust into Gervase's belt. "You have found a murder weapon—and I have lost one. Wistan wants revenge."

It was the last place that they would dream of looking for him. Northey Island had given him a temporary refuge but they had flushed him out with dogs in the end. No hounds would sniff him out here. For the first time since he had been a fugitive, Wistan felt supremely safe. Gervase Bret had shown him unexpected kindness and Oslac the Priest had even taken the boy into his own house, but neither man understood the imperatives that drove him on. What they had done was to create some time for him in which to find his bearings before he moved on elsewhere. Gervase had used a word that had had no real meaning for him before. Sanctuary. He had spoken of the church as offering sanctuary to the runaway boy. Wistan learned quickly. Oslac's house was a comfortable enough hiding place but there was only one building in the town that could provide true sanctuary and that was why he had made his way to Maldon Priory.

When he thought of the priest, he felt both guilty and relieved. Oslac had taken a great risk in protecting the boy and had shared his own home with Wistan, but the hours he had spent there had troubled him as much as they had restored him. The priest had a wife and four children who lived happily together in the cosy humility of their little house. They drew him to them and gave freely of what they had. Wistan was washed, fed, dressed in clean apparel, and shown to a mattress under the eaves. Their love had revived him but their very togetherness had pushed him apart from them. He was sorry that he had to hurt them but he was also helping them by leaving. His presence there put them in danger and they would now be safe. Oslac had created a well-knit family but Wistan had nobody else now, and it underscored another difference between the two of them. The priest had a reason to live: The boy was ready to die. It gave him an inner strength, which would sustain him through his last few days on earth. All he had to do was to stay alive long enough to avenge his father's murder and then he would happily join him in the grave. That was the only kind of family reunion that was now open to him.

Wistan had sneaked out of his bed in the night and stolen the sword and the food. Running to the priory in the dark, he had shinned up its wall and dropped into the garden. Shrubs and bushes ran along one side and there was thick cover for him. He was even sheltered from the worst of the rain. Wistan resolved to stay in his place of sanctuary until nightfall, then make his way to Blackwater Hall to see if there was any hope of gaining access. In the meantime, he would lie low at the priory while the hunt still continued for him outside. He was in a most privileged position. He could watch.

The first thing he noticed was the bell. It was chimed at regular intervals and its doleful clang called the holy sisters to the chapel for the sequence of offices. Wistan could hear faint voices raised in song but the Latin words were indecipherable. When the nuns eventually came out into the garden, he drew back into the burrow he had scooped out in the soft earth behind the bushes. They did not even throw a glance in his direction. He was thirty yards or so from the priory and his corner of the property held no interest for the women that morning. They were too busy with their appointed tasks.

Wistan was enthralled. He had never even seen a nun before. When the priory was first erected, there had been a lot of crude jokes made about its occupants by the slaves on the demesne, and he had duly sniggered at things he only vaguely grasped. One leering peasant had even boasted what he would do to all eight women if he could spend a night at the convent. Wistan's experience of a night there was very different. Climbing into the place out of necessity, he found a haven of peace and was given a brief insight into a world that was utterly spellbinding.

They actually worked. Saxon noblewomen, who had always had servants on hand in the past to perform any chores, were now doing those same chores themselves without any sense of shame. They brought wooden buckets and filled them from the well, they set up a line between two posts and hung up their washing, they even picked up tools to labour in the garden. Wistan was moved. He had watched his own mother engaged in constant toil in their tiny hovel, but they were slaves on the estate of a Norman lord and drudgery was the lot of such women. The holy sisters had been exempted by social position from such mundane work, yet they were doing it with apparent readiness. Wistan could not have been more surprised if he had seen Matilda FitzCorbucion felling a tree or hauling in fishing nets from the river. Ladies did not do such things.

The silence also intrigued him. They worked together but they did not speak, communicating instead with nods and smiles and gestures. One of them let out a suppressed giggle from time to time but she was instantly subdued by the warning finger of the stoutest of the nuns, a solid woman with her face almost completely obscured by her wimple. Another feature of the community struck the boy. They liked each other. There was the most extraordinary sense of union between them as if they really were sisters in one happy family. Even the stout nun was loved and cherished in the pervading atmosphere of shared joy. Wistan picked out the prioress as soon as she appeared because the gracious figure inspired such affection and obedience in the others.

Entranced by it all, he watched as the stout nun went back into the priory once more. The chapel bell began to chime and the holy sisters immediately abandoned their work and filed in through the door. One of them lingered for a moment as if unsure whether to stay or to follow, torn between conflicting loyalties and needs. She was a young nun whose grace of movement had already caught his eye and whose sweet smile rarely left her face. Wistan wondered why she was hesitating, then he gasped in dismay as she began to walk straight towards him. He had been seen. The holy sister was heading in his direction with a look of quiet determination on her face, as if she was prepared to grab the intruder for daring to trespass on the enclave.

His first impulse was to run but he saw the danger in that. If he was to be caught, he would far sooner face a nun with Christian benevolence than a search party with weapons. Wistan crouched down in his burrow and waited for her to part the bushes and accost him. But discovery did not come. A few yards short of his refuge, the young woman came to a halt, knelt down on the ground, and then lowered herself forward so that she could kiss the earth. He was totally mystified. There was such an aura of respect and devotion about her that he felt completely humbled. Sitting back on her haunches, she looked upwards and began to chant something to herself. She did not remain there for long. The prioress glided out of the building as if knowing exactly where to find the errant member of her little community.

"Sister Tecla!" she called gently.

The nun was too caught up in her ritual to hear.

"Sister Tecla!"

A note of command was injected this time and it earned a prompt response. Sister Tecla rose quickly to her feet and flitted across the grass towards the prioress before following her meekly into the building without a word of protest.

Brother Simon worked with the cheerful frenzy of a man who had at last discovered his true mission in life. Everything now depended on him and it was such a unique situation for the unassuming monk to be in that he savoured every moment of it. On the rare occasions when he paused to take a sip of water or to sharpen his quill with a deft knife, he offered a silent prayer of thanks to God for calling on him at last to render a service of such magnitude. Brother Simon was in an ecstasy of true humility. He sat behind the table on which so many succulent dishes had been set out for their delectation. It was now covered in writs, charters, and tenurial contracts, in grants and bequests, in lists of names and inventories of possessions. The gaunt monk was gorging himself with ruinous self-indulgence on a banquet of the finest parchment.

Ralph Delchard was still not satisfied with progress.

"Make him work faster, Hubert," he urged.

"Calligraphy is a painstaking art, my lord," said Canon Hubert. "If you hasten the pen, you end up with scribble. Brother Simon is already working much more quickly than he would normally do. Only a steady hand will suggest authenticity."

"Crack the whip over him at least."

"He is a holy brother," said Hubert, "and not a galley slave who is lashed to his oars. You speed up his pace at your peril." He adjusted his paunch in disapproval. "I will not urge him on. I still have the most serious reservations about this whole enterprise."

"Why?" said Ralph.

"You are encouraging Brother Simon to act as a forger."

"Perhaps that's why he is enjoying it so much."

"He is being led astray from the straight and narrow."

"A small crime is justified by a heinous one."

"That is unsound theology," argued Hubert. "And I do not accept that forgery is a small crime. Brother Simon may be selling his soul at that table."

"No," said Ralph. "He is saving Miles Champeney."

Canon Hubert's opposition was voiced rather than felt. Although he was obliged to register a token objection, he knew that they were taking the only option that presented itself. Hamo FitzCorbucion was stooping to the most disgraceful act of blackmail in order to gain the upper hand over the royal commissioners, and so a slight dip from their high standard of moral probity was perhaps permissible. Although he would never confess it openly, Hubert was entering into the spirit of the deception as willingly as any of them.

"One more is finished," announced the drooping monk.

"Give it to me, Brother Simon."

"Yes, Canon Hubert. It concerns four hides on Osea."

"Let me see."

Hubert combed the document for errors of detail and instances of erratic handwriting. None appeared. He dried the ink by shaking sand over it, then laid the paper out on the floor. Brother Simon winced as his beautiful penmanship was subjected to the full weight of Canon Hubert's dirty sandals. When the latter reclaimed the document from the floor, it was scuffed and discoloured. He threw an explanation at his wounded colleague.

"This charter must look as if it is twenty years old."

"Of course, Canon Hubert."

"I have added wear and tear to your excellent work."

"Thank you," said Simon, brightening at the compliment. "I will continue with renewed zeal." He reached out for the next document and read through it. Panic seized him. "Oh, no! My hand rebels at this! I cannot write these words!"

"What is the problem?" said Ralph.

"The name of this subtenant, my lord."

"Where?" He looked over his shoulder to read a name which called for a shout of celebration. "It's Humphrey!"

"My quill would moult if I used it on such vileness!"

"Why?" asked Hubert. "What is the fellow's name?"

Ralph handed him the document. "See for yourself," he invited. "There he hangs—Humphrey *Aureis testiculi*!"

Canon Hubert reddened. "It is a dreadful mistake!"

"Perhaps they are silver and not gold," said Ralph.

"Do not force me to copy those words," begged Simon. "I will serve you in any way I can but I will not lend my pen to such sinful usage."

"It is a mistake," insisted Hubert, flipping through the Latin alternatives in his mind. "Yes, I have it. Change that 't' to an 'r' then alter the 'i' and what do you have?"

"Humphrey Goldenbollocks!" announced Ralph.

"My lord!" said Brother Simon in scandalised horror.

"Humphrey Goldenropes," corrected Hubert primly.

"Ropes!" Ralph spluttered. "Golden—*ropes*!"

"*Resticula*—a thin rope or cord."

Ralph guffawed. "Humphrey is even more remarkable than I thought if he has golden ropes where his testicles ought to be." He passed another document to the monk. "Forget this one. It belongs to me. You copy the next one instead."

Brother Simon croaked his gratitude and attacked the less offensive Latin of the next charter. The outraged canon was still vainly trying to cover Humphrey's shame with the fig leaf of an alternative translation when Gervase Bret came striding into the room to ask why he had been summoned back to Champeney Hall. Ralph took him by the arm and led him off to a chamber where they could talk in private.

"Whatever is Brother Simon doing in there, Ralph?"

"Breaking the law."

"In what way?"

"He is feeding the ravens at Blackwater Hall."

Ralph explained the situation and the action he had taken to meet it. Gervase was alarmed at the development but in total agreement with the response. While anxious to help their host, however, he was disappointed to hear that Gilbert Champeney might actually have robbed his guests.

"The poor man was distraught," said Ralph in mitigation. "Put yourself in his position, Gervase. His son falls into the hands of his sworn enemy. There is no other way to secure his release. What would you have done?"

"Taken my complaint to the sheriff."

"Peter de Valognes would not wish to get involved."

"I would not have stolen someone's property, Ralph."

"There speaks a lawyer! You value your charters as much as Humphrey values his golden *testiculi*."

"Theft is unforgivable."

Ralph was more pragmatic. "That depends on what you take and from whom you take it," he said. "But do not lose complete faith in Gilbert. My guess is that he would not have been able to go through with it. He was a very halfhearted thief. Forgery is much more to his taste."

"Let us hope that it deceives Hamo."

"We will soon know, Gervase. I have sent word to him to appear before us in the shire hall at ten in the morning. If he thinks he has relieved us of much of our evidence, he will not miss the chance to gloat."

"What of Miles Champeney?"

"He will be set free."

"Is his father angry with him?"

"Infuriated. He'll have stern words for his son."

"I'll add a few of my own," said Gervase. "He has caused us an immense amount of unnecessary trouble."

"Come now. You would do exactly the same as he."

"I think I would have more sense."

"Sense has no place in a love affair," said Ralph easily. "If Alys were imprisoned in that house instead of Matilda, you would not hesitate to try to rescue her. Show some fellow-feeling for Miles. I admire the lad."

Gervase gave a nod. "So do I, Ralph," he said, taking a more charitable view. "And he has helped us in a strange way. Our hand has been forced but we may have found the ideal way to lure Hamo within reach of the law." He rested against the table. "What else have you learned?"

"A most curious connection."

"Between what?"

"The chalice and the raven."

"St. Benedict's emblem?"

"Do you remember the cup I saw at the priory?" said Ralph. "I believe it may have belonged to Guy FitzCorbucion. Someone stole it from Blackwater Hall. Hamo was ranting about it when the sheriff called on him yesterday. It was a family heirloom, it seems, and much prized."

"Then how did it end up in Maldon Priory?"

"Lady Mindred told me that it was part of a dowry that was paid to the priory by one of the nuns, and I assumed that she must be talking about Sister Tecla. But I was deliberately misled, I think. I warned you that nuns could tell lies, Gervase. It seems that they might be capable of other sinful acts as well." He raised an eyebrow. "Our prioress has a wandering hand."

"A holy thief?"

"You have seen the way she guards that chalice," said Ralph. "It is very precious to her. We know that she is fond of jewelry that she is not supposed to wear. I saw that gold bangle on her arm. Perhaps she also has a passion for silver. Vanity dies hard behind the veil. Lady Mindred needs to wear bright adornment and to have valuable possessions about her."

"I cannot believe that she would steal anything."

"Then we must settle for the other explanation."

"What is that?"

"The prioress is a witch," said Ralph with a wink. "Sister Gunnhild is her familiar. She turned that Danish nun into a raven and sent her to fetch the chalice back in her beak like a true Benedictine. How does that idea sound?"

"Ludicrous!"

"Find me a better one."

"I will," promised Gervase. "In time. If that chalice at the priory really is the one from Blackwater Hall, then it opens up many new lines of enquiry. But let me give you my news first." He produced the knife from his belt and handed it over. "Do you know what this is, Ralph?"

"I have a feeling you are about to tell me."

"The murder weapon used on Guy FitzCorbucion."

Ralph inspected it. "Where did you find it?"

"Tovild the Haunted gave it to me."

He told his story once more, described his visit to the cutler, and spoke of how Oslac the Priest had reacted to the same tidings. Ralph was not pleased to hear that Wistan was once again on the run. A boy of fifteen would not have enough guile to outrun Hamo FitzCorbucion's men for long, especially as they had now been joined in the search by the sheriff's officers. Gervase had wanted to question him further in order to help him more effectively, but Wistan clearly felt that justice was something that he would have to dispense himself. The boy was a worrying complication.

Ralph and Gervase went through all their evidence with meticulous care but it still did not give them the name of the murderer. Tovild's riddle might help them but it was still unsolved. Gervase shifted the angle of approach.

"Perhaps we should be asking another question."

"Go on."

"What was Guy FitzCorbucion doing there?"

"In the marshes?"

"He must have had a good reason to go to such a place."

"Unless he was taken," said Ralph. "That is more logical. He may have been killed elsewhere and then carried to the water's edge and dumped in."

"I doubt it. Think of his wounds. He had been stabbed many times. There would have been a trail of blood and the killer would also have been covered in it." Gervase tapped his finger on the table. "I believe he went to that place to meet someone. That same person had chosen the spot with care because it was ideal for his purposes."

"Who would Guy have gone to see? And why?"

"Let us try a process of elimination," said Gervase. "We know that Wistan is not the murderer."

"Nor is Miles Champeney."

"Perhaps not."

"You were wrong there, Gervase."

"We had to look at every possible suspect."

"Does that include Tovild the Haunted?"

"I fear that it does. And Oslac the Priest."

"Oslac?"

"His behaviour was most odd," said Gervase. "And he has as much reason to hate the FitzCorbucions as anyone. Hamo took his land after the Conquest. Hamo holds the advowson of his church. Hamo has killed more than one of his parishioners. Oslac is a strong man." He saw that Ralph was unconvinced. "Yes, I know. Oslac is a true Christian and believes that the taking of a human life is anathema. But look at Canon Hubert and Brother Simon. Nobody could be more devout than they, yet they are condoning this forgery of ours in order to expose a much larger act of fraud."

"Oslac killed in order to prevent more killing?"

"Guy FitzCorbucion was a symbol of oppression."

"So is Hamo," said Ralph. "Why murder the son when the father's death would remove an even worse tyrant?"

"Hamo is too wily and well guarded. He would never have gone off alone to a secluded spot in the marshes. The killer waited until he was out of the way before he set to work on Guy."

"And you think that Oslac could do that?"

"I'm not sure," said Gervase uncertainly. "But I wonder about the sword that Wistan stole from him. Why does a man of God have a weapon of war in his house? And what I do know is that Guy would have trusted him. If the priest had arranged to meet him at that spot, he would have gone without fear of danger." He took the knife back and held it up. "Until he saw this."

"Oslac still seems an unlikely assassin to me," said Ralph. "But you are right about one thing. Guy would only go to that place to meet someone he knew and trusted."

"That rules out Wistan and Miles completely."

"Who does it leave?"

They sifted through all the names once more but they could not agree on any one of them as the perpetrator of the crime. Gervase wondered if it was time to widen their search.

"Guy FitzCorbucion is killed," he said. "*Cui bono?*"

"*Cui bono?*"

"Who stands to gain by his murder?"

"Every man, woman, and child in the town."

"But who will gain *most*?" asked Gervase. "Perhaps we have been looking in the wrong place, Ralph. We have only considered enemies of the family instead of the family itself. That would certainly give us motive. And there would be ample opportunity."

"The family itself?"

"Think back to our first afternoon at the shire hall," he said, moving around the chamber as he developed his argument and becoming more and more persuaded by it. "He went out of his way to challenge us. Remember how cool and assured he was? Did you see how eager he was to assert his authority? Did you notice how important it was for him to put us in our place?"

"Jocelyn FitzCorbucion?"

"Who else?"

"But what did he stand to gain?"

"Power."

"The younger son," mused Ralph. "Weary of staying in his elder brother's shadow. More intelligent and gifted than Guy but forced into the background."

"Biding his time. Waiting to fulfill his own ambitions."

"He was certainly a self-possessed young man."

"Indeed, he was," said Gervase. "Consider the position he was in that afternoon. His father was away, his brother was lying on a slab at the church, his sister was agitating about Miles Champeney, and there was still bad feeling among his slaves as a result of Algar's death. Jocelyn had much to do. There was a search party to organise and a huge demesne to administer, yet he rolls up at the shire hall as if he did not have a care in the world. What does all that tell you, Ralph?"

"Put his name at the top of our list."

"*Cui bono?*"

"Joceyln FitzCorbucion."

Jocelyn FitzCorbucion fretted quietly in a corner while his father guzzled his way through his food. He felt cheated of his fair reward. Thanks to him, Matilda was imprisoned in her chamber at the top of the house while Miles Champeney was languishing in the dungeon below it. He had discovered the planned elopement and been instrumental in stopping it. The political marriage, which Hamo had arranged in Coutances for his daughter, could now take place without the hindrance of a rival. But something else rankled even more. Jocelyn had taken considerable pains to prepare a solid defence against the accusations of the royal commissioners. Blackwater Hall would be saved by his mastery of detail and brilliance as an advocate. Hamo had swept him aside uncaringly and chosen a much quicker and cruder method of defying his enemies. It was galling. Jocelyn was deprived of his chance to prove himself in legal debate and robbed of the glory, which he was convinced he would have won.

Hamo swilled down his food with some wine and belched.

"He will not come," decided Jocelyn.

"Gilbert *has* to come. Give him time."

"He would never steal from his guests."

"He is not stealing," said Hamo, sitting back in his chair. "He is merely borrowing a few documents."

"They will be missed. He will be caught."

"Gilbert Champeney will do exactly what I told him."

"But suppose that he does not, Father?"

"He has no choice."

"Suppose he does not?" repeated Jocelyn, crossing to face him. "You will need my skills then. You will have to rely on my advocacy in front of the commissioners. I have prepared a stout defence with walls as thick as those of Colchester Castle. We would be invincible in battle."

Hamo was unimpressed. "When Gilbert follows his orders, there will *be* no battle. Why waste all that time in a draughty shire hall when we can send these idiots packing in less than an hour?" His fingers ran over the fruit bowl and settled on an apple. "You still have much to learn, Jocelyn,"

"Nobody has studied harder."

"Study is only part of it. Instinct is the key."

"I have that, too."

"Not like me. Not like your brother, Guy. He had real instinct. Guy knew how to find out a man's weakness."

"It was usually his wife!" said Jocelyn ruefully.

"Don't you dare speak ill of Guy!"

"No, Father."

"He was twice the son you are!" yelled Hamo.

He stifled a rejoinder. "Yes, Father," he said.

Hamo bit into the apple and chewed it noisily. It was early evening and the sun was still putting a bright sheen on Blackwater Hall, but its rays had failed to penetrate the house itself and to thaw out the cold fury of its master.

"Where did they search today?" he snarled.

"To the north, Father. As you directed."
"That boy has to be here!"
"After all this time? I doubt it."
"Where else could he go?" demanded Hamo. "He has no money and no horse. Everyone is out looking for him. I've put such a high price on his young head that even his father would have turned him in for the reward."
"Perhaps he is already dead. Drowned in the estuary."
"He is still alive. I *feel* it."
"Then they will find him eventually."
"Tomorrow, I will ride out with them myself."
"But we are summoned to the shire hall, Father."
"That business will not detain us long," said Hamo through a mouthful of apple. "I'll go along to spit in the eye of the commissioners then join the hunt for my son's killer. They'll have no case against me."
"Only if Gilbert Champeney does your bidding."
"He will, Jocelyn. Mark my words."
"So many things could go wrong," warned his son. "My way is slower but more secure. Let me explain how I would go about it, Father. I have taken the measure of these royal commissioners so I know precisely what to expect from them. First of all ..."
Hamo ignored him. He had heard something else and it got him up from the table and across to the window. He let out a throaty chuckle and tossed his apple core to Jocelyn.
"I told you that Gilbert would come."
He led the way to the main door and went down the stone steps and into the courtyard with an irritated Jocelyn a few paces behind him. Gilbert Champeney had brought two of his knights as an escort and they waited near the gate. Fulk the Steward was giving him a welcome and holding the bridle of his horse while the visitor dismounted. Gilbert was in a feisty mood. Jocelyn recognised the satchel that he was carrying. It belonged to one of the commissioners and had lain on the table at the shire hall when Jocelyn had gone there to confront them.
"I knew that you would see sense!" said Hamo.
"Where's my son?"
"He is quite safe, Gilbert. I give you my word."
"Where is he? I wish to see him."
"You are in no position to haggle."
"Neither are you, Hamo." He put a foot in the stirrup once more. "I will return these documents to their owners."
"Wait!"
Gilbert stayed ready to mount. "Well?"
"Show me what you have and you will see your son."
"Where is he?"

"He can be brought here very quickly."

"Then send for him." Gilbert was firm. "Send for him now, Hamo, or I ride out of this accursed place."

Hamo regarded him with a mixture of contempt and admiration, then he gave a signal and Fulk went towards the ground floor of the house. Gilbert consented to let go of the saddle and remove his foot from the stirrup. Hamo held out a hand and his visitor reluctantly opened the satchel and took out a sheaf of documents. Jocelyn came forward to peer at them. Gilbert would not surrender anything until he had been assured of his son's safety but he did let the two of them see the first parchment. It was an abstract of all the charges that were to be levelled against Blackwater Hall on the following morning. They would be forewarned about the whole prosecution case. Jocelyn read through it carefully and nodded to his father. The document was authentic.

Fulk reappeared and waited until he got another signal from Hamo then he gestured in turn to somebody inside the building. Through the open door, two sturdy guards brought a dishevelled Miles Champeney, who was squinting in the unaccustomed light. His hands were bound with ropes and the guards had a firm grip on him but he seemed otherwise unhurt. Gilbert started forward towards him but quickly controlled himself. There was more bargaining to do.

"I want the servant as well," he said.

"What servant?"

"The one who carried the message between them. If he stays here, you will only beat him to death or starve him to a skeleton. Give him to me, Hamo."

"He is my servant."

"I will buy him from you."

Miles had adjusted to the light well enough to see his father. As he tried to lunge forward, the soldiers held him.

"Father!" he called. "Help me."

"Be patient, Miles."

"They threw me in a dungeon!"

"I have come for you. Hold still a little longer."

"What is this nonsense about my servant?" said Hamo.

"I am trying to prevent a murder." Gilbert would not budge on the issue. "No servant, no documents."

"And no son."

"Keep him, then," said the father. "He ran away from me and forfeited my love. I want him back to chastise him as much as anything else, but Miles comes with the servant or you can sling the pair of them back into your dungeon."

"He is bluffing!" sneered Jocelyn.

"Put me to the test." Gilbert patted the satchel. "You have seen what thunderbolts they mean to hurl at you tomorrow. Do you really think you could withstand them without the help that I have brought you?"

"Yes!" insisted Jocelyn.

"Be quiet!" said Hamo.

"We don't need him, Father."

"Stand aside!"

Hamo shoved his son out of the way and walked up to Gilbert until they stood face to face. The visitor had none of the other's dark ferocity but his gaze did not falter. Hamo stared at him for some minutes before he came to a decision.

"What is a miserable servant between friends?" he said with a grim chuckle. "Take the rogue. He is no use to me now except to provide sport."

"Give me a price."

"You pay it with that satchel."

He tried to grab it but Gilbert drew it back and shook his head. Hamo turned to signal to Fulk once more and the steward went into the building. He soon returned with the servant who was walking stiffly after his confinement and blinking in the glare of the sun. Both prisoners were now brought down into the courtyard by the guards and another voice joined in the bargaining.

"Miles! You're safe! Thank God!"

Matilda was watching from her window. As her beloved moved away from the building, she caught sight of him for the first time and screamed her anguish and her relief. He lifted his bound hands in a gallant wave.

"I'll come back for you, Matilda!"

"No, you won't!" shouted Gilbert.

"Help me, Miles! They've locked me in!"

"Silence that noise!" roared Hamo.

The guard entered the chamber above them and a protesting Matilda was dragged away from the window. When Miles added his own protests and tried to lurch towards the house, his father restrained him and gave him a stark choice.

"Me or her," he said crisply. "Which is it to be, Miles? Come with me and be free. Or stay here with Matilda and rot in the dungeon. Which is it going to be?"

Miles looked despairingly at the empty window. Then he lowered his head in submission. Only if he were released would he have any hope of saving Matilda. He had to bow to the force of circumstances.

"Now it is my turn," said Hamo gruffly. "You have your son and you have my servant, Gilbert. Give me my documents."

With a show of reluctance, Gilbert handed them to him. Jocelyn stepped forward again but his father waved turn aside and instead passed the satchel to Fulk. The steward was swift in his appraisal. Taking everything out, he read the list of charges, then checked to see that he had the documents that related to each of those accusations. Jocelyn, meanwhile, was livid at this public rebuff. His expertise was being discarded in favour of the steward's opinion. Hamo's blackmail had struck a fatal blow at the commissioners and it had also undermined his son.

"They are all there," said Gilbert shamefacedly.

"What took you so long?" asked Hamo. "Guilt?"

"Those people are my guests—my friends!"

"Not any more."

"You forced me to steal from them."

"And you did just that," agreed Hamo. "Bear that in mind, Gilbert. You are a thief. If I showed this satchel to the commissioners and told them who gave it to me, they would call the sheriff and have you arrested."

Gilbert lowered his head in disgust and Hamo was happy. He had made his enemy do something that caused him the greatest pain of all. A generous host had been forced to rob and betray his distinguished guests. Gilbert had been humiliated and his son had been taught a painful lesson. The Champeneys would not cause any more trouble at Blackwater Hall. Pulling a dagger from its scabbard, Hamo cut the rope that bound the prisoner's hands.

"Get off my land!" he said to Miles. "If you come within a mile of my daughter again, nothing will save you." He glared at the servant. "Take this offal with you! I want no traitors under my roof!"

Gilbert mounted his horse while Miles and the servant pulled themselves up into the saddles of the two horses which had been brought from Champeney Hall during the night. Joined by the two soldiers, they rode abjectly away. Gilbert had rescued his son and the servant but Hamo FitzCorbucion still felt that he had the best of the bargain. His mocking laughter pursued them. Fulk joined in his scornful mirth but Jocelyn remained morose and silent. Everybody seemed to have gained something from the transaction except him.

Oslac the Priest celebrated Mass at the priory with the silver chalice and the paten. Prioress Mindred and her seven holy sisters received Communion in the tiny chapel and were greatly sustained. The prioress herself knelt in an attitude of total self-abnegation. Sister Gunnhild felt a quiet exultation as she took the wafer of unleavened bread upon her tongue. Sister Lewinna expunged all thought of Aesop and brought her utmost concentration to the ceremony. Sister Tecla listened to the Latin words and translated them into a more familiar and comforting language.

"The Blood of Our Lord Jesus Christ, which was shed for thee, preserve thy body and soul unto everlasting life. Drink this in remembrance that Christ's blood was shed for thee, and be thankful."

Oslac gave her the chalice and she peered at her reflection in the dark red wine before sipping it. When he tried to take the chalice from her so that he could wipe its rim with a cloth and hand it to the next person, she kept her fingers locked tightly around its base. The priest put a hand on the top of her head in blessing, then detached the cup very gently from her grip. Sister Tecla did not try to resist his pull. She simply folded her hands in prayer but kept her eyes on the chalice as it made its way along the line of communicants.

"What else has happened, Father Oslac?"

"Peter de Valognes is in the town, my lady prioress."

"Has he joined the hunt for the boy?"

"He is conducting his own investigations into the murder. My lord, Hamo, is not pleased to have him here but a sheriff has duties that cannot be shirked."

"What else?"

Prioress Mindred was alone in her quarters with Oslac. Like the two other priests who came to celebrate Mass, he was her window on the town of Maldon and she enjoyed the chance to gaze through it and keep abreast of affairs in the wider community. Although her vocation encouraged her to look inwards, she had particular reason to look outwards as well. When Oslac hesitated, she searched his face with shrewd eyes.

"What else?" she repeated. "I can see that you have something important to tell me and I would like to know what it is. Do not try to soften the tidings because we are friends. Speak bluntly. You have come to warn me, I think."

"Yes, my lady prioress."

"The royal commissioners?"

"They are astute men."

"What have they found out?"

"Enough to make them extremely curious."

"Will they come here?"

"In time, they may. You must be ready for them."

"I am under no obligation to receive them," she said with a lift of her chin. "They have no right to intrude here. I will invoke the privileges of my station. They will be turned away."

"That would only increase their suspicion."

"How, then, may we allay it?"

"I do not know, my lady prioress," he admitted. "I seek only to alert you. These men are like terriers. They will not give up their search. They will find their way here."

Prioress Mindred felt a mild sensation of fear but she mastered it at once and drew herself up into a posture of dignity. "I am not ashamed of anything I have done," she said proudly. "If I were in that position again, I would act in precisely the same way. I made a stand for Christian love and righteousness. God himself guided me."

Oslac gave a nod of acquiescence but remained anxious.

"We may need His guidance even more now," he said.

Gervase Bret sat at the table where the documents still lay scattered. Brother Simon had used up nearly all the fresh parchment, but his colleague found one small scroll on which he could write and draw. He cudgelled his brain for an hour or more with only moderate success. When Ralph came sweeping into the hall, Gervase was still crouched over his conundrum.

"They have arrived back!" announced Ralph.

"Miles is safely returned?"

"He is returned, I know that, but his safety is very much in question. Gilbert is lashing him even now. Our kindly host has a most blistering tongue."

"But the exchange was effected?"

"It worked like a charm," said Ralph. "Hamo took the documents and released both Miles and that servant. Gilbert took me aside to tell me how delighted he was. He has not told his son that we were involved in the deception and that the documents are forgeries. Miles still believes that his reckless behaviour turned his father into a thief." He walked to the table and began to sift idly through the documents. "It will not hurt to maintain that illusion for a short while. Gilbert wants to make him suffer the pangs of remorse before he tells him the truth."

"What of Matilda FitzCorbucion?"

"She is still under lock and key."

"Will not Miles try to rescue her once again?"

"He will not get the chance. Gilbert will hover over him like a falcon and swoop at the first sign of movement." Ralph heaved a sigh. "In some ways, it is a pity."

"Why?"

"Because he would have a much better chance now."

"Of reaching Matilda?"

"Yes," explained Ralph. "They would never expect a second attempt. Last time they were waiting for Miles and he was a sitting target. They are off guard now and the girl will be watched with less vigilance. In addition to that, Miles has a valuable accomplice."

"Accomplice?"

"The servant who was released with him. That man would have died in Hamo's dungeon if Gilbert's kind heart had not pried him loose. He will be more than happy to strike back at his old master."

"And he knows the inner workings of the household."

"Exactly, Gervase. If I were the lover and she were my lady, I'd have Matilda out of Blackwater Hall within a day."

"How?"

"There is always a way. Every problem has a solution."

"This one does not!" said Gervase, looking down at the parchment in front of him. "I have been at it since you left me here and I am none the wiser."

"Are you still struggling with Tovild's riddle?"

"Yes. I have remembered all I can and set it down."

"Show me." Ralph looked over his shoulder at the paper. "What are these weird creatures?"

"They are drawings of the things Tovild mentioned."

He pointed a finger. "Is this a swallow?"

"It is supposed to be an eagle."

"This one looks like a bullock."

"It is a goat, Ralph."

"Now, this one I do recognise," said Ralph, jabbing his finger at another sketch. "It is a mouse."

"A dog."

"I can see why you are in difficulty, Gervase."

"This is all that I can recall of the riddle," admitted Gervase, indicating each drawing as he spoke. "Dog, goat, and grey eagle. Then goose, hawk, and gull. He also mentioned a war-bird but I am not sure what he meant."

"What are these letters?' asked Ralph, pointing to them.

"Another clue. He said they formed the name."

"G,A,R,I. An Anglo-Saxon name? Gari?"

"No, there were other letters but these are the only ones of which I am certain. I was playing around with others when you came in just now."

"G,A,R,I ..."

"*Gar* is a Saxon word," said Gervase. "It means spear."

"That would point to Tovild himself as the killer."

"How would a spear sing like a bird?"

"When it whistles through the air."

"How would it produce the noise of a goose?"

"When it is thrust through the body of an enemy," said Ralph. "He will squawk just like a goose, I can assure you."

"There were two or three other letters. Was H one of them?"

"Could it give us another word?"

"*Garholt*, perhaps. If we lost the I."

"What does it mean?"

"Spear-shaft."

"That weapon again. It must be Tovild himself."

"He certainly sings the song of gull."

"And he is an old goat who can bark like a dog."

"No, Ralph," said Gervase, writing the letters in a different order with gaps between them. "Raig? Argi? Grai? They are meaningless."

"Try that H once more. Change the letters round."

"Harig ... gahir ... rihag ... ?"

"What else did Tovild the Haunted say? Apart from the riddle? The clue we are missing may lie elsewhere."

"I do not think so. I have been over it time and again. Tovild said that the raven was killed in the marshes. The name I want is locked in the riddle."

"Who would kill a raven?"

"Anyone who farms the land."

"Someone on the Blackwater demesne?"

Gervase stared hard at the letters on the paper, then back at the drawings. He thought of Tovild the Haunted and of the glee with which he had told his riddles. A grey eagle. A goose, a hawk, a gull. A war-bird. And was there not also a mention of a kite? He dipped his quill into the inkwell and scribbled some new letters before sitting back with a shout of triumph.

"I have solved the riddle!"

"How?"

"Who would kill a raven?"

"That was *my* question."

"I have the answer, Ralph. Another bird."

"A bird?"

"If I put an O with these letters, what do I get?"

"God knows!"

"*Higora!*"

"Who?"

"*Higora!*" Gervase thrust the paper at him. "Take a look. The letters all fit. That must be right. *Higora!* He has given us the name of our killer, Ralph."

"And where do we find this *Higora*?"

"With the rest of its kind."

"Stop it!" yelled Ralph. "You've solved one riddle. Do not couch the answer in yet another one."

"*Higora* is the Saxon word for a magpie or a jay."

"Guy FitzCorbucion was killed by a bird?"

"Tovild was a witness. He told me exactly what he saw in the marshes. A raven killed by a magpie."

"Stop talking in riddles. Give me a name!"

"We must find that for ourselves," said Gervase, "but at least we know where to search now. Among the magpies."

Chapter Nine

Even a sanctuary had disadvantages. Wistan soon realised that he had been too hasty to congratulate himself on choosing his new refuge. It guaranteed him safety but only at a price. To begin, he had to stay virtually immobile behind the bushes when the nuns appeared. This was quite often because they used the garden, not only as a place to grow fruit and vegetables, but as their cloister garth. This introduced an unforeseen problem for the boy. The wants of nature eventually had to be satisfied and Wistan suffered the most acute embarrassment when forced to relieve himself—albeit out of sight—in the company of holy sisters. It seemed like an act of desecration and he had the same sensation of guilt that had afflicted him when he stole the sword from Oslac the Priest. Religious people unsettled him. Their goodness was quite beyond his comprehension.

Boredom also crept up on him. Things that had intrigued him were dulled by constant repetition. The nuns led a strange and apparently contented life but it seemed so barren to him. Why did they not speak to each other? Why did one sit on a bench in meditation while another walked around the perimeter of the garden with her head in a book? Who was the stout nun and why was her face hidden? Who was the graceful sister who had crouched on the ground near him and kissed the earth? Only one of the holy sisters had any spirit about her, but her sudden giggles were immediately suppressed by the stout woman whenever they broke out. Wistan became restive. He found the passivity of the nuns weighing down on him. Northey Island had been a far more dangerous place to hide but it had also been more varied and interesting. There was an excitement in the chase even if he had been the quarry. Maldon Priory was sapping his vitality and taking the edge off his vengeful urge.

As evening shaded slowly towards night, he found himself wishing that he had selected another hiding place. Wistan had entered a forbidden realm, bizarre and stimulating at first, but ultimately a handicap. Holiness distracted him. It made him think twice about what he planned to do and question his right to do it. He needed to get away.

Light failed by degrees until the whole garden was dappled with shadow. Wistan was not afraid. Darkness was becoming his natural element now, the only time when he had any freedom of movement. Something else kept fear at bay. He had the sword.

The implement, which he had stolen from the home of Oslac the Priest, gave him a sense of power and importance. A sword was the most prized weapon of Saxon warriors of old and few men below the rank of thegn had possessed one. The spear was a far more common weapon. Swords reflected status. This one had a broad, two-edged blade that had grown rather blunt but he could sharpen it on a stone when time served. There was a shallow groove down the centre of both sides of the blade to lighten the dead weight of the iron but it was still heavy. The hilt had a grip of wood, bound in leather, and a three-lobed pommel to counterbalance the weight of the blade. The long guard curved downwards. The scabbard consisted of two thin laths of wood covered in leather and protected at the mouth and tip by a metal strip. The inside of the scabbard was lined with fleece.

Wistan had grabbed the sword and carried it away from the house. Now that it was time to leave, he decided to wear it properly. A thegn would have slung the scabbard on his left hip from a baldric over the right shoulder or on a waist belt. All that Wistan had was a piece of rope knotted around his midriff but the sword could just as easily and as proudly be worn on that. He stood up and tied the scabbard in place before pulling out the sword. It seemed to fit his hand and his purpose completely. Its balance was perfect. Wistan was no longer a runaway slave trying to defend himself with a crude knife. He was a Saxon thegn with a fine sword in his hand and a noble heritage behind him. For a brief moment, the boy was at one with Tovild the Haunted.

A door opened in the priory and he became a startled animal, dropping to his knees and peering with anxiety through the leaves. A figure was coming towards him across the grass and the graceful movement told him that it was Sister Tecla, but she did not reach his corner of the garden this time. The stout nun came bustling out after her and took her gently by the arm. There was a slight altercation as Sister Tecla pointed in the direction she had wanted to go but the older woman was firm. Tecla's shoulders drooped in resignation. The other nun kissed her tenderly on both cheeks then led her back into the building by the hand.

Wistan was puzzled but glad to be left alone again. He waited another five minutes to make sure that the holy sisters had retired for the night, then he moved across to the wall and pulled himself to the top of it. There was nobody in sight. He was over it in a flash and running with a long stride up the hill. Maldon was largely in darkness now with only the occasional flickering light showing through a window or under a door. He met nobody as he hurried along High Street with his left hand holding up the scabbard so that it did not swing against his legs. After being hemmed in for so long at the priory, it was a joy to be free again and on the move.

He needed to recapture the full sense of anger that impelled him and there was only one place to do that. Therefore, when he reached the Church of All Souls', he paused to make sure nobody was around, then went through the little wooden gate and into the churchyard. Eerie and still, it was shrouded in gloom but the sword was his comfort. He drew it out and held it in front of him as he picked his way among the graves. Algar had been buried in sloping earth in a mean corner of the churchyard. Guy FitzCorbucion, by contrast, had been given a prime position and his last resting place would be marked in time by some monument. Wistan went first to the spot where his father lay and he offered a mumbled promise of revenge. He remembered the ague-ridden old man who had no strength to defend himself properly against the cruelty of his young master. The hatred began to bubble inside him again. Wistan also recalled the warrior after whom he had been named. That hero had taken his toll of a much stronger foe before he fell with honour. The boy would now do the same. With rancour in his heart and the sword in his hand, he felt ready for any trial that lay ahead.

After paying homage to Algar, he moved away from one grave in order to attack another and hack at the mound of earth that covered his father's killer. But there was someone on guard. He sensed the movement before he saw anything and it made him check his stride and approach with more caution. Clouds hid the moon and the place was in almost total darkness but somebody was definitely there at the graveside. Wistan became possessed of the idea that it might be Hamo FitzCorbucion, keeping a lonely vigil over his dead son, kneeling beside him, unarmed and vulnerable. The boy wasted no sympathy on him. Raising his weapon, he ran the last few yards to the grave and lashed out viciously with the sword, only to be forced back in alarm as a whole flock of ravens took wing in front of him, flying into his face with screeches of outrage before perching on the church itself to hiss their curses down at him. The grave had its own guardians.

Wistan fled at once and he did not stop running until he was clear of the town and on the Blackwater demense. He slowed down to catch his breath and exercised more caution as he got closer to his destination. The hall came out of the darkness to stop him like a mountain that had been dropped in his path. Like Miles Champeney, he knew better than to enter by the courtyard. The wall at the rear of the building was high but he scaled it with moderate ease and dropped down onto the soft ground beyond. He was now at the very heart of

FitzCorbucion territory and his hand tightened on the hilt of the sword.

Moving with a stealth that had now become natural, he crept up to the back of the house and walked its full length in search of a mode of entry. The one door was securely locked and the windows were barred. Those on the first floor were well beyond his reach. He came furtively around the side of the house but that offered no possibility either. He was about to double back and try the other side of the building when he heard a resounding clatter as a troop of men came riding into the courtyard to rein their mounts. Wistan got down on his knees and inched his way to the angle of the house so that he could peer around it and watch.

A few torches had been lit to welcome the latecomers and a few grooms came running. Hounds, which had been used to track down Wistan on Northey Island, barked in their kennels or poked out inquisitive heads. The stone trough where Algar had met his death was clearly visible. Everything about the scene stirred the boy's loathing. Fulk the Steward came out of the house and down the stone steps. He addressed the captain of the troop.

"You are very late."

"My lord, Hamo, sent us as far north as Kelvedon."

"But with no success?"

"None, Fulk. Nobody has seen a glimpse of the boy."

"We'll search again tomorrow."

"What is the point?" said the captain. "The lad must be far away from here by now. He's had days on the run."

"That is my feeling but he will not listen to me." Fulk raised his voice so that all could hear. "My lord, Hamo, will lead you tomorrow. He and his son have to visit the shire hall at ten o'clock. Some paltry business that will not take long. Be ready to leave soon after that."

Moans of protest were mixed with sighs of relief that they would not have to be out again at first light. It was a minor blessing but a welcome one for men who had been in the saddle for the best part of a day. Fulk had delivered his message and went back into the house. Wistan had heard him clearly. Hamo and Jocelyn FitzCorbucion would be going to the shire hall in the morning. The boy might not have to find a way to get into the house, after all. If he was in the right place at the right time, his enemies would come to him.

He climbed back over the wall and trotted happily away.

Canon Hubert knew how to put a man right off his breakfast.

"I am all in favour of branding and mutilation," he said airily as he slurped his frumenty. "A brand marks a man for life and a missing ear or nose is a reminder that he is never allowed to forget. Be just but merciless, I say. One must make the punishment commensurate with the crime."

"Could we talk about something else?" asked Brother Simon queasily. "The subject distresses me."

"It must be discussed."

"Why, Canon Hubert?"

"Because I have chosen it."

"Of course, of course ..."

"And because it is germane."

"So how would you punish Hamo?" asked Ralph Delchard.

"Most severely," said Hubert.

"Branding or mutilation?"

"Both, my lord. I'd brand him a criminal and cut whole pieces of his demesne away to give back to their rightful owners." Hubert was vindictive. "I'd also throw the rogue into prison to cool his heels. Nobody is above the law. Not even Hamo FitzCorbucion."

"Nor even the King's own brother," noted Gilbert Champeney. "Odo has been behind bars for years now and he was Earl of Kent."

"He is also Bishop of Bayeux," added Gervase Bret.

"Yes," said Ralph brightly. "That fact delights me most. A reverend Bishop thrown into prison. The Church must bow down to the law of the land." He beamed at Hubert. "How would you sentence Odo? To the branding iron or the knife?"

"We are wandering from the point, my lord."

It was early morning and the six of them were having breakfast together. Canon Hubert and Brother Simon were preparing themselves for the encounter with Hamo at the shire hall, Ralph Delchard and Gervase Bret were taken up with the related problem of the murder, and Gilbert Champeney was trying to make amends for his near-betrayal of his guests by an even more excessive show of hospitality. He had cajoled his son to come along and Miles was far more ready to join in the banter. He had now been told about the deception practiced on Hamo and it had given him a degree of consolation. But the woman he loved was still locked away in Blackwater Hall, so he had a personal interest in the outcome of the morning's session at the shire hall.

"No punishment could match Hamo's crimes," he asserted. "I think he should be tried and executed for what he has done."

"Come now," teased Ralph. "You are being very harsh on your future father-in-law."

"He has held this town to ransom for too long."

"We will put a stop to that," said Hubert. "He will be dealt with accordingly. We can unleash the full rigour of the law upon him."

"But it is Norman law," reminded Gervase, "and it falls short of your own preference, Canon Hubert. A moment ago, you were advocating the use of branding and mutilation. That is nearer to the Danish code. King Cnut also favoured such savage law."

"Do not compare me with the Danes!" said Hubert querulously. "They were heathens!"

"Cnut became a devout Christian," returned Gervase. "Like you. That is what surprises me about your attitude. The Christian ethic surely has no place in judicial castration or the blinding of felons. King Cnut even prescribed mutilation for women taken in adultery."

"God save us!"

Brother Simon had heard enough. Clutching his stomach, he ran into the courtyard to spew up what little food he had managed to eat that morning. The idea of taking a knife to a woman by way of punishment was too revolting to contemplate. He began to pray for an early return to the bosom of his monastery where the only thing likely to offend his sensibilities was an overheated debate about a passage from the Scriptures.

Ralph Delchard was amused by the monk's sudden exit.

"Brother Simon is too easily upset," he observed. "It has been a bad morning for him so far. He had a fit when I suggested to him that a more appropriate manor for Humphrey *Aureis testiculi* would be that of Goldhanger."

Gilbert hooted with laughter, Gervase smiled, and even Miles cracked his face, but Canon Hubert pretended not to have heard and returned to the fray. Even over breakfast, he refused to be beaten in argument.

"Law must be fair but firm," he insisted. "A visible justice is the most effective of all. Every thief who has his hand cut off is a warning to others. Every traitor who is hanged helps to keep the rest of the subjects loyal. Crimes committed in private must meet with public retribution."

"Your retribution is legal vengeance," said Gervase.

"Yes," agreed Gilbert. "Look to the Saxons. They can teach us in this as in so many other ways. Their law was based on compensation rather than on mutilation. The only crimes carrying a death sentence were treason, cowardice, and desertion." He gave a nervous laugh. "And unnatural vice."

"They were a warrior people," said Ralph. "Every soldier was a valued asset. Why kill him or cut him up when he can be used to fight for you?"

"That is my contention," resumed Gilbert. "Examine the laws of King Ethelbert of Kent and you will see a list of fines for everything from murder to fornication. Thieves did not lose a hand that could be used in battle. They paid compensation for their crime."

"Compensation is not enough," said Miles hotly. "To fine a man like Hamo FitzCorbucion would be to fly in the face of every principle of justice."

The dispute continued for a few more minutes before Canon Hubert shifted its basis in order to assert himself.

"When we deal with Hamo," he said, "we move from the realm of crime into that of heinous sin. Evil must be burned out in the flames of Good. I will ignite the torch in the shire hall today."

It was a timely reminder. Although the session was still some hours away, there was much to prepare and rehearse. Ralph and Gervase got up from the table, Miles excused himself and drifted away, and Canon Hubert had one last mouthful of food before going off in search of Brother Simon. Whatever their individual views about the nature of punishment, they first had to convict Hamo of his crimes and that was by no means a foregone conclusion.

"Do not underestimate his guile," warned Gilbert. "We may have deceived him with forged documents but he will not concede defeat. Hamo will fight tooth and nail."

"So will we," reassured Ralph.

"The evidence against him is too strong," said Gervase.

"That is what your predecessors thought."

"Trust us, Gilbert," said Ralph. "We will fetter this tyrant for you. And if we do, I will ask for a favour in return. Do not deny me now."

"You may have anything you choose."

"Anything at all?"

"Name it."

"The truth about Humphrey. Is that a bargain?"

"It is, Ralph," said the chuckling Gilbert. "And I will even give you a hint to whet your appetite. Look again at Humphrey's holdings."

"Both of them?"

"I speak of his land."

"But he has no more than three hides."

"You forget his beehives."

"Beehives?"

"I say no more," said Gilbert. "But take note of his honey render and you will get closer to his name."

"We must leave it there," said Gervase briskly. "You may worry about Humphrey but there are much more serious issues to decide first. We must put all our documents in order and then we must ride off to our appointment."

"Appointment?" said Gilbert.

"We are hunting birds."

"Ravens?"

"Magpies."

Advance warning had been sent to the priory as a courtesy. Prioress Mindred therefore had time to consider her response and take appropriate action. Oslac the Priest was summoned at once to give his advice and they talked for a long time. When he left, the prioress called Sister Gunnhild into her quarters and told her about the imminent visit of the royal commissioners. Gunnhild listened with impassive interest.

"What will you tell them?" she asked.

"The truth."

"The whole truth?"

"I will tell them what I judge needful, Sister Gunnhild. But I require your help. Nobody else here must know of their visit or suspect for one moment its purpose. You will greet them and bring them straight to me. Is that understood?"

"Yes, Reverend Mother."

"On no account must Sister Tecla be informed."

"She will be kept in ignorance."

"I know you have her best interests at heart."

"None more so."

Mindred gave a hesitant smile. "Have you been able to sound the depth of her spiritual commitment?"

"She is responding well."

"Good."

"I have commended the works of St. Aldhelm to her."

"*De Virginitate?*"

"We will study it together."

"That is ... pleasing to hear," said the prioress with muted enthusiasm. "You are her mentor now. We must work hard to win her soul. I have tried to show her certain privileges to draw her more completely to us. Sister Tecla brought that sacred earth back from Barking Abbey with me. I permitted her to transfer it to the reliquary as a sign of my faith in her. Then we both prayed to St. Oswald. He saved our lives once."

"Let us hope the blessed saint still watches over us."

The bell rang and the prioress braced herself. Sister Gunnhild went swiftly out to the front door and returned with Ralph Delchard and Gervase Bret. The black habits of the nuns were offset by the startling whiteness of their caps, so that there was indeed a superficial resemblance to magpies, and the visitors knew only too well that magpies belonged to the same family as ravens. Gunnhild gave a noncommittal bow then backed out and closed the door behind her to ensure their privacy. Prioress Mindred exchanged pleasantries with her guests, then invited them to sit. She lowered herself into the high-backed chair and waited. Her manner was as gracious as ever and it forced them to wonder if their suspicions could possibly have any real foundation. Gervase was the spokesman.

"We have been looking into the murder," he explained.

"It was a horrific event," she said. "Father Oslac has told me something of the details."

"He discussed the case with you?"
"Only in passing."
"And what did you conclude, my lady prioress?"
"That the murderer was deeply wicked," she said with a slight grimace. "To take life by violent means is a most dreadful crime but this went beyond that. Mutilation was practised. The body was disfigured. Only a man consumed by an evil and bitter hatred could do that."
Gervase was surprised. Oslac seemed to have confided in her things that he had only divulged to them under pressure and that suggested a closer relationship between priest and prioress than he would have assumed. It helped to confirm the doubts he had been having about Oslac.
"You are in close touch with Father Oslac?" he said.
"He is one of three priests who visit us regularly. They come to celebrate Mass but they also bring in gossip from the town."
"Oslac seems to have told you more than gossip."
"I like to think that I am a trusted friend."
"He speaks highly of you, my lady prioress."
"I can return that compliment."
"Would you call him a true man of God?"
"Without question."
"A lover of peace and humility?"
"Of course. He is a Christian."
"Then why does he keep a sword at his house?"
"A sword?" Mindred was visibly taken aback but she collected herself with admirable speed. "I do not see what this has to do with your enquiries, Master Bret. Why are you asking me such an odd question?"
Ralph Delchard tried to speed up the interrogation.
"Let us go back to our meeting with you," he suggested.
"Very well, my lord."
"You and Sister Tecla were returning from Barking Abbey, were you not?" She nodded. "Why did you go there in the first place?"
"It is our motherhouse. I visit regularly."
"Did you not have a special reason this time?"
"That is a matter between me and Abbess Aelfgiva."
"Is it?" he probed. "Or between you and Sister Tecla?"
"Tecla ...?"
Her dismay was more evident this time and Gervase moved in swiftly to take over once more. He had hoped to coax the truth out by patient questioning but Ralph's impulsiveness had now made that impossible. Gervase had brought the murder weapon, which had been reclaimed from the marsh, because he believed it might belong in the convent. The prioress was on the defensive. She was clearly prevaricating. It

was time to confront her with the blend of evidence and supposition that had guided the two of them there. Gervase leaned forward on his stool.

"I believe that you possess a fine silver chalice."

"We have more than one here."

"This cup is rather special," said Gervase. "It has delicate engravings around four inset rubies. It is extremely valuable. You told Canon Hubert and my lord, Ralph, that it was part of a dowry that was paid to the priory by one of the holy sisters."

"That was true," said Mindred uncertainly.

"It was used to celebrate Mass?"

"When it had been approved and blessed."

"Then why did it leave here?"

"Leave here?"

"Yes," said Gervase. "I believe that you and Sister Tecla took it with you to Barking Abbey." She shook her head vehemently but he pressed on. "I believe that chalice came originally from Blackwater Hall. That is why the ambush was set for you. Those men were knights in the FitzCorbucion retinue. They were sent to take that chalice back to its rightful owner. Is that not true, my lady prioress?"

She lowered her head. "No, no," she whispered.

"Can you hear what Gervase is saying?" said Ralph. "Your chalice was the property of Guy FitzCorbucion. That links this priory very clearly with his murder."

"No, my lord!" she protested, rising to her feet with her eyes blazing. "You are wrong!"

"Tell us why," said Gervase quietly.

"I am unjustly accused here!"

"Defend yourself, my lady prioress. We will listen."

She glanced at the door then wrung her hands for a few moments before returning to her seat. When she had composed herself again, she looked from one to the other.

"I did not go to Barking Abbey with Sister Tecla," she said. "I returned with her, as you saw, but I travelled alone with my escort. The purpose of my visit was to collect her."

Gervase was perplexed. "How long had she been there?"

"Some weeks."

"For what reason?"

Mindred bit her lip. "Spiritual recuperation."

"What is that in layman's terms?" said Ralph.

"Sister Tecla had been unwell," explained the other. "It began as a physical illness but it took on serious emotional and spiritual connotations. She sank rapidly. She began to lose her faith. I was too inexperienced to handle something of this magnitude and sought help from our motherhouse. Abbess Aelfgiva interceded personally. Sister

Tecla was sent to Barking Abbey for the care and sustenance that only they could offer. When she was sufficiently recovered, I travelled there myself to bring her home."

"With that chalice in your pouch?" said Gervase.

"Yes," she confessed.

"Why?"

"It had immense significance for Sister Tecla," she said softly, "though I still do not fully appreciate why. She brought it here as part of her dowry. It was a most welcome gift. She begged me to let her clean and polish it each day so that she could handle it. Abbess Aelfgiva wrote to tell me that Sister Tecla had pined for that chalice and that her mind would be more fitted to return here if I took it to Barking Abbey with me." A smile of almost maternal fondness played around her lips. "When I gave it to her, she was like a child with a doll. It was touching."

"What of those men who ambushed you?" said Ralph.

"They were trying to steal it."

"To take back to Blackwater Hall?"

"I do not know, my lord," she said. "I give you my word that I had no idea that it had been stolen from there. Sister Tecla assured me it had been in her family for many years."

"A Norman chalice in a Saxon household?"

"Strange things sometimes appear in strange places," she said. "You asked me why Oslac the Priest has a sword in his house. It is indeed an unusual item for him to have but it is not as sinister as you imply."

"Where did he get the weapon?" said Gervase.

"I gave it to him."

"You?"

"It belonged to my husband," she said, straightening her back and tilting her chin. "Before the Conquest, he owned half of this town. That sword was used in battle." She lapsed back into a more modest posture. "Father Oslac was kind and helpful to me. Without him, I would never have been able to found this priory. That sword was a gift of thanks. It was one of my husband's proudest possessions but it had no place in a convent. Father Oslac deserved it. He is a priest but he still has something of a warrior spirit."

Gervase felt abashed. Theories that had seemed quite sound when he and Ralph had discussed them earlier now began to fall apart, and he was reminded with an uncomfortable lurch that their case rested on the word of Tovild the Haunted. What if they had got the wrong solution to the riddle? Or the right solution and the wrong magpie? The prioress had been evasive but with good reason. The nun who she was accompanying back to Maldon had been through some kind of personal crisis and needed to be kept away from any form of disturbance. Prioress Mindred and Sister Tecla were miles away from the town when the murder was committed but the chalice did in some way connect them to it. Gervase pinned everything on that detail.

"Before she took the veil," he said, "did Sister Tecla live in Maldon?"

"No, she came from Woodham. Not far south of here."

"Did she have any connection with Blackwater Hall?"

"I do not believe so."

"Think hard, please."

"She never mentioned it to me."

"Yet that chalice came from the hall," said Gervase. "How do you suppose it got into Sister Tecla's hands?"

"I have no idea."

"Did she deliberately mislead you?"

"I intend to question her about that."

"Could she have stolen it herself?"

"No!" denied the prioress. "Sister Tecla has suffered much but she is not capable of theft. If she *said* that the chalice was hers, she must have believed that it was. She is young and very fragile. Her mind has been disturbed. You must make allowances."

"We cannot excuse theft," said Ralph. "Especially when such a valuable item is involved. I think we had better take a look at this chalice once more, if you please?"

"That is no possible, my lord."

"Why not?"

"Until yesterday, I did not know it had belonged to Blackwater Hall. We used it in good faith to celebrate Mass. There has been no deception on my part because I was myself deceived. I swear that, on the grave of the holy St. Oswald!"

"How did you learn that the cup might be stolen?"

"From my lord, the sheriff," she explained. "He paid us a courtesy visit yesterday evening and happened to mention that a chalice was missing from the manor house. I did not at first link it with ours—why should I?—but the very possibility kept me awake last night. This is a religious house and we will not harbour stolen goods."

"So where is the chalice now?" asked Gervase.

"On its way to Blackwater Hall."

"You sent it back?"

"Naturally," she said, and a note of vindication came into her voice. "You were unjust in your suspicions of us. We are holy sisters who serve God to the best of our poor abilities. We are prone to human frailty but we are not criminals, and we resent being regarded as such." She rose to her feet with dignity to signal their departure. "I bid you good day, sirs. Look elsewhere for your thief and your murderer. You will find none here."

Oslac the Priest tethered his horse in the courtyard and ascended the steps at Blackwater Hall. He knocked on the door and was admitted by a servant. Hamo FitzCorbucion was summoned from his chamber. He was puzzled to see the priest and even more mystified when the visitor handed him an object, which was wrapped in fine linen.

"What is it?" he demanded.

"Something that you will be pleased to see, my lord."

"The head of that boy, Wistan?"

"No," said Oslac. "It is a missing heirloom, I believe."

"The chalice!"

Hamo tore off the linen and held up the object with delight. He scrutinised it carefully to make sure that it had not been damaged in any way. The chalice was clearly very dear to him. It had belonged to his wife who had herself inherited it from her own mother before passing it on to her eldest child. Thrilled to have it back, Hamo was also anxious to punish the thief who took it away in the first place.

"Where did you get this?" he asked.

"It was left on the doorstep of the church, my lord."

"By whom?"

"I have no idea," said Oslac. "But I heard that a cup of this description was missing from Blackwater Hall and so I brought it to you immediately."

"You did well. I am very grateful."

"It is a beautiful chalice."

"My wife bequeathed it to Guy."

"Who will inherit it now?" wondered the priest.

Hamo seemed oddly discomfited by the question. Still hugging the chalice, he pressed his visitor for details of how and when it was found. Oslac stuck to his story because it had a strong element of truth. Counselled by him, Prioress Mindred had agreed to part with the chalice at once. One of her nuns had been deployed to place the object at the church door but Oslac had insisted that he not be told whom. When he faced Hamo, he wanted to have as few lies as possible to pass on to such a searching inquisitor. Although the priest promised to make further enquiries, he vowed inwardly that he would protect the priory. The link between the chalice and the convent had to be tactfully suppressed.

Hamo clapped him on the shoulder in gratitude and offered refreshment but Oslac politely refused.

"No, thank you, my lord," he said. "You have business at the shire hall today, I believe, and I will not hold you up any longer. I came but to return the chalice, but since I am here ..."

"Yes?"

"I would like to see my lady, Matilda."

"Why?"

"This is a house of mourning. I can offer comfort."

"Matilda has taken to her chamber," said Hamo.

"That is a bad sign, my lord. She should not be left to brood alone for long periods. I was able to give her much consolation when she mourned the death of your dear wife, and I am sure that I can help to sustain her again. Permit me some time alone with her and I will do what I may to revive her spirits."

"She may not wish to see you."

"Let her be the judge of that."

Hamo glanced at the chalice and back at him. Oslac had done him a great favour by returning the object to him. It was a good omen for the day ahead. Two vital tasks awaited him. He had to confound the royal commissioners and find his son's killer. Matilda was an irrelevance now. Her planned elopement had been scotched and Miles Champeney had been driven away forever from the estate. Hamo felt in an almost bountiful mood for once and he reasoned that a priest could do no harm. Even if his daughter were to moan about the loss of her beloved, Oslac was powerless to do anything more than express sympathy. Matilda was still locked in her chamber, tearful and mutinous by turns, but no longer a problem to her father. He decided that a visit from the priest might actually calm her down.

"Very well," he agreed. "Matilda is in need of comfort. Spend a little time with her and do what you may."

"Thank you, my lord."

"Tell her about the chalice. It may cheer her up."

It had taken him a long time to find a way into the shire hall. Wistan did not wish to break a window or force a door because that would have led to a thorough search of the premises to see what had been taken by the intruder. Instead he opted for the infinitely slower process of cutting himself a way in under the eaves, skewering out the reeds with the end of his sword until he made a hole just big enough to squirm through. Once inside, he stuffed the displaced thatch back into position to cover the hole. It would not survive close inspection but he was hoping that those who came into the shire hall would be far too busy to worry about some minor damage to the roof.

When daylight began to peep in at him, he was able to choose his hiding place with care. It was high in the roof beams and right at the back of the hall. Squeezed in under the thatch, he would be completely invisible. His view was obscured by the rafters but he could hear everything. When Hamo FitzCorbucion and Jocelyn came in, he would know. The sword was out of its scabbard and resting beside him on a thick beam. He had merely to grab it and the death of Algar could at last be avenged in the only fitting way. The noise of a key in a lock made him prick his ears and tense his muscles, but there was no cause for alarm. It was the town reeve. He came in to check that everything was in order. Servants brought in refreshments and set them out on the trestle table before scurrying back out. The reeve himself soon left. Wistan was satisfied with his vantage point. They could not see him.

It was not long before two other figures entered. Their voices were raised in argument as they made their way towards the table at the far end of the hall.

"That is the last time I put faith in riddles, Gervase!"

"I still think that we were on the right track."

"Follow it on your own!"

"Tovild witnessed that murder."

"Yes," said a peeved Ralph. "At the Battle of Maldon."

Gervase reflected. "Magpie. I am certain the answer was magpie. What else could it be, Ralph?"

"I have no idea, but I am not barging in there again like that. It was an ordeal!" He pointed a finger. "There I was, waiting for you to pull out that murder weapon and thrust it under her nose so that she would confess—and what happens? You never even got the chance. She was plainly innocent of everything of which we accused her. We were made to look complete fools, Gervase. We were wrong about her, wrong about Sister Tecla, wrong about the knife, wrong about Oslac, and wrong about the whole stupid idea of magpies!" He perched on the edge of the table. "What, in God's name, did we actually get *right*?"

"That chalice."

"It takes a lot to make me blush—but I did!"

"That *must* have been the reason for the ambush."

"A nun embarrassing me! It's unthinkable."

"All we have to do is to find out how that chalice got there in the first place and why Guy FitzCorbucion—it had to be him—was so keen to get it back." He turned to Ralph. "You're not listening to me."

"No, Gervase. I've had enough for one morning."

"But we have picked up the trail."

"It leads straight back to mad old Tovild!" yelled Ralph. "This is all a game that he's playing with us. Hunt the Magpie! The only bird that comes into this is a great black raven named Hamo."

"Calm down, Ralph."

"The chalice is back with the raven again! Hamo can don a cowl and pass himself off as St. Benedict!" He went off into a mirthless laugh then gave a sigh of apology. "I am sorry, Gervase, but I hate to be caught on the wrong foot like that. The chalice was the essence of our case but the prioress denied all knowledge of its true ownership. And I believe the noble lady. You heard her. She swore on the grave of St. Oswald."

"Indeed, she did ..."

Gervase Bret stared straight ahead with eyes glistening and mouth agape. He was deep in contemplation. He thought about the spiritual collapse of a young woman. He thought about a child playing with a doll. He thought about the ambush, a pile of holy earth, and two nuns chanting a Saxon charm in a church. He thought about a discussion that morning of the nature of crime and punishment. He thought about a murdered man and a chalice and the one certain thing that might connect them. He punched Ralph in his excitement and let out a cry of delight.

"St. Oswald!" he exclaimed. "St. Oswald!"

"What about him?"

"Saxon nuns would revere a Saxon saint."

"Where does that get us?"

"St. Benedict was an Italian."

"Even I know that, Gervase."

"It was St. Oswald who saved them from that ambush!"

"I like to think that we gave Oswald a spot of help."

"*He* is the link with Blackwater Hall."

"Who?"

"St. Oswald! Do you not see? We chose the wrong saint!"

Ralph was more bewildered than ever but Gervase was not able to enlighten him. Canon Hubert and Brother Simon came in with satchels of documents and a sheaf of complaints. A crowd was forming outside. The intention had been to examine Hamo FitzCorbucion on his own before bringing his accusers in on the following day to confront him, but word had got around about that morning's session. Saxon burgesses and Norman barons alike wanted to be there to view Hamo's disgrace. Gilbert Champeney had also come along in the hopes of being admitted to the proceedings. The pressure to change their original plans and to allow a more public debate was intense.

Brother Simon was against the idea on principle and Canon Hubert was even more determined to keep the self-appointed spectators at bay. Gervase slowly persuaded them by pointing out that the contest between good and evil, which Hubert had set up, deserved the largest possible audience. Hamo FitzCorbucion should be both humiliated and *seen* to be humiliated by the people over whom he had ridden roughshod for so many years. Canon Hubert had trumpeted the virtues of a visible justice only that morning over breakfast. He should be ready to open the doors to anyone who wished to come in. Ralph Delchard added his support to this argument. They had come to Maldon to clean up the filth of Hamo's tyranny. The town had a right to watch them do it.

Hubert relented, Brother Simon withdrew his opposition, and the town reeve was given new instructions. The public would be admitted. As the commissioners settled down in their chairs, eager faces came streaming in through the door and the benches were rapidly filled.

Ralph had time for only the briefest exchange with Gervase, who sat next to him.

"Do not leave me hanging in the air!" he said.

"We will talk about it later, Ralph."

"At least give me some idea. The wrong saint?"

"St. Oswald is our man."

"But why? What is so special about him?"

"His emblem."

"Emblem?"

"Do you know what it is?"

"If you tell me it has a magpie on it, I'll go berserk!"

"No magpies, Ralph, I promise you."

"Then what?"

"A raven and a ring."

"I thought you would condemn me for disobedience," she said.

"Why should I do that, my lady?"

"A father has a right to choose my husband."

"You have a right to be consulted."

"He does not see it that way."

"No," agreed Oslac, "I imagine that he does not. Your father is so used to making decisions that he will not stand for any objection to them. You and he have very different ideas about marriage. My lord, Hamo, is selecting a husband so that he can join family to family and not heart to heart."

"Miles Champeney is the man I want."

"I marvel that the two of you managed to get so far."

"We have exchanged vows."

"True love thrives on adversity."

They were in Matilda's chamber at the top of the house. Oslac had been taken along the gallery by a servant. The guard had been removed from outside but the door was still locked and the priest soon understood why. Having come to console Matilda over the death of her brother, he found her mounting the loss of the man she loved. He was shocked to hear of her incarceration in her own home and of the brutal treatment of Miles Champeney. It was a situation in which he felt he ought to offer practical assistance.

A shout took them both to the window. Down in the courtyard, Hamo FitzCorbucion had mounted his white destrier and pulled out his sword. He was wearing full armour and looked a most striking figure. Jocelyn was with him and so was Fulk the Steward but they were lost in the armed escort. Hamo was bristling. If the commissioners dared to call him before them, he intended to arrive at the hall with forty knights at his heels in a display of naked force. The visit to Coutances had not just produced a potential son-in-law. It had rekindled the hot blood that ran in his veins. Hamo envied the chaos of Normandy where barons like himself built castles without license and conducted their private wars unimpeded. That was the spirit that was needed in England. He would answer to no man and bend the knee to no king. With another loud yell, he led the full troop out of the courtyard and towards the town. Victory was assured.

Matilda watched them go, then stayed at the window for a few minutes. When she turned to Oslac, her eyes were moist.

"You must think me very callous," she said.

"Why?"

"My brother lies in the churchyard and all that I can do is to talk about myself." She dabbed at her eyes with a handkerchief. "But I do care about Guy. He had many faults but he did not deserve such a hideous death. I have been ashamed, Father Oslac. I should be weeping for a brother's death and praying for his soul. I should be hoping that they will soon catch his murderer."

"And do you hope that, my lady?"

She shrugged. "I do and I do not."

"Your mind is too full of Miles Champeney."

"Father threw him into the dungeon!"

"It was an unkind way to welcome a suitor," said Oslac with mild irony, "but it is not altogether unusual. Fathers often disapprove of the men whom their daughters favour as husbands. They may not all go to the extent of flinging an unwanted son-in-law into a cell, but they can make their opposition very clear." He gave a nostalgic smile. "I know that to my cost."

"You?"

"I was young once, my lady."

"Of course."

"And even a priest may fall in love."

"I have met your wife. She is a charming woman."

"Her father did not think me a very charming man," he said. "In fact, he found me unsuitable in every way and made no bones about telling me so to my face. He swore that he would not let his daughter marry beneath her. His opinion of priests was not high. It was a trying time for us."

"Yet the marriage went ahead."

"Eventually."

"How?"

"It is not for me to put ideas into your head, my lady."

"Ideas?"

He studied her for a moment. "You are right to reproach yourself," he said seriously. "It is only fitting that you should grieve for a brother who has passed away. I think it might help if you were to visit the churchyard and pay your respects at his grave."

"But Father will not allow me out of this house."

"He is not here to enforce that decree."

"There was a guard outside my door."

"He is not there now," said Oslac. "You watched the troop ride out. My lord, Hamo has taken all his men-at-arms with him."

"There are still servants in the house."

"A lady may command a servant."

"What if they try to stop me?"

"Tell them that I am escorting you to the church. They would not dare to stand in the way of a priest, would they?" His eyes twinkled. "The decision must be yours, my lady."

The shire hall was now so full that latecomers had to stand pressed against the walls. Ralph Delchard's men-at-arms could barely find room for themselves at the rear of the building. Up in the rafters, Wistan could hear the noisy jostling and feel the sense of expectation. The whole of Maldon seemed to have come along to witness the encounter but one of the disputants had failed to turn up. Was Hamo FitzCorbucion scorning the summons of royal commissioners? If he did not come, did they have the means to compel him? Gervase Bret's acuity and Canon Hubert's gravitas had impressed all the witnesses who had appeared before them and they had also admired Ralph Delchard's brisk authority. But none of these things could be brought into play if the lord of the manor of Blackwater ignored their warrant. As the appointed time came and went, murmurs of doubt began to swell. The summons was being spurned.

Then the door of the hall was thrown open. Every head turned and every eye expected to see Hamo FitzCorbucion come storming in but the spindly character who pushed a way past the guards was Tovild the Haunted. Carrying a spear and wearing his mottled armour, the old man gazed around in wonderment. He had not gone down to the bank of the river to quote his poem that morning. With the instincts of a true warrior, he knew that the real Battle of Maldon was being fought in the shire hall. The taut silence gave way to laughter and the mockery soon came. Tovild was a figure of fun to Saxons and Normans alike and they taunted him happily, urging him to spear a few Vikings for them by way of entertainment. The commotion was quickly smothered beneath a louder and more menacing noise. A large troop of men could be heard cantering towards the hall and dozens of hooves clacked on the hard surface of High Street as the knights came to a halt.

This time Hamo FitzCorbucion did enter. Four men-at-arms came first to clear a way roughly through the crowd. Hamo walked after them like a conquering hero walking in triumph through a vanquished territory. Jocelyn FitzCorbucion and Fulk the Steward brought up the rear, each bearing a sheaf of documents. Seats had been left vacant in the front row and the newcomers settled into them with an arrogance borne of years of unchecked power. Hamo dismissed his soldiers with a flick of the fingers and then reached up to remove his gleaming helm before handing it to Jocelyn. He looked at each of the four men who sat in judgement behind the table and found nothing to trouble him.

He glared at them with total disdain.

"You sent for me, sirs," he growled, "and I have come."

"We sent for Hamo FitzCorbucion," said Ralph.

"I am he!"

"What proof do we have of that?"

"Every man here will know me!"

"We do not."

"I am the lord of the manor of Blackwater!"

"Then why do you act like a renegade baron?" challenged Ralph. "Why do you arrive here with a troop of men and force your way in? Why do you appear before us in armour? Why do you try to threaten us with the trappings of your power and to pervert the course of justice?" His voice crackled with sarcasm. "We recognise a lord by his demeanour. We look for dignity and a natural authority. We expect an honourable man. When you come charging in here like this, all that we see is a marauding soldier."

Hamo leapt up. "I am hunting my son's killer!"

"You will not find him here."

"Do not provoke me, sir!"

"Resume your seat."

"I am here before you. State your business."

"Only when you sit down again." Hamo remained on his feet to show his defiance. Ralph was peremptory. "Very well. We will adjourn this session, if you wish, and call you again tomorrow. On that occasion, the sheriff himself will be sent to fetch you. Show him the contempt you are showing us and you will not find him so lenient. Peter de Valognes would be only too happy for an excuse to place you under arrest."

Hamo put a hand on the hilt of his sword but Jocelyn and Fulk quickly restrained him. They had a whispered conference with him and held up the documents that they carried. It was madness to institute a brawl when they had come to take part in a legal dispute that they were bound to win. Ralph Delchard was deliberately goading Hamo to bring out his choleric streak and throw him off guard. The most effective reply was to subject the commissioners to a crushing defeat in front of the whole town.

"Will you take your seat again, my lord?" said Ralph.

"He will," said Jocelyn, tugging at his father's arm.

"We wish to begin the proceedings."

Smouldering with anger, Hamo finally resumed his seat.

Ralph formally introduced each of his colleagues then called on Gervase Bret to read the list of charges. It was long and complex and it drew murmurs of approval from every part of the hall. The commissioners had been exhaustive in their researches. Hamo and Jocelyn listened with motionless expressions but Fulk could not resist a sly smile. The accusations were exactly those set down in one of the documents in his sheaf. Gilbert Champeney had done them a good service when he robbed his guests of their satchel. Blackwater Hall could be attacked with words but there were no writs and charters to lend them any bite.

"This concludes the list of charges," said Gervase. "As you have heard, it affects a large number of people in the town. If we can substantiate all these claims against my lord, Hamo, there will be restitution and compensation of a high order."

The promise drew a muffled cheer from the audience but Hamo cut through it with a snarled accusation of his own.

"You have no evidence!"

"Canon Hubert will take up that point," said Gervase.

"Where is your proof?" demanded Hamo.

"The burden of proof is upon you, my lord," said Hubert at his most stern and fearless. "When charges are levelled against you by royal commissioners, it is incumbent on you to answer them. *We* are not on trial here—you are. I realise that you are not closely acquainted with the law, because you have broken it in a hundred different ways ..." He paused to allow the general laughter free rein. "... but it does impose a strict code of behaviour on you. We ask the questions. You will answer. As and when directed."

"This idiot will keep us here all day!" moaned Hamo.

"Are you referring to me?" said the indignant Hubert.

"No," said Jocelyn, seeing the chance he wanted. He had come to demonstrate his skills and not just to sit there with his father's helmet on his lap. His voice rang out. "You must forgive my father. He is anxious to continue the search for my brother's killer. Beside that outrage, these claims of yours are petty and absurd. They can be dealt with very quickly."

"I beg leave to doubt that," warned Hubert.

"Let us take the first charge in your list."

"We intend to."

"It concerns the annexation of three hides of land formerly owned by Robert of Verly," said Jocelyn without even referring to his documents. "We can refute this insulting allegation at once. That property was not annexed at all. It was given to us by deed of gift."

"It is still held by Robert of Verly's subtenant."

"Produce him and he will swear in our favour."

"I am sure that he would," agreed Hubert. "Under duress. Fear will make a man swear to anything and we have found a lot of fear in Maldon. But we do not need to rely upon the testimony of a subtenant when we have the charter that originally granted this land to Robert of Verly."

"Show it to us," challenged Jocelyn.

"If you can!" said Hamo with a grin.

"Give us a sight of this famous document."

"We will."

Canon Hubert picked up the rolls of parchment that lay scattered before him and pretended to search through them. He nudged Brother Simon and the two of them hunted for the relevant charter with increasing dismay. Hamo was now chuckling aloud and Fulk sniggered but Jocelyn retained his poise. He was growing into his role with every second and determined to make his impact felt. Disappointment and discontent spread through the hall. They had come to see the ravens of Blackwater caged by the law, not to be set free with even more ravenous appetites. Obviously, the charter could not be found. The hunt became more frenetic.

Jocelyn leaned forward with a smile of polite mockery.

"Would you like us to help you in the search?"

"There is no need," said Gervase Bret, bringing a sheet of parchment from the satchel that lay at his feet. "I have the appropriate charter here."

"But that is impossible!" exclaimed Jocelyn.

"Examine it if you doubt its authenticity."

"It bears the royal seal," indicated Canon Hubert. "We were given it by Robert of Verly himself."

"Step forward and see it for yourselves," said Gervase.

"Yes," added Ralph with a smirk. "Compare it with the version that you carry in your own satchel. I think you will find that they match each other word for word. But we have the genuine charter and not the clever forgery."

Hamo stirred, Jocelyn blanched, and Fulk began to stammer. All three of them swung round to search the ranks of faces behind them for the one that had so comprehensively betrayed them. Gilbert Champeney stood up obligingly and gave them a cheerful wave. Instead of stealing documents from the commissioners, he had been working in collusion with them. Hamo FitzCorbucion was caught in a trap from which even his son could not rescue him and it made him seethe with fury.

"Forgive the delay," said Canon Hubert, taking control once more. "Here is the charter, as you may see. We have documentary proof of every illegality that has taken place and sworn statements to support them. Twenty years of theft and fraud have been uncovered here and it will take time to go through each instance. Bear with us while we do so and a great oppression will be lifted from this town." He used his pulpit voice. "Good always triumphs over evil in the end."

A cheer went up and Canon Hubert acknowledged it with a lordly smile. He performed best before an audience and felt he had been right to allow the public into the session. Hamo was now impaled by the law in front of him. It was time to exact full and uncompromising punishment.

"To return to the first charge ..."

"No!"

Hamo jumped to his feet, pulled out his sword, and used it to sweep all the charters from the table. He was not going to sit there quietly and listen to the catalogue of his crimes. He would do what he had always done and fight his way out of trouble. Turning on the audience, he swung his sword in a circle above his head.

"Out of my way!" he yelled. "I'll kill the first man who dares to block my path!"

Panic ensued. Benches were knocked over, heads cracked, and bodies sent flying. Everyone fought to get out of his way. A gap opened up down the centre of the hall and Hamo stalked up it with his weapon still flailing. No man was brave enough to stand in his way.

"Stop!"

A boy of fifteen had all the courage that was needed. He dropped onto the floor from the rafters and held up his sword. Hamo halted in astonishment then let out a bellow of rage as he recognised the sturdy figure who confronted him.

"Wistan!"

"Yes," said the boy proudly. "Son of Algar."

"Wistan!"

The swords clashed immediately. Hamo saw the killer of his son and Wistan saw his father's persecutor. As the metal clanged and the bodies grappled, everyone else pushed away in blind terror. Ralph Delchard tried in vain to get to the combatants to separate them but even his strength could not force a path through the swirling crowd. The fight, in any case, was soon over. Wistan had youth on his side and a burning need for revenge but they were not enough to overcome the skills of a veteran soldier. Hamo held the boy in a grip of steel, spat in his face, twisted the sword from his hand, then flung him to the floor. The boy lay spread-eagled helplessly as Hamo lifted his sword in both hands in order to jab it down with full force into his chest. But the weapon never reached its target.

"Wistan!"

The name had been enough to ignite the spirit of Tovild the Haunted. When his brave compatriot fell, he had to fight on to keep the invader at bay. Saxon pride compelled him to win the Battle of Maldon once and forever.

"Wistan!"

With every ounce of his remaining strength, he thrust with his spear at the advancing enemy. Hamo was about to bring his sword down for the kill when the point of Tovild's blade went clean through his unguarded neck and out through the back. Blood spurted wildly. There was a loud gurgle of pain and outrage, then the lord of the manor of Blackwater fell backward to the floor with terrifying finality.

Resignation was alien to the character of Miles Champeney. He could never simply accept defeat with a philosophical shrug. His harsh reception at Blackwater Hall had hurt his pride but it had not weakened his determination to rescue Matilda from her imprisonment in her own home. He wanted to go straight back to the house and force his way in, but common sense told him that this was a forlorn hope. He had to be far more careful next time. Although he had nobody to take a message to his beloved, he had her servant to give him advice about the habits of the household and the best way to penetrate its defences. The man had even more cause to help him now. But for the kind intercession of Miles's father, the servant would still be locked away in what might well have turned out to be his tomb. Loyal to Matilda, the man also owed allegiance to the Champeneys.

Loyalty was something that now troubled Miles himself. His father's opposition to the match had been distressing but it had also strengthened his resolve. When he had ridden out from Champeney Hall in the night, he had experienced few qualms at turning his back on a man who was so hostile to his choice of bride. Filial duty had been cast aside by the urgency of his love. Now it was different. Gilbert Champeney had shown a father's devotion when he came to bargain for the freedom of his son. Given the fact that he was also bearing forged documents, he had acted with considerable coolness and tenacity, even to the extent of securing the release of the blameless messenger. Yet Miles was planning to betray the old man once again, to steal away in the night in order to free Matilda from custody.

There seemed to be no way to reconcile the conflicting loyalties. His love of his father was strong but it paled beside his devotion to Matilda. She was being blamed for the faults of her family. The name of FitzCorbucion was like the mark of a leper upon her. Miles shook off his feelings of guilt. His own needs were paramount. He had to devise a plan to get into the house at a time when they would least expect him and that required the connivance of the servant. A plan had to be set in motion at once. He went off in search of the man but could not find him anywhere in the house. Miles came out into the courtyard and crossed to the stables.

He was about to call out for the servant when he was distracted. A lone figure was riding slowly towards the house in the middle distance. He thought at first that it must be his father, returning from a morning at the shire hall, but the posture of the rider and the gentle gait of the horse soon changed his mind. It was a woman. When she got closer, Miles saw that it was a young woman. For a moment, he could not believe what he was looking at and blinked in wonderment. He could recognise her profile, her attire, even her palfrey. She waved to him. He had spent all that time trying to plot her rescue and Matilda FitzCorbucion was now coming towards him. It was the answer to a prayer. Miles let out a gasp of joy and sprinted across the grass to meet her, grabbing the bridle of her horse, then catching her in his arms when she dropped down to him.

They held each other in a fierce embrace and kissed away the long separation. Miles Champeney did not know whether to laugh or cry as he clutched her to him.

"How on earth did you escape?" he asked.

"I went to church."

"Church?"

"Yes," she said. "Father Oslac looked the other way."

Prioress Mindred was in her quarters with Sister Lewinna when the bell rang, trying to still the nun's waywardness with some kind words of advice and suggesting that the homely wisdom of Aesop's *Fables* should be supplemented with a study of Aldhelm's *De Virginitate*. Visitors were not expected. Sister Lewinna was sent to answer the door and returned breathlessly with the news that Ralph Delchard and Gervase Bret were insisting on another interview with the prioress. Mindred composed herself and told the young nun to conduct the visitors in to her. Sister Lewinna obeyed at once then left the three of them alone.

The guests were invited to sit down and the prioress lowered herself into her chair. Having believed that she had routed them, she was disturbed by their return and by the quiet determination of their manner.

"We are sorry to intrude once more," said Ralph, "but it was unavoidable. We believe that what we are seeking is within the walls of this convent, after all."

"I thought I dealt with all your enquiries," she said.

"You did, my lady prioress, but there was something that you held back from us, something of crucial importance." She shifted uneasily on her chair. "Before we come to that, however, there is something you should know because it has a bearing on our visit. Hamo FitzCorbucion is dead."

"Dead!" She was aghast. "When did this happen?"

Ralph gave a terse account of events at the shire hall that morning and explained that Tovild the Haunted had been taken into custody by the sheriff. The circumstances had forced a postponement of their own deliberations and enabled them to address themselves to a related problem. Hamo had been killed by a mad old man, but his son's murderer was still at large and had to be brought to justice. Prioress Mindred listened with evident discomfort and steeled herself.

"St. Oswald brought us back here," said Ralph. "He has helped us just as he once helped you. Gervase will explain."

"That chalice gave us a link with Blackwater Hall," said Gervase. "When we put a chalice and a raven together, we had the emblem of St. Benedict and that seemed to sit easily on a Benedictine house like this. But St. Oswald has an emblem as well."

"Raven and ring," she said dully.

"That is what the chalice was," said Gervase. "A ring. It was a token of love given by Guy FitzCorbucion to Sister Tecla. It was the most valuable thing he possessed and he offered it to her in order to win her favours. Other ladies succumbed readily to his charms, it seems, but Sister Tecla—or Tecla, as she then was—held him at bay until he gave her a promise of marriage."

"The chalice was that promise," said Ralph.

"A ring to mark their betrothal," continued Gervase. "When she submitted to him, he soon tired of her and demanded the return of his gift. Tecla refused but she knew that she could not hold out against a FitzCorbucion. She fled to the only place of refuge—this priory."

Mindred let out a cry of alarm and crossed herself.

"There was a slight complication," said Gervase softly. "She was carrying his child. I do not know what happened to it, but I suspect that she lost it. You spoke earlier of her physical collapse and of her spiritual deterioration. I believe that came in the wake of the baby's death."

"Go on," she murmured.

"The chalice had been a ring to confirm her betrothal but Guy had forsaken her. It then became the baby she had lost. She pined for it at Barking Abbey. When you took the chalice to her, she was like a child with a doll."

Tears formed in the prioress's eyes. She did not sob with anguish on her own account but wept quietly for the pain of another. She stood up and crossed to the window to gaze into the garden. After a moment she beckoned them across with a gesture and they came to stand beside her. The picture that they saw supplied its own explanation. Sister Tecla was in the far corner of the garden. It was the place where Sister Gunnhild had found her sleeping one night and where Wistan had watched the young nun kiss the ground. Tecla was kneeling at the same spot again now and watering it gently with a can.

"The child miscarried," explained Mindred. "We buried it where Sister Tecla now kneels. It was a difficult time." She turned to face them. "We saved her life. If she had not come to us, Tecla would have died of grief. She told me about the child but she would never admit who the father was. I accepted that chalice in the belief that it was her own." She glanced through the window again. "In a sense, it was. I see now why Tecla revered it so much. She clung to it so desperately because it was the only proof she had that he had once loved her. When he was killed, the chalice took on even more significance for her. Sister Tecla has been desolate since it was sent back to Blackwater."

"It had great significance for Guy FitzCorbucion as well," said Gervase. "His mother bequeathed it to him. He knew how angry his father would be if it was found to be missing. He sent his men to ambush you and steal that chalice. Before they returned, he was murdered."

"I do not understand," she said with a shrug. "How did he know that I was travelling with that chalice?"

"Someone told him," explained Ralph. "It was the same person who arranged to meet him in the marshes. She felt there was only one way to rid Sister Tecla of the menace of Guy FitzCorbucion. She killed him."

The prioress shuddered. "*She?*"

"Sister Gunnhild," said Gervase. "With this."

He produced the knife, winch had been given to him by Tovild, and held it out to her. Mindred started. It looked very much like one of the priory's own kitchen utensils. She fought hard to rebut the idea that one of the holy sisters could actually commit a murder, but the evidence was too strong and it could be buttressed by things that she herself had noticed about Sister Gunnhild—not least the Danish nun's obsessive attachment to Sister Tecla. Shame would descend on the convent if it were known to harbour a murderer but Prioress Mindred did not hesitate. She snatched up a little silver bell from the table and opened the door. When she shook the bell hard, the urgent noise brought Sister Lewinna hurtling along the passageway.

"Go and fetch Sister Gunnhild!" ordered Mindred.

"She is not here, Reverend Mother," said Lewinna. "When I told her who your guests were, she ran straight out through the door. It was most unseemly behaviour for someone who has always criticised me."

The two men came quickly across to her.

"Which way did she go?" asked Ralph.

"I do not know, my lord."

"She cannot hope to outrun you," said Mindred.

"I'll get my men and start a search," said Ralph. "She is very distinctive and they will soon track her down."

"No," said Gervase, thinking. "She is not trying to escape."

"Then where has she gone?" asked Ralph.

"I will show you."

Sister Gunnhild was on the point of exhaustion by the time that she reached the marshes. She felt no contrition for what she had done and even had a momentary sensation of triumph when she came to the place where it had happened. Sister Tecla was a young and vulnerable woman who had been yet another victim of Guy FitzCorbucion's lust. The young nun would refuse to name the father of her child but Gunnhild had discovered who it was. She was in charge of the convent while the prioress was travelling to Barking Abbey where Sister Tecla had been taken to recover from her traumas. Guy FitzCorbucion had arrived at the priory and demanded the return of his chalice, threatening to ransack the place if it were not handed over. She was forced to tell him where it was and her resentment had boiled over. It was not the first time she had suffered at the hands of an aggressive man.

Gunnhild walked to the bank of the river estuary. It was there that she had arranged to meet Guy FitzCorbucion. She knew that he would have to come. Her letter had been explicit. If he did not obey her summons, she would tell his father about the use to which the precious family heirloom had been put. Guy responded at once to the threat of blackmail, intending either to bully her out of it or buy her off. The last thing he was expecting was a murderous attack. Gunnhild smiled as she looked at the place where she had thrown him in.

A harsh sound shattered through her reverie. Two horses were galloping towards her. Sister Gunnhild jumped into the river and waded through the reed beds before flinging herself forward into the deeper water. Weighed down by her sodden habit, she sank quickly beneath the surface. Ralph Delchard was the first to reach the scene, reining in his horse and leaping from the saddle to run to the bank. Overcoming his hatred of water, he plunged straight into the river and threshed his way towards her. In an emergency, Ralph could indeed swim. The nun had already swallowed a lot of water and was failing fast but she still had one last reserve of strength left. As Ralph came splashing up in an attempt to save her, she lashed out an arm to fight him off. He tried to overpower her but he was encumbered by his attire and could not master her sudden ferocity.

In the hectic struggle to subdue her, Ralph grabbed hold of her wimple but she twisted her head violently away from him. Hood and wimple came away in his hands and her whole head was exposed to view. Ralph let go of her in surprise. Sister Gunnhild was almost totally bald. Tufts of grey hair ran down the sides of her head but they could not hide the ugly wounds where both ears had been cut completely away. She sank beneath the water again and he tried to pull her back to the surface. Gervase had now swum out to assist him but their efforts were too late. When the mutilated head reappeared above the water again, Sister Gunnhild had the smile of a woman who had finally escaped from the ordeal of men.

Epilogue

Canon Hubert was sad to leave the town of Maldon. He had eaten so well at Champeney Hall, and with such wanton self-indulgence, that his donkey brayed in protest whenever he mounted it. But his regrets were not confined to the kitchen of his genial host. Their visit had been almost wholly satisfactory. They came to attack the rank injustices that had been exposed by their predecessors and they had done so in the most signal way. All was now concluded. A decent interval had been left for the family to bury Hamo FitzCorbucion but two deaths at Blackwater Hall did not absolve it of its crimes. It was Jocelyn who had been arraigned in the shire hall and who had been destroyed there by the commissioners, and Hubert felt that his personal contribution in that arena had been vital. Large amounts of land had been restored to their rightful owners or tenants. Compensation on a massive scale was to be paid out by the new lord of a much-depleted manor of Blackwater.

Brother Simon's memories of the town were more mixed. His brilliant forging of the documents had been a decisive element in their campaign—even though he still had doubts about its moral validity—and he could look back on it with some pleasure. He looked back with less enjoyment on discussions of mutilation and the nickname of a local magnate, and he was praying that their homeward journey would not oblige them to enter a house of nuns again. The revelation that it was a holy sister who had butchered Guy FitzCorbucion confirmed his most deep-seated fears about the opposite sex. On balance, he was relieved when they finally took their leave of Champeney Hall and wended their way towards Chelmsford. Chastity was a comforting thing.

Ralph Delchard and Gervase Bret led the cavalcade. It was a bright day and the open road beckoned. They were moving at a rising trot through sporadic woodland.

"Our stay was much longer than we anticipated," said Ralph. "But our efforts were very worthwhile. If it had not been for us, Hamo's reign of terror would still be continuing."

"Yes," said Gervase. "Jocelyn will be a much more amenable lord of the manor now that we have cut him and his demesne right down to size. His sister will profit as well."

"How so?"

"The marriage in Coutances will be called off," he predicted. "When it was arranged, she was the daughter of the mighty Hamo and brought a rich dowry. That situation has been altered dramatically. Her elected husband will think twice before allying his family to that of the FitzCorbucions now."

"Miles Champeney may yet come into favour, then."

"In time, Ralph. In time. My guess is that Jocelyn will warm to the idea eventually. Now that his wings have been clipped, he needs friends in Maldon."

"Gilbert will soon mellow as well, I think."

Matilda FitzCorbucion's escape from her house had not led to the idyllic reunion she had hoped. Miles Champeney had been delighted to see her and immediately saddled up his horse to ride off with her, but the news of her father's death arrived before they could depart. It changed everything. Overcome with remorse, she went back to Blackwater Hall. It was her father's domineering personality that had held the whole demesne together and that quickly became clear, even to Jocelyn. He would never exercise the power or the influence of Hamo and he would need all his energies to administer a demoralised estate. Jocelyn and his sister had reasons to hate each other but they were reconciled by the adverse circumstances. By the same token, Gilbert and his son came to a deeper level of understanding. With the death of his rival, Gilbert was able to take a slightly more accommodating view of the FitzCorbucion family. Miles, too, had learned the importance of blood ties. As the son of a prominent lord, he would now have something to offer Matilda. Hard reality had made a romantic elopement impossible but the passage of time would bring the lovers ineluctably together.

"Did you see who else was waving us off?" said Ralph.

"Wistan."

"Gilbert has taken the lad under his own wing."

"There is no place for him at Blackwater now."

"Wistan had the courage to take on Hamo in single combat," recalled Ralph. "The boy is lucky to be alive. He has Tovild the Haunted to thank for that."

"And his own father, Ralph."

"His father?"

"Wistan was named after a brave warrior who fought in the Battle of Maldon." He smiled wryly. "That was what brought Tovild to his aid. If the lad had been called Ralph or Gervase, he would now be lying dead in his grave."

"Too true."

"He will now have a kinder lord to serve."

"Yes!" said Ralph with mock horror. "Gilbert is half-Saxon."

"There is nothing wrong with that," said Gervase.

Ralph started to rhapsodize about the virtues of Sister Tecla and to wonder if he could not have rescued her from the strictures of convent life. Cold fact then intruded. Hers was indeed a sad condition but Maldon Priory would be a more secure and loving environment for her now that its darker element had been purged. He could never offer her the peace and spiritual companionship that she needed to help her to recover from all she endured. Whatever his faults, she had loved Guy FitzCorbucion once and cherished the gift that he had given her. His murder was a blow to her. The fact that it had been committed by one of her holy sisters was even more devastating.

These thoughts steered him around to a question.

"Tell me, Gervase," he said. "What first gave you the idea that Sister Gunnhild might be the killer?"

"Canon Hubert."

"*He* suggested it?"

"No," said Gervase, "but he did start that argument we had over crime and punishment. Hubert seemed to have a soft spot for mutilation, even though he was indignant when I pointed out that he shared the same attitude as King Cnut."

"Well?"

"Sister Gunnhild was a Dane."

"And old enough to have lived under Cnut's reign."

"I remembered the mutilation of Guy FitzCorbucion."

"That's something I choose to forget!"

"Why should someone castrate him?" said Gervase. "You thought it might be a vengeful husband whose wife had been seduced by Guy, but I wondered if it might not be something else. Cnut enforced his legal code rigorously, and when he died, its spirit lived on. Especially among the Danish communities that remained here. Gunnhild was the victim of those laws. They cut her ears off."

"The punishment for adultery."

"She was fortunate not to lose her nose as well," said Gervase. "You can understand why she wanted to hide her disfigurement. Even Prioress Mindred knew nothing about it until she discovered Gunnhild taking a bath one night. The truth finally came out. The prioress confided it to me."

"That fat old woman committed adultery? Never!"

"She was young and thin once, Ralph," he said, "and was even betrothed. Then a trusted neighbour came to see her and forced himself upon her. He was a married man. They were caught in the act. The man fled but Gunnhild was left behind to face me judgement of her elders. Nobody believed her when she told the truth, not even the man to whom she was betrothed. He spurned her along with all the others. She had committed adultery, it was said, and they mutilated her. Where else could she turn but to a convent?"

"No wonder she hated men so much!" observed Ralph.

"She inflicted the punishment on Guy FitzCorbucion that she felt the man who defiled her should have suffered. She saw herself and Sister Tecla as fellow victims of lust."

"Yes," said Ralph soulfully. "I sometimes think that you Saxons are primitive enough but the Danes could be barbaric."

"Hamo was both," reminded Gervase, "and he was Norman."

Ralph conceded the point with a grin then swung around in the saddle to take a valedictory look at Maldon. The hill was no more than a distant mound on the horizon now and it aroused a welter of memories for him. One dominated.

"I was thinking of Humphrey Goldenbollocks."

"At least, you know the truth about him now."

"I wish that I had not asked," said Ralph bitterly. "I was much happier believing that his overweening desire had earned him the name of *Aureis testiculi.*"

Gervase smirked. "In a sense, it did."

"Before I was told, I envied the man. Not any more."

"Does it not make you want to keep bees?"

"I'll never eat honey again as long as I live!" vowed Ralph. "A man is entitled to his pleasures, is he not? All that Humphrey did was to take a fair fat wench into the long grass on a summer's afternoon. I have done the same myself a score of times but I will be more careful in the future."

"You do not have beehives, Ralph."

"That was his undoing. They resented him stealing their honey. The bees did all the work and Humphrey came along to take the fruits of their labour." Ralph gave a shudder as he recounted the tale, which Gilbert Champeney had told him. "When they found him lying naked in the grass, they took their revenge. Did they attack his arms, his legs, or his back? Did they concentrate their venom on his bare buttocks? No! They stung the poor fellow where it would hurt most. No wonder he was dubbed *Aureis testiculi.* By the time the bees had finished with him, his bollocks were as big and golden as two oranges." He gave a groan of sympathy. "What a grotesque punishment!"

"Do not mention it to Canon Hubert," joked Gervase, "or he will incorporate it into his own legal code. It sounds painful enough to have great appeal for him."

"Testicular torture! The monastic ideal."

They shared a laugh, then kicked their horses into a gentle canter. Maldon was behind them but other assignments awaited in Winchester.

So did Alys. Gervase was lifted by the thought that he would see her again before too long. Ralph was still having wistful longings about Sister Tecla. Brother Simon was meditating on a passage from the Gospels. Canon Hubert was speculating on the quality of his next meal. The men-at-arms were chatting happily.

A lone raven came out of the sky ahead of them and landed right in their path. It put its head to one side and peered at them impudently. They cantered towards it. The bird soon repented of its audacity and flapped its wings noisily before flying out of their way and into the trees.

They liked to think that it had recognised them.

Lightning Source UK Ltd.
Milton Keynes UK
18 August 2010

158607UK00001B/56/P